P9-DHT-903

"Come on out of the dressing room, Hannah."

Will kept his voice low. "I want to see you," he went on.

Reluctantly, she peeped around the corner, and seeing no one else in sight, stepped out. The salesclerk had provided her with a pair of black heels, and Hannah teetered a little as she walked.

He stared at her for a moment before saying, "Wow."

She gazed down at the floor. "Will, this isn't really me. I don't think—"

He gave her a thorough appraisal. "Whoever it is, I'm taking her out tonight. You look incredible."

She looked up and saw the admiration shining in his eyes. Suddenly she knew that tonight would be *the night*. The night that would have to last a lifetime.

ABOUT THE AUTHOR

Inglath Caulder's fascination with romance novels started the day her mother first took her to the local bookmobile. "A librarian handed me a Janet Dailey Harlequin Presents, and I've been hooked ever since." It was only natural that Inglath would bestow the same passion for books upon her heroine, Hannah Jacobs.

Inglath lives in Virginia with her husband, Mac. She'd love to hear from her readers and invites them to write to her at: P.O. Box 973, Rocky Mountain, VA 24151-0973

Inglath Caulder

Truth and Roses

Harlequin Books

TORONTO • NEW YORK • LONDON
AMSTERDAM • PARIS • SYDNEY • HAMBURG
STOCKHOLM • ATHENS • TOKYO • MILAN
MADRID • WARSAW • BUDAPEST • AUCKLAND

If you purchased this book without a cover you should be aware
that this book is stolen property. It was reported as "unsold and
destroyed" to the publisher, and neither the author nor the
publisher has received any payment for this "stripped book."

ISBN 0-373-70609-X

TRUTHS AND ROSES

Copyright © 1994 by Inglath Cooper.

All rights reserved. Except for use in any review, the reproduction or
utilization of this work in whole or in part in any form by any electronic,
mechanical or other means, now known or hereafter invented, including
xerography, photocopying and recording, or in any information storage
or retrieval system, is forbidden without the written permission of the
publisher, Harlequin Enterprises Limited, 225 Duncan Mill Road,
Don Mills, Ontario, Canada M3B 3K9.

All characters in this book have no existence outside the imagination of
the author and have no relation whatsoever to anyone bearing the same
name or names. They are not even distantly inspired by any individual
known or unknown to the author, and all incidents are pure invention.

This edition published by arrangement with Harlequin Enterprises B. V.

® and TM are trademarks of the publisher. Trademarks indicated with
® are registered in the United States Patent and Trademark Office, the
Canadian Trade Marks Office and in other countries.

Printed in U.S.A.

To Mac, for believing
and
to Mama, for always being there

PROLOGUE

New Orleans, Louisiana

THE BALL FLEW out of the quarterback's hands, whistling down the length of the Superdome field like a missile. A missile aimed at Will Kincaid.

From his spot on the fifteen-yard line, he narrowed his gaze, willing the oncoming ball to land in his waiting hands. Nothing existed except this moment. There were no fans lunging to their feet, no vendors hawking popcorn and Cokes in the stands, no TV cameras zooming in on him. There was only the knowledge that within his reach hung the brass ring.

The moment he'd waited for all his life. The Superbowl. A single chance in which to make his mark in history. He could taste the victory, feel its reassuring caress through the sweat and grime that covered his face. His. It was his. Before his eyes flashed an image of his father's face....

"I know you'll make me proud out there, son. Never given me reason to be ashamed yet. I know you won't start tonight."

And then his goal was within sight. Winning. Nothing else mattered. With an almost inhuman grunt, Will lunged to the side, reaching...

The ball landed solidly in his grasp, and he was off. A hand grabbed for his shoulder, missed and reached again. As Will's feet crossed the line, the safety tackled him, taking him down, slamming him into the unforgiving turf. His right knee twisted and took the full impact of his weight.

The resounding crack echoed in his ears. It was over.

Will Kincaid lay there, not moving. The cheers of thousands of fans roared in his ears, hero worship for a young man who, at twenty-nine, had reached the top. Nausea rose inside him, swift enough to draw a groan from his midsection. Then the blackness overtook him, and everything else faded—even his father's unreadable frown.

CHAPTER ONE

HANNAH JACOBS had long been aware that most of the people in Lake Perdue considered her a mystery. They thought it odd that a young woman would go months without showing her face at a public function. Odd that she seemed content to work in a small-town library week after week, month after month, year after year, when most of her peers had moved away to make their fortunes.

What they didn't know was that the old brick building with its slate roof and musty memories of the flood of '64 suited her. It no longer mattered that she'd once entertained other dreams. The library had become her solace. Her refuge. Books did not question or judge. They made safe companions.

As assistant librarian, Jenny Dudley did not share Hannah's passion, but she went about her work with singular efficiency and enthusiasm. In the past six years, she had become Hannah's closest friend. But even Jenny didn't know what made Hannah tick. She avoided talking about anything personal, preferring, instead, to discuss topics associated with the library—which books had received favorable reviews in *Publishers Weekly,* how many they could order and stay within budget.

But today their conversation did not run toward anything so dry. Hannah would have given a day's pay to be arguing the merits of stocking the shelves with extra copies of Faulkner. Avoiding Jenny's eyes, she reached for the *L* encyclopedia and shoved the volume into its proper spot with more zeal than necessary. "The idea seems a bit ridiculous to me," she said.

"That's not the point. It'd do you good to get out for a change. A parade would be just the thing," Jenny argued. "Live a little." At forty-five, Jenny followed her own advice, coming in with a new hairstyle every week. Keep the men guessing, that was the trick. She followed the ritual religiously, convinced it would find her the man she'd been searching for in the twenty-odd years since she'd lost her husband.

"I don't have time today."

"Don't you ever get tired of the same old routine? You're here every day except Sunday. And every night you head straight for that old mausoleum you call home. I mean, look how you live. You're the only person I know whose spice cabinet is alphabetized. Not to mention that you've read ninety-five percent of the books in this library. Books and reality are two different things, you know. What you *need*, Hannah Jacobs, is something to ruffle your feathers a bit."

Hannah closed her eyes and rubbed a hand across the back of her neck. She'd heard it before, how the romance of spinsterhood had gone the route of the wooden icebox. "Jenny, don't start this again—"

"A young woman like yourself ought to be getting out more."

"Jenny." The word was a warning.

"And I can't understand why you insist on playing down your God-given good looks. It's like you're trying to hide them or something. Why on earth don't you—"

"We've been through this before, Jen. Please."

Jenny muttered something about the folly of a woman hiding her light under a bushel, then made a mock salute of truce. "All right. But it's not as if a local hero comes home to roost every day of the week." With a what's-this-world-coming-to sigh of exasperation, she urged the metal book cart down the aisle and said, "You really aren't going?"

"It's February," Hannah said, hoping to divert Jenny's mission. "How can you have a parade in February?"

Jenny shrugged. "No one ever complains about having the Christmas parade in cold weather. What's the difference?"

A gust of wind caught a limb of the pine tree outside the front window, slapping it against the pane. Hannah flinched, then reached for another book. "Parades are for soldiers coming home, retired war veterans, even Santa Claus. Not football players," she added with a shake of her head.

"For goodness' sake, Hannah, you act like Will Kincaid's an ax murderer or something. He *won* the Superbowl."

"And the rest of the town is acting like he's the messiah."

"Oh, that's hogwash. You know he's just a local boy made good. What's wrong with giving him a little pat on the back?"

"Certainly a contribution to mankind." Hannah aligned the row of encyclopedias in soldierlike precision, despite the fact that the two-thirty school bus would drop off a dozen or so hands to interpose *A* with *H* and *P* with *Z*.

"Come on. Sandy will be here after school to work the front desk. We could slip out for a few minutes—"

"I have a dental appointment at four." For all the sorrow in her voice, she could have been announcing her imminent departure for Tahiti.

The corners of Jenny's mouth puckered in a frown. "I guess I'll go by myself, then."

Hannah didn't take the bait. "I'm sure you'll have plenty of company."

"Well, then, you might just be sorry," Jenny said, attempting one last tack. "He's awfully good-looking, if all those magazine articles are anything to judge from."

Smoothing the front of her dress, Hannah grabbed the remaining books from the cart, sending her co-worker a look that said it wouldn't have mattered if he'd been Mel Gibson's twin. "I need to run a few errands before my appointment. I'll see you in the morning, Jenny."

Hannah slipped the last three volumes into their appropriate spots, then walked to the front desk. She opened the bottom drawer and pulled out her purse, humming as she went, an apparent portrait of indifference.

THE YELLOW TWENTY-FIVE-miles-an-hour sign warned would-be speeders of the hairpin curve marking the entrance into the Lake Perdue town limits. Will Kincaid took note of it, then dismissed it much the same as he'd once dismissed his ninth-grade algebra teacher.

He knew today the same reckless uncertainty for his future he'd known then.

Downshifting, he sent the car accelerating into the curve. The new red Ferrari hugged the pavement at well over double the sign's advised speed. The tires squealed in protest before the car hummed on, fourth gear, back to fifth, leveling off with a purr that was to the auto enthusiast what Rachmaninoff might have been to the New York Philharmonic patron.

Limits. Life these days revolved around them.

Will didn't have time for speed limits today. He was late. Late for this damn parade his father had planned. He'd wanted nothing more than a few weeks to recover. A few weeks to put body and soul back together again. To forget about football. And Grace. To convince himself he'd done the right thing in walking away from both of them.

The Superbowl. The high point of his life. It had shattered not only his knee, but all sense of direction, as well, leaving him with no idea of where to go or what to do.

Not that he hadn't had his share of well-meaning friends and relatives intent on showing him the way. *Head for Hollywood. New York's the place for you. Come home for a while, son. Do not pass go. Do not collect two hundred dollars.*

Despite the barrage of well-intended advice, Lake Perdue had beckoned and won for the time being. Will's father had wanted him to move back home, an option totally out of the question. He'd rented a house in Tarkington's Cove, instead. Close enough to visit. Far enough away to secure the space he needed.

Although so far, physical distance hadn't been a deterrent for his father. John Kincaid had still managed to talk Will into sitting on some ridiculous float and being pulled around town like a monkey in a cage. "How can you turn them down, son?"

"I'm tired, Dad."

"It's just an hour or two. Surely that's not too much to ask from someone who's made it as big as you."

Guilt. John Kincaid played it better than anyone Will had ever known. No one had pushed him harder toward his success in the NFL. No one had reminded him of it more often.

Will had relented finally, certain by the end of their discussion that his father would get more pleasure out of the event than anyone else in Lake Perdue.

He hadn't exactly dressed for the occasion, a fact his father would be certain to point out. Will had never been much for Armani suits and the like. Designer jeans had battled for their share of the market without ever making it to a hanger in his closet. His taste had remained constant over the years. He still preferred Levi's, the kind that had been washed so many times they'd gone soft and white. Today he'd paired them with a denim shirt and a worn-looking leather jacket that cost more than a lot of used cars. He wore equally well-worn loafers on sockless feet. He hated socks.

He reached forward and popped in a CD. The sound of Wagner's Die Walküre split the air, blasting away at the edges of his impatience. He sighed and ran a hand through his hair, while he controlled the steering wheel with the other. The car had been a bonus from Hank Calhoun, owner of the team on which Will had played wide receiver. A farewell present for a job well done. And maybe a bit of a bribe, as well, Will had later realized. For him to consider going back to work for Hank in some other capacity. To reconsider not forgetting Hank's daughter once he left L.A.

"You and Grace make a fine couple, Will," Hank had said the last time they'd talked. "There aren't too many men I'd hand my daughter over to, you know." Will knew it was true. But it had taken him three years to realize he wasn't the man for that particular honor.

Like the rest of the world, Hank had known Will's career was over. Unlike Bo Jackson's case, no one seemed willing to dispute the evidence that he would never again play football. "With the number of injuries you've had on that knee, this was just the final straw, Will," one of the doctors had said. "The average playing time is four and a half years," another had consoled. So he'd had more than most. But that didn't make the verdict any easier to accept. A verdict he'd sentenced himself to years ago. Time to pay the hangman.

Using his left foot, Will braked to a halt at the first of the town's three stoplights.

No one had understood why he'd left the West Coast mecca of wealth to come back to a town where the population hovered around five thousand. He wasn't sure himself. He just knew that home was the place for him to recover—both physically and mentally.

With one wrist draped over the wheel, he glanced at his surroundings. Things had changed since his last visit. Progress had stuck its big toe into Lake Perdue. Aaron Tate's General Store, which had since risen to One Stop Gas & Go status, still sat on the corner of Second and Main. A pizza joint had been wedged in between it and Kawley's Drugstore, more than likely giving Simpson's Ice Cream, the old high-school hangout, a run for its money. On the other side of the street, Ethel's Fine Fashions had been replaced by a shop that looked as though it belonged on Fifth Avenue in Manhattan, a concession to the customers coming in from some of the lake's new developments.

Disappointment shot through him. Nothing stayed the same. The rest of the world was beginning to discover Lake Perdue, the quiet little town that had been his refuge in the years of traveling from one big city to another.

The light turned green. He put his foot to the accelerator and continued along Main Street, dodging the potholes and passing a car and then a truck. He didn't know either of the drivers, but he lifted a hand in greeting, anyway. Here, everybody waved. Will pictured himself cruising down Sunset Boulevard, waving at every car he passed. He shook his head and smiled to himself for the first time that day. At the very least, he'd have been pulled over and given a Breathalyzer.

Tom Dillon, an old friend and now a town deputy sheriff, stood just ahead in the middle of the street, directing traffic for the parade. Will rolled down his window and lifted a cautious hand in greeting. The two had been buddies in high school, but had had a falling-out just before graduation. Will hadn't forgotten it.

Tom apparently had. He grinned and yelled, "Hey, Will, how's it going?"

"How ya doin', Tom?"

Tom blew his whistle and motioned a lane of traffic forward, shouting over his shoulder, "Come on out to Clarence's when you get a chance. Buy you a beer."

With a half nod and a wave, Will swung off Main onto McClanahan for the First Baptist Church. He checked his appearance in the mirror and then glanced up just in time to see a stop sign ahead that hadn't been there the last time he'd been home.

Brake lights flashed as the car in front of him rolled to a stop. Nothing short of a miracle would allow him to miss it. Tires squealed, rubber smoked against asphalt as the Ferrari plowed into the back of the stopped car.

The seat belt was all that kept Will from going through the windshield.

"Damn!" He slammed a palm against the steering wheel and leaned forward to get a closer look at what he'd done. The brand-new Ferrari now sat with its nose tucked under the ancient relic in front of him.

The car was the color of his aunt Fan's grasshopper pie. It appeared to be a good thirty feet long, sporting twin pointed extensions just above each taillight. He recognized the make—a 1962 Cadillac Sedan de Ville. Had it been a convertible, it would have looked a lot like something Batman drove.

With another muttered curse, he climbed out of the car, pulling his leather bomber jacket close against the February chill. He cast a glance at the damage and decided it might not have been as bad as he'd thought. A few scratches maybe if they were careful about separating the two cars. Not worth calling the police.

Lips pressed together, he limped across the pavement to the other driver's door. A woman. He should have guessed. Judging from the antique she was driving, she probably hadn't been on the road in fifteen years.

Will knocked on the window and leaned forward. The woman sat there, staring straight ahead as if in a trance. Alarm stabbed at him. What if she was hurt or...

Before he could complete the thought, the car door opened, barely missing his nose. The woman slid out of the front seat, sidestepping him until they stood a good four feet apart. Focusing to the left of his shoulder, she asked in a frigid voice, "Was there a problem with your brakes?"

The question sounded innocent enough. But her tried-and-convicted tone rankled Will. He took a step back and arched a brow, taking in the wool cap pulled so low on her head that she appeared not to have any hair, the round glasses that seemed to dwarf her small face, the scarf wrapped around her neck and tucked under her chin. From the way she'd mummified herself, he could barely see where the hat ended and the scarf began.

"Hey, I'll be the first to admit this was my fault. But I don't mind saying I've seen snails move up to an intersection faster than you do."

The woman kept her eyes averted and appeared to be searching for words. Her response, when it finally came, was calm and reasonable. "McClanahan wasn't exactly made for drag racing."

He slid his sunglasses down his nose and stared at her, his eyes narrowed. Something about the woman seemed familiar. Only he couldn't see her well enough to figure out what. He stepped back and frowned at her. "Do I know you?"

The woman hesitated. Then she quickly pushed past him and slid into the car to shuffle through some papers she pulled from the glove compartment. "I have an appointment in a few minutes, so if you don't mind, I'd like to get this over with. I assume you have insurance.''

Will couldn't remember the last time a woman had given him the cold shoulder. Maybe he'd gotten spoiled, but her attitude ticked him off. "I do," he snapped. "And I'd rather not get the police involved in this. I've had a hell of a day, if you'll pardon the language. Your damage is minimal. I'll take a chance on mine. I'm late for something myself."

Her eyes widened. "Fine. If you could please give me your company's name—" She kept her gaze on the notepad in her hand, pen poised in midair.

"Better yet," he said, his voice softer now, "how about if I just pay you for the damage? We could make a reasonable estimate, and if it's more, you can get in touch with me later."

"I'd prefer to keep this within the law."

"I wasn't suggesting anything illegal, just—"

"Convenient. You're interested in convenience." She nodded impatiently. "All right. We'll do it your way."

"Sounds reasonable enough." He turned and made his way back to the Ferrari, deliberately taking his time. Reaching for the wallet inside the glove compartment, he pulled out several traveler's checks and signed each of them with a slow, precise hand. That ought to do it. He doubted the whole car was worth that much.

Favoring his right knee, he ambled back to the woman's car and leaned inside to hand her the checks along with a few insurance papers. "It's all there. With a toll-free number. I don't imagine you'll need it, though. These should cover it."

The woman glanced down at the checks. "Traveler's checks?"

His mouth tightened. "Anything wrong with that?"

"A personal check would be fine."

He looked away, then forced himself to meet her questioning gaze. "I don't have one with me. Look," he said, "I made what I thought was a generous guess. If it's too much, keep the rest for your trouble."

"Fine," she said again. With surprising strength, she yanked the door closed, leaving him staring at her through the window.

He took a hasty step back and then grimaced when a pain shot through his leg. Suddenly he realized he hadn't told her he'd disconnect the two cars himself. It would need to be done carefully, just right in order to—

He reached out to pound on the window just as she fired the old clunker, jerked it into gear and surged forward.

Speechless, Will stood there watching her as she floored the old heap and roared through the intersection at a speed that couldn't possibly be described as a snail's pace.

IT WAS WELL AFTER FIVE when Hannah pulled into her driveway on Wilmington Street. Turning off the ignition, she leaned forward and glanced up at the old white house. The towering maples stood naked and gray in the front yard. Jenny was right. With only one person to fill its rooms, the house *was* a mausoleum. Built in 1910, it had been designed for a family, not a woman alone. But Sarah had loved the house. And Hannah loved it, too. She'd grown up here in a childhood filled with books and classical music. And books with endings where Mommies and Daddies didn't leave their little girls.

This house was home to her with its front porch and rocking chairs that invited one to sit and relax. It was the same front porch on which Sarah had sat watching Hannah play in the front yard. The same porch from which aunt and niece had stood hand in hand as Hannah's father had turned to say, "'Bye, Hannah Banana, see you soon," as they'd climbed into their car. Two young parents who'd met up with responsibility too soon and handed their daughter over to Sarah long enough to sow a few wild oats. Unaware that they would never see either Sarah or Hannah again.

In front of the white rail porch grew Hannah's treasured Madam Butterfly tea roses. Featherless peacocks now in the last throes of winter. Hannah's mother had planted the bushes more than twenty-five years earlier, when she and Hannah's father had first married and lived here with his older sister, Sarah. Hannah tended them now, pruning and pampering, awaiting their arrival each spring as one awaits the return of old friends.

She climbed out of the car, reached for her purse and shut the door with a clunk. After letting herself into the house she leaned against the door and closed her eyes. In this house, at least, everything remained in order. Dishes were stacked neatly in the kitchen cabinets. Towels were folded precisely on the bathroom shelves. Books lined the walls of the small den. She felt better just being here.

The house had its own familiar scent. Years of lemon-scented furniture polish; winter afternoons of chocolate-chip cookies and summer Sundays of blackberry cobbler. Home. For the first time in an hour and a half, Hannah allowed herself to relax. She felt as if she'd been holding her breath since she'd glanced in her rearview mirror to find Will Kincaid ramming into her car.

Will Kincaid. She'd known he was coming back. But meeting up with him face-to-face had been the last thing she'd anticipated.

She sank to the floor and rested her head in her hand. In the few seconds she'd had before he stalked up to her car, she'd wrapped the scarf around her neck and yanked the hat down on her head, praying he wouldn't recognize her. And he hadn't.

To her surprise, the realization had brought her no sense of satisfaction. In fact, she'd found herself fighting the crazy impulse to shout at him. *Don't you know who I am? Have I changed that much?*

But then, she knew the answer to that.

She scrambled up to stand before the cherry mirror that hung in the hallway. She yanked off the hat and the glasses she wore for driving. Ten years had brought about more than a few changes, she knew. She'd all but given up makeup. Fine lines had appeared in places where once there'd been none. She didn't smile much anymore and tended to stay about five pounds underweight.

She stared at her reflection in the mirror. She'd gotten what she wanted this afternoon. Will hadn't recognized her. And she'd driven away without having to endure the awkwardness of that recognition. She had no desire to start digging up the past. She should be glad. She was safe.

Laughter bubbled inside her at the irony of it. Her eyes grew moist and the laughter died. Ten years. And she'd never forgotten Will Kincaid or his smiling face.

She'd never forgotten him. He hadn't recognized her.

HANNAH WENT TO WORK at the Lake Perdue Library each Saturday morning from eight to twelve. This Saturday should have been no different.

She left her house at seven forty-five just as she always did. But this morning as she scraped the frost from her windshield, she sent a cursory glance up and down the street before climbing into her car. Turning off Wilmington onto McClanahan, she searched both directions for a flash of bright red.

She was being ridiculous. As if he'd be waiting for her. She doubted he even remembered the accident had taken place. He'd been so nonchalant about the whole thing he'd probably already replaced the car with a new one.

Determined to put the incident behind her, she climbed out of her car and shut the door. Halfway through the library parking lot, she turned and looked back at the sorrowful sight of her aunt's cherished old jalopy. It had been one of Sarah Jacobs' eccentricities, and she'd been reluctant to part with it long after such gas-guzzlers had gone out of style. Along with everything else she owned, Sarah had left it to Hannah when she'd moved into Meadow Spring a year ago. Hannah didn't know why she'd kept the car other than that she couldn't see herself in some flashy little import. And it ran perfectly. Why replace it when the entire trip to and from work rolled the odometer forward a mere ten miles a day? The car suited her just fine. She'd see about having it fixed first thing Monday morning and send Will Kincaid a check for the difference.

She'd barely gotten through the door before Jenny Dudley scooted around the front desk and strong-armed her to the drawer where they stored their purses. Two fingers graced the line of her jaw as she cocked a hip and said, "I won't candy-coat it and say you didn't miss out. Because you certainly did. You should have been at that parade, Hannah. You should have come."

"So tell me what was so exciting."

"Why, Will Kincaid, of course." She took Hannah's sweater and hung it on the coat rack behind the desk. "Let me get your coffee and I'll tell you all about it. You really missed..." Her voice trailed off as she stepped into the back room.

Hannah let out a deep sigh. Will Kincaid again. So far, overlooking his impromptu visit to Lake Perdue had proved impossible. Neither he nor anybody else was about to let her forget it.

Jenny clicked back to the desk and handed Hannah a mug of coffee.

"Thanks, Jen. You didn't have to do that." She took a sip of the strong brew and then reached for a stack of books that had been returned the previous afternoon, flipping through the brown wood box for the appropriate card. The library had yet to be computerized, but she preferred it this way. For the most part, she did not welcome change. Aware that Jenny was waiting, Hannah decided it was time to face the music. With a look of resignation, she said, "All right. I'm all ears. Tell me what I missed."

"I wouldn't be the first to point out that those pictures in the magazines didn't do him an ounce of justice. The man is downright delectable."

"Delectable." In her mind Hannah conjured up the image of the wide-shouldered man who'd appeared at her car window.

"And so athletic," Jenny said in a winsome tone, bending over the desk to rest her chin on one palm. "I just *love* a man who takes care of his body."

"He's an athlete all right." The brown leather bomber jacket he'd worn had done little to hide the well-honed body beneath. A body he was paid to hone, of course.

"And that smile. Why, half the women on Main Street were beside themselves. Swooning, practically."

"Really?"

"Imagine Lake Perdue turning out a man like that! He's as famous as any movie star," Jenny declared with an assertive nod.

"Think so?" Yes, he had turned out to be quite a man. A man who'd grown from a charming boy who could convince anyone to do anything into a man whose mere physical presence threw women like Jenny Dudley into swoons. Women like Jenny Dudley, not women like Hannah Jacobs.

Jenny straightened and sighed. "I know so. All you have to do is take one look at him to see that."

Hannah slid a card into a book and slapped the cover closed. "Then he shouldn't be lacking for female company while he's visiting."

"If I were ten years younger, I'd march out to that house he's renting in Tarkington's Cove and introduce myself. Rumor has it he might be staying awhile.

According to Kay Lynn over at Kelly's Realty, he took out a six-month lease on the big house—you know, the one the developer built to spec for himself and then decided to rent—"

"Six months?" Hannah looked up in surprise.

"That's what Kay Lynn said. They don't expect him to ever play pro ball again. Hurt his knee real bad in that game."

Hannah focused on the cards before her. "How do you know all this stuff, Jen?"

"I read about it. Lake Perdue doesn't have many famous residents."

"I guess not." Hannah's hand shook as she shoved a card into the last book and then grabbed a rag and scrubbed at the countertop. She knew exactly how Jenny knew. She'd been following the same accounts of his career, unable to help herself.

"Funny thing was, Kay Lynn said she was over at the First Baptist Church when Will pulled in yesterday. The front end of his fancy car had been crunched up like last week's newspaper. Tom Dillon had just seen him on Main Street and the car was fine. Darnedest thing, but he wouldn't say what happened."

Hannah scrubbed furiously at a nearly invisible ink spot. "Really?"

"A car like that. You'd think he'd have been hopping mad."

Before Hannah could reply, the front door opened. Henry Lawson stepped inside, his bulky frame catching Jenny's attention. Thankful for the diversion, Hannah said, "Morning, Mr. Lawson. How are you today?"

"Fine, fine, Miss Jacobs. Keeping busy as usual." The big man took off his hat and doffed it in Jenny's direction with a quick nod. "Mornin', Miss Dudley."

"Mr. Lawson," Jenny said, blushing. Henry Lawson's appearance put the subject of Will Kincaid on hold. She moved around the desk and said, "Can I get you anything to read this morning?"

Twisting his hat in his hands, he said, "Naw, I don't reckon. I'll find something interesting, no doubt."

Jenny nodded and cleared her throat. "Then you let me know if I can help you."

Hannah sighed. Thank goodness for Henry Lawson. "I think I'll go work on some of those torn bindings, Jenny. Call if you need me."

She quickly made for the back room before her friend had a chance to remember what they'd been discussing.

CHAPTER TWO

WILL KINCAID AWOKE on Saturday morning to the certainty that a marching band was playing inside his head.

Sunlight streamed in through his window, high enough in the sky to indicate ten o'clock had come and gone. He groaned and rolled over, pulling the feather pillow over his head. That last scotch had done it. God, he hated scotch. But it had been the only thing he could find in the boxes still packed in the basement. And after the day he'd endured, it had seemed the appropriate tonic for a much-desired bout of self-torture.

Drinking alone. They said people who drank alone had big problems. He supposed he qualified. In the last month his life had all but fallen apart.

It should not have been that way. He hadn't thought the Superbowl would be the end. Who the hell retired at the age of twenty-nine? Except for his damned knee, he'd never been healthier. What if he lived to be seventy-eight or, God help him, became another George Burns? What would he do with all those years in between? Live his life as a has-been? Yesterday's news?

With a heavy sigh, he rolled over and stared up at the ceiling, one arm thrown behind his head. One

thing he knew for certain. He couldn't stay in Lake
Perdue forever. Not with his father.

Sometimes he found it hard to believe that his father could always find something in him to be disappointed about. *Eight years of pro ball, but what about
that Superbowl, son? Finally a Superbowl, but you've
ruined it with that bum knee, son. Glad you made it
home in time for the parade, but what the hell happened to that hundred-thousand-dollar car, son?*

Will groaned. His eyes flew open, and he squinted
at the sunlight now bathing every corner of the room.
He'd forgotten all about the car. When he'd come
home last night intent on beginning his solo drinking
spree, the scotch had washed away all thoughts of the
incident. But he realized now it had been in the back
of his mind since yesterday afternoon. Not the car. But
the woman he'd run into. He recalled her face and realized he'd seen it in his dreams last night. The wool
cap pulled low over her forehead. The oversize glasses
that hid her eyes. And still there was something about
her, something so familiar, yet so different. He knew
her. She was a plainer, skinnier version of someone
he'd once known....

Hannah Jacobs.

The name hit him hard, a blow low in the stomach.
It had been Hannah. No doubt about it.

But what had happened to...

In the getup she'd been wearing, she'd looked
nothing like he'd remembered her. Before he had time
to reconsider, he got up and gingerly made his way to
the basement. There, he shuffled through five or six of
the boxes he'd had sent back from L.A. before pulling out his high-school yearbook, the red cover
scuffed, the edges worn. His right leg stretched out in

front of him, Will sat on a crate by the washing machine and flipped through the index for her name. Hannah Jacobs. Page 123.

He licked a finger and then leafed through the pages until he found her picture. Long honey-blond hair. Wide hazel-green eyes that, as he remembered, had a way of changing shades depending on what she wore. High cheekbones. A full generous mouth. Lips that tended toward red without the enhancement of lipstick. Lips he'd once discovered were infinitely kissable.

He rubbed a thumb across the picture and frowned. Lake Perdue High had boasted more flamboyant girls than Hannah Jacobs, but in his mind, she'd always had something that set her apart. Something appealing. Up until the last couple of months of their senior year, she'd always had a shy smile for him.

Shyness had been a part of Hannah the way brashness had been a part of the girls who had run around with Will's crowd. A crowd to which Hannah had never belonged. While other girls concentrated on cheerleading and dating, Hannah had spent her time studying. Everyone knew Hannah Jacobs made the highest SAT scores. She was smart. So smart that Will had felt like a real jerk trying to talk to her. But she'd been the only girl in school to look at him with eyes that seemed to see through to that spot deep inside him that even he refused to examine. That small spot he'd subdued until it no longer existed.

He stared at the washing machine in the corner and let her name play through his mind. Hannah Jacobs. God, it had been what, ten years? Ten years. A lifetime. And yet, it seemed like only yesterday that he'd mustered up the courage to walk by her locker on the off chance that some miracle would occur and he'd find a reason to talk to her. *Ah, you left your purse in class. Mrs. Smithers asked me to give you this book.* The excuses came flooding back as if he'd invented them yesterday.

Of course, that was before Tom Dillon had beaten him to the punch and asked her out first. Before Tom had told him all about his night with Hannah. Will had been dumbstruck. He couldn't believe that after the day he and Hannah had spent together at the lake she would . . .

He cut the thought off there, still strangely unwilling to let himself think about it.

He thought instead about the day he'd finally cornered her at school after a week of looking everywhere for her. He'd had no idea what he would say, simply that he had to know if what Tom had told him was true. Hannah had been facing her open locker, staring at a book on the top shelf, her back straight, her shoulders rigid.

His steps had slowed as he approached her, the words stuck in his throat. He touched her shoulder with one hand.

She whirled around as if he'd burned her, stumbling back against the locker.

The look in her eyes caught him off guard. "Hannah, I . . . I didn't mean to scare you."

She stared at him for several uncomfortable moments. And then without saying anything, she grabbed her book and slammed the door shut. Without looking at him again, she took off down the hall.

Something propelled him after her. He reached for her arm and pulled her to a stop. "Why have you been avoiding me, Hannah? Did you not have the guts to admit you were going out with my best friend?''

He watched the color leave her face. She swallowed visibly, then wrenched her arm free from his grasp. "Don't touch me, Will! I don't ever want you to touch me again!"

Beet-faced, he'd stood there staring after her. At that moment, all the doubts he'd had about himself and the likelihood of someone like Hannah being interested in him were confirmed.

Will got up from the crate, his cheeks burning with the memory. During the last two months of their senior year, they never spoke to one another again. But in the ten years since, he hadn't forgotten that incident. A person never forgot some things, whether it was a decade or half a century.

So why hadn't he recognized her yesterday? Something told him this Hannah Jacobs was not the Hannah Jacobs he'd taken to the lake that spring afternoon all those years ago. The young girl who'd laughed and teased when they'd given in to a little craziness and gone swimming together.

There had been no laughter in this Hannah's eyes. She'd made herself plain. Plain as most women her age would never think of doing. Camouflaging herself. Making herself as unnoticeable as possible. And that car. How many young women drove something that looked like that?

And for some reason, she'd pretended not to know him.

That was the part that really burned.

He knew as surely as he was standing there that the best thing he could do was forget he'd ever seen her.

Put the memories back in the past where they belonged.

But he also knew he couldn't do that. He wanted to know what Hannah Jacobs had done with her life.

With a sense of purpose he hadn't felt since the night he'd ruined his knee, Will made for the stairs, heading for the one place in Lake Perdue where everybody knew everything.

AN HOUR OR SO LATER, Will made his way into town at a more sedate pace than he had the afternoon before. He now sat behind the wheel of a new Jeep Cherokee. After the parade he'd called the local dealership and learned they only had one four-wheel drive left on the lot. He'd told the surprised salesman he'd take it.

And if the truth were known, he preferred a Jeep over that temperamental piece of Italian finery Hank Calhoun had insisted he accept. He flipped on his signal light and wheeled into Tate's One Stop Gas & Go, coming to a halt beside the pumps.

The teenage boy ambling out of the store spotted Will and hightailed it across the lot with a grin on his face. "Hey, Will! How ya doing?"

He climbed out of the vehicle and said, "Don't tell me you're Carl Johnson's boy."

The boy nodded, his grin widening. "That's right. Tim."

"You've done a little growing in the last few years. If you don't watch out, you're gonna be taller than your daddy."

Tim shrugged, his grin broadening. "Nah."

Will pointed to the Jeep and said, "How 'bout filling this thing up for me?"

"Sure thing, Will."

He watched for a moment as the boy eagerly yanked the nozzle from the pump and scurried for the tank. He felt as if he was seeing himself as he had been ten years ago, pumping gas for Aaron Tate every summer, carefree and maybe a little cocky, certain that regardless of his other shortcomings, football would be his "Let's Make a Deal." Behind the first few doors, he'd found more than most people ever dreamed of finding. Behind the last one, however, he'd found a bum knee and a road to nowhere.

"Aaron around, Tim?"

"He's inside."

Will headed across the gravel lot toward the old white clapboard store. Climbing the concrete stairs, he stepped inside to find that here, unlike the rest of the town, nothing had changed at all. The old cash register still sat to the left of the door—the kind you punched in by hand with a lever to open the drawer. Taped to the register hung the rules by which everyone who entered Tate's had abided for as long as Will could remember. Yellowed by the years, it read:

Granny Tate's Rules of Order

Grandma doesn't approve of:

smoking
drinking alcohol
bad language
conduct unbecoming to a lady or a gentleman

Will smiled every time he saw it. To the right of the register sat an old Coke cooler. The room smelled of fresh-baked ham and homemade bread, no doubt for the sandwiches local workers came in to buy at lunchtime. The same group of old-timers sat around the wood stove in rickety chairs, chewing tobacco and sharing the latest gossip. "Mornin', boys," he said.

A chorus of greetings went up as they all turned around at his voice.

"Well, hey, Will."

"Heck of a game, Will."

"Welcome home, boy. Glad to have you back."

A round of hand pumping and back thumping followed. Aaron Tate stepped out of the back storeroom just then, customary pipe in hand, his tobacco-rasped voice bellowing out a welcoming "Well, I'll be damned. Will. Good to see you, too, boy. Wondered when you'd come by."

"How's it going, Aaron? Damn, it's good to see you."

Aaron reached up to give Will a loose hug and a few welcoming slaps on the back. "Doing fine. You been gone too long. Here to stay awhile, I hope?"

Will shook his head and shrugged. "Don't really know yet. Have to see how things go."

Aaron made for the old cooler and pulled out a grape Nehi, wiping it across his overalls before slipping the neck of the bottle into the opener and popping the top. "Believe that used to be your drink of choice."

Will accepted the soda with a laugh. "Don't you know the rest of the country's quit selling these things in bottles?"

"Don't taste the same in cans far as I'm concerned."

Will guzzled half the bottle, then wiped his mouth with the back of his hand. "Sure don't."

The corners of Aaron's mouth lifted in a grin that revealed a missing molar. "Since you were her most famous student, Betsy's kept up with your comings and goings in the papers. I'd say you deserve a vacation if anyone ever did. How's the knee?"

Will relaxed for the first time since he'd been back. Why was it that he'd always felt more at home in this old store, among these people, than in his own father's house? "Better."

"Glad to hear it."

Will cleared his throat and lowered his voice so that only Aaron could hear. "Wanted to ask you a question, Aaron."

"Shoot."

"Don't know if you heard about it, but I had a little accident yesterday afternoon."

"Yeah, yeah. In that fancy car."

Of course Aaron had heard. Nothing stayed secret in Lake Perdue. Especially if it made it to the Tate grapevine. "Ran into the back of Hannah Jacobs. I need to talk to her. Any idea where I can find her?"

Aaron hooked his thumbs through the straps of his overalls. "Still lives over on Wilmington. But she works down at the town library. 'Spect she's there right now. It's open on Saturday morning. Till noon, I believe."

"Great. Thanks, Aaron." Will gave the man a fond slap on the shoulder.

"You come on back when you can stay and talk awhile."

"I'll do that," Will said. With a wave at the others in the store, he set off for the Cherokee.

AT EXACTLY ONE MINUTE past twelve, Hannah and Jenny, along with Henry Lawson, stepped outside the library doors. Hannah pulled a set of keys from her purse and closed the glass door, yanking at it to make sure it had locked. Fishing through the ring for her key, she glanced up to see the blue Cherokee parked beside her car. Her eyes widened at the sight of the man sitting behind the wheel. The steps that propelled her toward her car were no longer slow and ambling. She scrambled to get the key in the lock, pretending not to have seen him.

But Will Kincaid got out of the Jeep and crossed the asphalt. He was standing beside her before she'd opened the car door.

"Hannah."

Shock surged through her at the sound of her name on his lips. So, he'd finally remembered.

"Hannah, wait. I want to talk to you."

"I—I really have to go. I don't have time to—"

He caught hold of her wrist and turned her to face him. He looked down at her in confusion. "Why didn't you say who you were yesterday?"

She bit her lip and for the first time let herself really look at him. She'd avoided doing so the day before, telling herself she didn't want to see the ways in which he'd changed. Now, she realized, the changes had been for the better. The years had hacked away the boyishness of his high-school days, leaving in its place a man with nothing boyish about him. Those eyes— how could she have forgotten? Intelligent eyes in the face of a boy who did everything possible to present a very different image. Eyes she'd always had trouble meeting. Eyes that drew people to him.

As she recalled, it had always been that way with Will. Gazes followed him, lingered, assessed, yearned. Boys and girls alike had watched him, perhaps trying to determine the source of all that arresting charisma. And ten years ago, Hannah had been no exception.

Shaken now by the reality of the man who stood before her, she blinked once and said, "*I* recognized *you.*" The accusation in her voice sounded ridiculous even to herself, especially when she'd deliberately made herself unrecognizable.

Will let go of her wrist, then raked a hand through his hair. "It's been a long time, Hannah."

"Ten years." Although her hands were shaking, her voice held no trace of the turmoil inside her.

"You looked different. With that hat and those glasses...." Will gave her a look of bewilderment. "What are you doing, Hannah?"

"Going home for the day." She was so calm. So cool. So surprised by this indifference she'd dredged up from within herself.

He sighed and said, "That isn't what I meant. What have you been doing with your life?" He waved a hand in the direction of the old Cadillac and then up and down the plain navy wool jumper revealed beneath her open coat. "This isn't the Hannah Jacobs I knew."

"You never knew Hannah Jacobs." The assertion was soft and certain. She turned back to the car and tried once again to insert the key in the lock.

"What is this? I haven't seen you in ten years and you... Wait a minute," he said as she went on fumbling, giving a cry of frustration when the key refused to go in.

"Hannah, wait. Please."

His voice had gone soft. She heard the note of compassion in the words. And for the first time in years, sorrow welled inside her. If she didn't get away from him now, she would make a fool of herself. That couldn't happen. She wouldn't allow it. She closed her eyes for a moment and searched for words cutting enough to make him leave. "What made you come here today? Was it the realization that not everyone might have fared as well as you? Did you want to gloat?"

Will's eyes grew wide and he stepped back. He stared down at her and then held up a hand. "Okay. I can take a hint. Sorry I interfered," he said in a careful voice. "I can see you've got everything under control. I don't know what I was thinking. What you do with your life is none of my business."

Her chin tilted a fraction of an inch, and she pressed her lips together to keep from replying.

"Let me know if that's not enough money to fix your car. I'm staying down at Tarkington's Cove," he added as he backed away from her. He turned around and limped toward the Cherokee, slamming the door and then gunning it out of the parking lot.

The light wind pressed the boxwood hedges closer to the library walls. The breeze whipping at the bottom of her coat, Hannah wrapped her arms around herself and watched him go, eyes dry, swamped by feelings she'd thought shut away years ago.

THE REMAINING WEEKS of February were the longest Hannah had ever endured. A cold spell set in, and the temperature hovered just above freezing. She tried to forget the fact that Will was in Lake Perdue, living just minutes away from her, but restlessness tugged at her.

She felt as if she'd been on a bland diet for years, and someone had added a little seasoning to her food, making her aware of what she'd been missing.

Outwardly, she went about business as usual, getting her car fixed, going to work each morning, doing the children's hour at noon and chatting with Mr. Lawson on the days he came in. But inside she was a wreck.

Jenny persisted with attempts to discover the reason behind Hannah's pensive mood. Although Hannah assured her it was nothing more than the winter blahs, the other woman never let up. One Wednesday in March, Jenny fixed the two of them a cup of hot chocolate and brought it out front before saying, "The only way to lift your spirits, Hannah, is to get out a little more."

Hannah looked up from the desk where she had been alphabetizing a stack of past-due library cards. "I'm happy with my life as it is, Jen. Why would I want to change it?"

Jenny gave an unladylike snort. "You haven't looked all that happy to me lately. Anyway, it's not natural, I tell you. A young girl like you, never getting out and having fun. In the six years I've known you—"

"Twenty-eight hardly makes me a young girl," Hannah interrupted quickly.

"You've got your whole life ahead of you. Since Sarah moved into Meadow Spring, the only people you ever see are me and the people who come and go in this library."

Hannah made a note on one of the cards. "If that's true, then it's by choice. Besides, you ought to be working on your own social life. Shouldn't there be a man at home waiting for you every evening?'' The comment was more chastising than harsh.

The other woman rolled her eyes. "At least I'm looking. I've got my bingo game every Tuesday night. And then there's the ladies' breakfast every Thursday morning. How much looking is a woman supposed to do?''

Hannah thought of Henry Lawson. He was the only person capable of making Jenny Dudley tongue-tied. She smiled and said, "Maybe you aren't looking in the right places.''

"Maybe not. But we can look together on Friday. Mr. Tyree down at the county building called yesterday afternoon. There's a fund-raiser at the firehouse Friday night. He's expecting both of us to be there as a show of support.''

Hannah looked up from the cards she'd been sorting. "What?''

"Friday night. No ifs, ands or buts. It's perfect, if you ask me. You might actually enjoy yourself.''

Just then, eight-year-old Mary Jane Kelly scuffed up to the front desk in sneakers that squeaked against the linoleum floor and plopped her books on the countertop. Jenny smiled at the little girl, thanked her for returning the books and then continued on in a nonchalant voice, "At least it won't be boring. Will Kincaid's agreed to be there. Fire department's hoping to sell a lot of tickets that way. It's nice of him to donate his time, don't you think?''

Jenny's last words were lost on Hannah. She'd heard nothing other than that Will Kincaid would be there. He'd be there and she would not. "I don't think I'll be able to go, Jenny. I—''

"Oh, no you don't," Jenny said, wagging a finger at Hannah. "Mr. Tyree said attendance was mandatory. And I'm not going to cover for you. Do you think I'm passing up this opportunity to get you out of that house of yours? Uh-uh."

Hannah pressed her hand against her forehead. How would she face Will Kincaid after what had happened the last time they met? How many times since that afternoon had she relived the scene, berating herself for letting her emotions get so close to the surface? She couldn't see him again, she couldn't. But she didn't have a choice.

She didn't have a choice, and she could forget about any help from Jenny.

ON FRIDAY NIGHT, Will stood near the back of the Lake Perdue firehouse, surrounded by a group of men that included Aaron Tate and Tom Dillon. It was the first time he'd been out in public in weeks. He could now walk without limping, and although his knee was better, his attitude wasn't. The only time he'd left the house was to drive in to Roanoke to have an orthopedic specialist take a look at his leg. Other than that, he'd sat in front of the television watching tapes of some of his best games. And brooding. Brooding about a future he refused to contemplate.

And while he cursed himself for his own stupidity, he'd spent far too much time thinking about Hannah Jacobs. Replaying their conversation in the library parking lot. History had a way of repeating itself, so they said. Indeed, it had. And he'd helped it along with the same blind spot he'd been guilty of ten years before. Refusing to see her for who she was. Certain she wasn't the person Tom had made her out to be.

So he tried not to think about her. He went fishing one day and poked a hook in his finger when his thoughts strayed. Another afternoon he rented a boat over at the Lake Perdue dock, wrapped himself in a winter parka and cut waves up and down the lake, only to be reminded of an afternoon he'd spent with Hannah on this same lake years earlier.

And now the last thing he wanted to do was make small talk with Tom, who immediately brought Hannah to mind with less than pleasant memories. It was the first time they'd met face-to-face since the day Will had returned to town. As a boy, Tom had been an All-American Opie Taylor. But the years had thinned his reddish-brown hair to a thatch that resembled a rooster's comb. And his eyes were a little too close together, giving him an air of perpetual befuddlement.

Will had only run into Tom a couple of times in the past ten years. It had been just as well. By the end of their senior year, their friendship hadn't been the same.

As they'd slipped from boyhood into adolescence, Will had grown more and more uncomfortable with Tom's claims that Will had gotten more than his fair share of athletic genes and that the rest of them had been shortchanged. Will had forgotten all about that, until now. But Tom still seemed to think Will could walk on air. Will wished he knew how to tell him it wasn't so.

Aaron clapped Will on the shoulder and said, "See you later." The other men moved away, as well, leaving Will and Tom standing together against the cement-block wall.

"When you gonna get out to Clarence's for that beer?" Tom asked with a grin, one thumb hooked in his pants pocket.

"Been meaning to do that. Guess I haven't felt too much like socializing since I got back."

"Aw, I can understand that," Tom sympathized with a shrug that emphasized the folds of his now too-thick neck. "Heck of a bum rap, messing up that knee for good. Any idea what you'll be doing now that you won't be playing football?"

Will took a sip of lemonade, surveying the room over the rim of his glass. "Nope. Guess that's the problem."

"Be kinda hard to come back here after the life you must have had out in L.A."

"It had its drawbacks," Will said, looking toward the front of the room again.

"Who you looking for?" Tom's forehead wrinkled in a frown.

Will shot him a startled glance. "Nobody," he said quickly.

"Well, I'll be damned." Tom did a double take as he looked in the direction of the door.

Will's gaze followed Tom's across the room, and he knew then what he'd been looking for.

Something inside him jolted. She looked different tonight somehow. Maybe it was the conspicuous absence of the wool cap and scarf she'd been bundled up in the afternoon he'd run into her. Now she looked more the way he remembered her. Standing there in the crowd, Hannah reminded him of Michelle Pfeiffer. Although the likeness wasn't so much feature by feature, she had the same full, vulnerable mouth and that air of "There's a secret here, but I'm tough enough to handle it, so don't you worry about it."

But Hannah didn't have the bearing that came with being recognized as one of the world's loveliest women. And he knew she would never have believed anyone would make the comparison.

"Haven't seen her out in ages," Tom said when Will remained silent. "That friend of hers must have dragged her in by the ear."

Will frowned at Tom. "What do you mean?"

"She don't get out too much. Keeps to herself, you know."

"Why?"

Tom shrugged. "How should I know? Guess she likes being an old maid. What is this, anyway? Twenty questions?"

Tom's resounding laughter grated on Will's nerves. Suddenly he'd had enough of his old friend. But despite his desire to escape, he found himself asking one more question. The one that had been at the back of his mind for years. "Whatever happened between you and Hannah, anyway? Thought you were pretty hot and heavy for a while there."

Tom shrugged awkwardly. "Guess she decided variety might just be the spice of life." He chuckled, a just-between-us-guys sort of laugh.

Will stared at the other man for a long moment, straight-faced, wondering why the words didn't quite ring true.

"Not that it makes a whole lot of difference. Doesn't look the way she used to, does she? Too damn skinny for my taste."

Will frowned. It was time to put some distance between himself and Tom Dillon. He had no reason even to like Hannah Jacobs, and yet he found himself wanting to defend her.

"Suppose I ought to mingle a bit," Will said abruptly. "Be seeing you, Tom."

"You come on out to Clarence's, now. We'll see if we can't pick up your spirits a bit."

Ignoring the invitation, Will wound his way to the front of the room.

HANNAH PULLED her coat closer about her as she and Jenny stepped through the doorway and stopped on the edge of the crowd. From the looks of things, every citizen within the county limits had decided to show up tonight in support of the volunteer fire department. She'd never seen anything like it. The walls were lined with people.

The smell of barbecued meat vied with the odors of cigarette smoke and brewing coffee. Conversation rose like a lion's roar from every corner of the room, and Hannah had to read Jenny's lips when she suggested they go hang up their coats.

When Jenny saw someone she knew and went over to say hello, Hannah found a corner and parked herself. Perhaps if she pretended not to be there, no one would notice her. The technique had worked when she was a child. No reason it still couldn't.

Just as she began to relax, she spotted a set of wide shoulders moving toward her. She let her gaze travel up to the eyes that now stared directly at her. She stepped back as though the corner might somehow shield her. But it did not, and she stood there, panicking when no escape route materialized.

"I didn't expect to see you here tonight." The voice was low and controlled.

She straightened her shoulders and stepped forward, trying to smile but failing miserably. "Hello, Will. I understand you'll be speaking after dinner."

"Yeah." He shrugged. "Let's hope they're serving coffee after the meal. Wouldn't want everybody to fall asleep."

Hannah clasped her hands in front of her and looked down. "I'm sure you won't have to worry about that."

He watched her for a moment and then said, "I saw an old friend of ours a little while ago."

"We never had mutual friends." She kept the remark deliberately light.

"Yes, we did."

She looked up and said, "No, we—"

"Tom Dillon." He dropped the name like a water balloon from twenty stories, his eyes searching her face as if waiting for its impact.

She made sure she disappointed him, smiling when she said, "How nice."

"Guess you run into him pretty often?" he fished.

"Actually, no." This without elaboration.

He shrugged and then shot her a grin. "Hey, you wanna call a truce for the night?"

Trying to stay calm, she said, "Truces are for people with differences. And since we aren't likely to run into one another again, I don't really see how it would matter one way or the other."

The fire chief picked up the microphone just then and requested that everyone take a seat for the meal.

Will stared at her for a long moment, shifted his weight from one foot to the other. "Ahh...would you like to sit with me at dinner?"

She looked up at him in surprise. "What?"

He shoved a hand in his pocket, his voice a little gruffer when he repeated, "Would you like to sit with me?"

She remained silent for a full five seconds. The question had caught her off guard. She looked around the room. The only available chairs were at the table where Tom Dillon was sitting. She swallowed and found herself saying, "Well . . . I guess . . . all right."

Will's eyes widened when she agreed. He nodded once, then took her arm and led her to the front of the room where a couple of seats had been reserved in his honor.

CHAPTER THREE

A HALF HOUR LATER, Hannah began to feel a little less like she'd stepped into a dream. Jenny had spotted her at the front and given her a look that promised a whole truckload of questions at the first opportunity. She'd then moved to a table where Henry Lawson was holding her a seat.

Hannah and Will shared the table with six others, among them, Will's father, John Kincaid, who'd been shooting her curious looks from the moment they'd sat down. She knew little about the man except that he'd grown up in what amounted to a tar-paper shack outside town, had made a fortune in real estate and married the only child of what had once been one of the county's most prominent families.

It was obvious at a glance that Will was his son. Physically, anyway. Otherwise, she'd always heard there were many differences.

John Kincaid had acquired a reputation around Lake Perdue for his ability to convince others. He had charm, they said. But it was different from Will's. There was nothing boyish or innocent about it. The elder Kincaid's methods of getting what he wanted ran in a different vein. He left one with the impression that if it wasn't offered, he would simply take it.

Next to Kincaid sat Mayor Nichols, who reminded Hannah of a Mr. Potato Head with his oblong face, bushy brows and short protruding ears. He'd made a ten-minute speech to the rest of the room about how grateful he was to Will for making an appearance this evening.

Once the mayor had sat down, Will set out to make Hannah more comfortable. Although the men seemed intent on keeping him talking about football, he took every opportunity to turn to her and discuss such things as whether the library still ran its weekly bookmobile. The bookmobile had driven to different parts of the county once a week with a new selection of books for those who might not have a way to get into town.

"We had to stop running it last year," Hannah told him, surprised at his interest. "We ran out of funding."

The mayor looked up from his plate and shot them all a diplomatic smile. "Can't keep everything the same. Had to cut somewhere."

Will took a swallow of ice water. "I remember Aunt Fan used to take me out to meet it once a week. Dad was usually too busy to go into town, so it worked out better that way. Bet a lot of kids are in the same situation."

John Kincaid pulled out a cigarette. "Don't know why you wanted all those books, anyway, son. You never read them. Just looked at the pictures."

Will swallowed visibly and glanced away. When he looked back again, his smile held no indication that his father's words had bothered him. "Never was much of an academic, was I?" The remark was light, but self-deprecating, nonetheless.

"That you weren't," the older Kincaid concurred.

Hannah spoke up for the first time since they'd sat down. Her voice sounded surprising even to her ears. "Lots of children prefer looking at the pictures until they can read on their own. Children love being read to."

Will met her eyes, a half smile playing on his lips. "Aunt Fan always thought so. Couldn't see worth a darn, but she always made sure I had a story before I went to bed."

"As a single parent, I didn't have much time for that myself," John said defensively. The table remained silent for a moment before he added, "Looks like my boy made out all right, though, doesn't it?"

The table broke into motion again, faces smiling, shoulders shrugging, hands fiddling with forks. The mayor slapped Will on the shoulder. "Sure does. We're all proud of you, Will."

Hannah sensed that more had been said than she or anyone else might have guessed. Will looked up, his gaze meeting hers. For a brief moment, the faces and voices around them faded. In his eyes, she glimpsed something she'd imagined she'd seen once or twice in high school. Uncertainty. Vulnerability. The day of senior assembly when he'd been recognized as having won two senior superlatives: Best-Looking and Best Athlete. The day Mr. Wilks had bragged to the class about the chemistry project she and Will had completed.

She was startled to glimpse traces of that uncertainty and vulnerability now, when he'd made it to the top, as far as the rest of the world was concerned. She saw those things in herself. But to see them in Will Kincaid? Impossible. She'd imagined it. With his bounty of confidence, the idea of his being uncertain about anything seemed laughable.

She didn't have a chance to second-guess herself, though. The sudden smile that Will flashed her extinguished any traces of what might have been in his eyes moments before.

WHEN WILL HAD GIVEN his speech and thanked the crowd for inviting him that evening, everyone began standing up to leave. Hannah said goodbye to the other people at her table and cut a path for the front door. She'd gotten halfway through the crowd when Jenny caught her arm and said, "Wait up. Boy, do you have some explaining to do!"

Hannah turned and shot an uneasy glance over her shoulder. "Not now, Jenny. I'll explain later. Are you ready to go?"

But before Jenny could reply, Will stepped up to Hannah's side and put a hand on her arm. "There you are. Thought I'd lost you."

She looked up and tried to smile. She could feel her friend's eyes boring into her back, and so, against every instinct, she turned and said, "This is my friend Jenny Dudley. Jenny, Will Kincaid."

"Oh, my goodness!" Jenny exclaimed. "So nice to meet you, Mr. Kincaid."

"It's Will," he returned with a smile that Hannah felt certain would dissolve Jenny's insides.

"I've kept track of your career. It's so nice to have you back in Lake Perdue. Why, Hannah didn't tell me she knew you—"

"We can leave now, Jenny, if you're ready," she interrupted.

The other woman pulled her gaze away from Will and nodded with a frown in Hannah's direction. "All right. I'll get the car."

"Did you come here with Miss Dudley, Hannah?"

"It's Jenny," the older woman asserted. "And yes, she did."

"If it's all right with you, Jenny," he said, "I'll give Hannah a lift home. I'm going in that direction, anyway."

Hannah began shaking her head. "No, no. Really. Jenny goes right by my house."

Jenny looked at Will and then Hannah. Her face lit up. "That might be better. I'd like to hang around a bit longer and since you're ready to go..."

"I can wait," Hannah said quickly.

"I'm ready, too," Will said, taking Hannah by the arm and turning toward the door. "No sense holding your friend up. Be seeing you, Jenny. I'll get her home safely."

Hannah only caught a glimpse of Jenny's mischievous smile before Will had led her out of the room.

They had barely cleared the doorway of the firehouse when Hannah rounded on him, her shoulders stiff with indignation. "Why did you do that?"

"I offered to take you home. That's all." He shrugged, as though the gesture had been planned for months.

She looked away, then folded her arms across her chest. "I don't want you to take me home."

He nodded. "I know."

"You know?" Her chin jutted.

He nodded again. "Yes, I know."

"Then, why... what..."

He shoved a hand in one pocket. "From what I've seen since I've been back, you work pretty hard at looking as blank as that concrete wall behind you. It was worth the chance you might have me arrested for abduction just to see you with your feathers ruffled." His face broke out in a grin. "They're definitely ruffled."

"They're not ruffled," she denied vehemently, as if he'd just accused her of stealing food stamps out of Tate's cash register.

Will's smile grew wider as he soundlessly mouthed, "They're ruffled."

She tried to move her lips, but found that no sound came out. When the words came, they were calm, measured. "Now that you've cracked my composure, I'm supposed to call a cab?"

His shoulders shook with silent laughter. He took her by the arm and pointed her in the direction of the parking lot. "Nope. I have every intention of taking you home."

"A true gallant."

"I've been accused of worse."

"I don't doubt that for a minute."

He stopped in the grass just beyond the firehouse and looked down at her. An overhead streetlight illuminated them. They stood that way for long moments, studying one another with questioning eyes. Several people turned to stare at them, nodding amiably as if the town's very flashy, very famous pro football player standing on the lawn chatting with its very subdued, very unremarkable librarian was nothing out of the ordinary.

"Why don't you take me home before the whole town gets a chance to wonder if we're both crazy?"

His smile dimmed. "All right," he said. "But only if you agree to a cup of coffee first."

She wanted to hate him for the innate gift he had of convincing. In that respect, he hadn't changed in the past ten years. In that respect, neither had she. She was no different from the girl she had been. She could do nothing more than nod in agreement.

THE LAKE PERDUE CAFE was on Main, next to the courthouse. At some point in Lake Perdue's history, it had been a general store. In the years since, it had become a restaurant, its front windows accented by green shutters, the double wooden doors decorated with a grapevine wreath topped by a bow of the same color. The café was well-known for its homemade Southern-style biscuits. Gladys Carter had been making them three times a day for the past twenty-five years, serving them with anything from gravy to apple butter.

When Hannah and Will stepped inside the front door, most of the patrons seemed to forget about the food in front of them. Heads popped up, and the place fell silent.

Hannah swallowed the urge to turn and run.

Will, on the other hand, appeared not to mind in the least that the gazes followed them to the back of the café. She supposed he'd grown used to it. He smiled at Aaron and Betsy Tate, who looked as surprised as the rest of the crowd. Will raised one hand in greeting, keeping the other at Hannah's elbow, as if aware she might bolt at any moment.

He didn't know how right he was.

He helped her off with her coat and then stood as she slid into the booth, before taking the seat opposite her.

A waitress appeared immediately, menus in hand. When Hannah looked up and met Louella Hanes's gaze, she wanted to melt into her seat. She'd graduated with Louella, who now stood at the edge of the table, looking from Will to her as though certain she must be seeing things.

"Hannah Jacobs. Haven't seen you out in a coon's age."

Hannah cleared her throat and said, "Louella. How are you?"

"Not as good as you, obviously." The woman sent Will a knowing look. "How you doing, Will? Wondered when you'd get around to visiting us. Never thought Hannah'd be the one to bring you in."

"Yeah, well, she insisted, so..." He let the words trail off, casting an amused glance at Hannah, before he said, "You're looking good, Louella. Life must be treating you all right."

"Not as good as it's been treating you." She laughed and with her gaze still on Will, she added, "Nor Hannah, apparently."

A wave of heat blazed a path on Hannah's cheeks. She remembered only too well the torch Louella Hanes had carried for Will in high school. How dare he bring her here, subject her to the scrutiny of half of Lake Perdue, then act as if she'd initiated the whole thing? "I'll have some coffee, Louella," she managed through set lips.

"Regular or decaf?"

"Regular."

"How about you, sugar?" Louella directed at Will.

"The same. And a couple biscuits with apple butter to go with it."

Louella sent him another smile that could have melted the stainless-steel utensils set out before them. "Be right back."

As Louella headed for the counter, Hannah leaned back in her seat and crossed her arms. "What was that all about?"

"Those feathers again. I kinda like them ruffled."

She looked away and refused to let the smile tickling the back of her throat break past her lips. The man was unbelievable. "I don't know why I let you talk me into this."

Will played the confused innocent. "A cup of coffee?"

"Putting myself on public display for the whole town of Lake Perdue to gossip about."

His voice softened. "Why do you care what they say?"

She avoided his eyes. "I don't have to tell you that you're the hottest topic on record around here. I'd rather not give the likes of Louella any reason to link my name with yours."

He clasped his hands and leaned forward to force her to meet his eyes. "That would really bother you, wouldn't it?"

Taken aback by the chagrin in his voice, she said, "It's just... I'm a private person."

"So I've seen."

She looked up at the knowing note in his voice. "What do you mean?"

"Just... you keep to yourself."

"There's nothing wrong with that."

His head tilted. "Not if you're ninety-four and in poor health. But you're twenty-eight. And you look perfectly healthy to me."

Before she could reply, Louella returned with the coffee and biscuits. She set Hannah's down in front of her, sloshing some of the hot liquid over the side of the cup. She then turned to slide Will's across the table with an efficiency that kept the biscuits and apple butter firmly in place and every drop of coffee in the cup. She laid the check in the middle of the table and said, "Good to have you in, Will. You come on back again."

Hannah reached for a napkin and began soaking up coffee, resisting the sudden urge to laugh. When Louella sauntered to another table, she whispered, "And leave her at home."

Will glanced up with a startled look on his face. "She didn't say that."

"She didn't have to." Hannah took a sip of coffee, wondering where that remark had come from. And what difference did it make, anyway? "Don't worry. I know I'm not here as your date. And so does everyone else. Your efforts to head an old maid off at the pass are admirable. But I'm happy as I am."

"Anyone ever accuse you of being direct?"

"Louella's perfectly welcome to flirt with you all she wants. Whether I'm here or not."

He rolled his eyes and, picking up his knife, sliced the biscuit in two. "Louella was not coming on to me."

She gave him an appraising look. "I may not get out much, but I'm not blind."

"All right. So she was," he allowed with a shrug. "Since it bothers you so much, we can go somewhere else."

She fiddled with the edges of a napkin. "It doesn't bother me in the least."

"Could've fooled me," he said, a smile tugging at the corners of his mouth.

"I was merely pointing out that it was a mistake to bring me with you. You'd be freer to do as you choose—"

"Hannah," he interrupted, "I'm doing exactly what I choose to be doing tonight. And if you would just forget about Louella, maybe we could talk about something else. Besides, don't you think the term old maid is a little outdated?"

She shrugged indifferently. "Figure of speech."

"Twenty-eight is hardly an old maid."

She lowered her head and took a hasty swallow of coffee, scorching her tongue in the process. She pressed her lips together, her eyes squeezed shut.

He reached across the table and put his hand on top of hers, "Are you all right?"

She jerked back her hand, his touch more unsettling than the hot liquid that moments ago had singed her tongue. "I'm fine."

"No, you're not. Here, let me see."

An exasperated sigh accompanied her reply. "I am not going to stick my tongue out for your inspection right here under the noses of half the town."

"Then let's go. I'll look at it in the car."

He started to get up, but she reached out a hand to stop him. "Please, don't make a scene. I live here. You can create a stir wherever you go, because you won't be around to hear about it. That's not true for me. So, please—"

"Okay, Hannah." He sat back down, his tone gentle as he added, "Sure you're all right?"

"Fine."

Awkwardness hung in the air as she searched for a way to change the subject. She finally asked, "What are you doing here, anyway, Will?"

"Here, as in this very moment?"

"In Lake Perdue. You don't belong here anymore."

He cocked a brow. "That's blunt."

"You've been gone ten years. Lake Perdue must seem incredibly boring after living in Los Angeles."

"Things move a little faster there, I'll admit. But believe it or not, the change in scenery has felt good for the most part."

"Why *did* you come back?" The question wavered on her lips. The answer seemed suddenly very important.

"I could probably give you ten different reasons. Only problem is, I'm not sure any of them would be accurate."

"Try."

He surveyed her silently, then said, "One, it seemed like a good time to straighten things out with my father. Two, I was at a turning point and didn't know what else to do. And three, there's just something about home that you never find anywhere else, no matter how far you go." He paused. "Well, that was three, anyway."

She looked away, pleased for some reason to learn that Lake Perdue still appealed to him. "Are you . . . I mean, I guess you're trying to decide where to go from here."

"You could say that." He looked down at his coffee cup. "This injury sort of pulled the rug out from under me."

Her voice softened. "That unexpected, hmm?"

"I'd been warned it was a possibility. But absolutes are a lot harder to swallow than maybes."

"Then your playing days are definitely over?"

"That's what they tell me. I'd prefer to wait and see."

She sent him a surprised look. "What if you weren't able to walk on it again? You'd risk that?"

He sighed and slid lower into his seat. "On the days when I think about the future and wonder what I'm going to do with my life, yes, I'd risk it."

"But there are so many other things to live for."

"For other people, maybe. But when the only thing you know is football..."

She opened her mouth to disagree, but then closed it abruptly, looked down at her lap and said, "It's hardly my place to be giving you advice on how to spend the rest of your life. We barely know each other."

His voice dropped a note or two when he said, "We were always so different. And a lot of years have gone by. But I felt like I knew you then. I still do for some crazy reason."

She looked up at him. How many times had she felt the same thing? She could have counted on one hand the occasions they'd been alone together. But there had always been something there. Some instinct of self-preservation pressed her to deny it. "We lived in different worlds, Will."

"I'll admit that, but what about you, Hannah? I never thought you'd stay around here."

"And become an old maid?"

"That's not what I meant."

She tried to smile. "Sometimes the maps we draw for ourselves create their own detours."

"You went on to college, I heard. What happened to that Ivy League school you were headed for? Your plans to teach at a university, to write a book one day?"

She looked down at her fingernails and blinked back a short start of pleasure. He'd remembered the hopes she'd admitted on that long-ago afternoon by the lake. How could she tell him that writing about the problems and realities of other peoples' lives seemed impossible for someone who could not face those in her own? "I decided to go somewhere close by. I—I wanted to be able to help Aunt Sarah with things at home."

"And the book?"

"A person doesn't have to create them to enjoy them."

Will frowned and took another sip of his coffee. "I remember hearing your aunt at church one day, bragging about your being chosen class valedictorian. She seemed happy that you'd be going up north somewhere."

Hannah reached for a sugar packet. "Like I said, Will, things change."

"Yeah, I guess they do."

She slid her coffee cup toward the center of the table and said, "I need to be getting home now. It's late."

He watched her for a moment, looking as if he wanted to disagree. Finally he said, "All right, Hannah. If that's what you want."

WILL AWOKE earlier than usual the next morning, a tension headache pounding at his temples. Dreams punctuated his sleep, disturbing images of himself sitting in a reclining chair, white-haired and old without ever knowing again the fulfillment of doing something worthwhile.

Worthwhile. A lot of folks would debate the worthiness of a football career. Granted, he hadn't saved starving children or discovered a miracle cure for some serious illness. But football had been Will's reason for getting up every morning.

Now, he didn't have one.

The doorbell interrupted his bout of self-pity, the quick staccato sound making his head pound all the harder. Will closed his eyes and groaned. Who the hell...?

He swung out of bed, reached for his robe and made his way to the door. Jerking a hand through his hair, he unbolted the latch and yanked the door open, squinting against the sudden onslaught of sunlight.

"Dad. What are you doing here?"

John Kincaid stood almost eye to eye with his son. Dressed in pleated khaki pants and a starched white shirt with a red silk tie, he was a handsome man. He'd held his age well. With a casual shrug, he said, "Can't a father come visit his son once in a while?"

"A father would do well to call first," Will said wryly, waving him inside.

"Since when do I need an invitation?" Will let the question go unanswered as John Kincaid stepped in and closed the door behind him. His glance took in the pizza boxes stacked on the kitchen counter and the empty beer cans decorating the coffee table. "I see I took you by surprise," John said.

Will rubbed at his eyes. "You could say that."

"Looks like you could use Fannie's help out here."

Will went to the kitchen to pour himself a glass of orange juice, answering over his shoulder. "Aunt Fan doesn't need to come out and clean for me."

"Well, someone does," John Kincaid argued with a wave of his hand. "Neatness never was your strength."

Returning to the living room, Will took a gulp of juice and leveled a stare at his father. What *had* been his strength? "No one sees it but me. What's the big deal?" He crossed the room and sank into a chair.

John studied him as if he didn't quite recognize him. "You got a hangover?"

"What is this? An inquisition?" Will kept his voice even. Considering that he wasn't in the mood for this scene, it was an effort.

John answered the question with one of his own. "What are you doing, son?"

"Is this a loaded question?"

John ignored that. "What are you doing with your *life?*"

Will clasped his hands behind his neck and let his head fall back against the chair. A thread of irritation knotted its way up his spine. What right did his father have— He cut the thought off there. Funny that he'd asked Hannah the very same thing. "I don't think I can answer that. To be honest, I'm not too sure myself."

"You've been here a month now," John managed with just the right note of incredulity. "You must have some idea of the direction you're headed." He paused for effect. "Your mother would be disappointed to see you floundering like this."

"I'm sure she would, Dad." The response held a note of belligerence.

John Kincaid sighed and sat on the couch. "You have so many options. What about all the commercials you've been offered? Engagements you've been asked to speak at?"

"The last thing I want is to wake up in a year and see myself on TV telling someone why I prefer a certain type of underwear. Is that so wrong?"

John made a visible effort to curb his frustration. "Right now you could pick and choose what you wanted to do. And the money—"

"I don't need it. The amount I've made over the past few years is obscene. I couldn't spend it all if I tried."

"That's not the point, Will. You earned it."

"Yeah, and I've got a ruined knee to prove it."

"Is this pity I hear in your voice?" John asked gruffly. "My God, son, do you know how many people would give anything to be where you've been?"

"'Been' is the key word."

"Like I said, there are a lot of options open to you."

"Most of which I'm not interested in."

John sighed heavily. "So you'd rather hang around here doing nothing for the rest of your life? Escorting the likes of that Hannah Jacobs around town when you could be in California dating movie stars and models?"

The clock over the mantel chimed eleven and seemed to keep time with the pounding in Will's head. He pressed his lips together and remained silent until the last *dong* sounded. "I wondered when you'd get around to that."

"It looks absurd. She's the town librarian, for God's sake. Your mother—"

"—would have liked her had she known her," Will finished for him. "The years haven't shortchanged you on directness. My mother taught me to look beyond the surface. She once told me it was something she wished she'd practiced earlier in life."

The dig was unmistakable. John blanched. "I'm only looking out for what's best for you."

"Who I see while I'm in Lake Perdue is up to me. Hannah Jacobs is an old friend. And I'd appreciate your keeping your opinions to yourself."

John rolled his eyes. "What the hell do the two of you have in common, anyway? Most people think she's a recluse."

"Maybe most people don't know her."

John let out a sigh and gave Will a wide smile. "I didn't come here to argue with you. But it's time you got on with your life. Following the only path a famous football player can. Doing something worthwhile—"

"Being seen with the kind of woman you think I ought to be seen with," Will interrupted.

John shrugged.

Will made a tent of his fingers and leaned forward to rest his chin on them, pondering his father's words. A fragment of last night's dinner conversation ran through his mind. He did a mental backtrack and dwelled a moment on the idea that was spawned. It only took a second for the notion to blossom and grow, leaving him for the first time in weeks eager and curious. Only a fraction of that enthusiasm showed in his voice when he said, "You're right about one thing, Dad. It's time I did something worthwhile. Maybe I'll get started today. So, if you don't mind, I need a shower. I've got a few things to do."

"That's my boy. I knew you'd come to your senses sooner or later." John stood and slapped Will on the back. "You know I only want what's best for you, son. That's all I ever wanted. If I sometimes push a little too hard, it's—"

"Yeah, Dad, I know."

John shrugged into his coat and moved toward the door. "Let me hear from you."

Will stood at the door watching as his father climbed into his Mercedes and backed out of the driveway.

CHAPTER FOUR

AT TEN MINUTES past twelve, Hannah stepped outside and locked the library door behind her. She'd been on her own this Saturday. Jenny had awakened with the flu and called in sick. Although she'd felt sorry for Jenny, Hannah hadn't minded being given a day's reprieve from the barrage of questions the other woman would no doubt have in store for her concerning the Friday-night fund-raiser.

The Friday-night fund-raiser. Hannah had known some strange Saturdays, but this one topped the list. The morning had started off with Hal Downing coming into the library for the first time since she'd been working there. He'd been widowed for three years. And according to Jenny, he was looking for a wife.

He'd thumbed through a few books in the nonfiction section and then, picking one out, brought it up to the desk, greeting Hannah with a smile that emphasized the wrinkles around his eyes. All in all, he was an attractive man with work-roughened hands and an easygoing manner that gave him a certain appeal. "Reckon spring ought to be on its way anytime now," he said with a nod as he waited for her to stamp his card.

"I'm looking forward to it," she said, smiling at him.

Hal took the book from her and cleared his throat. "Saw you at the fund-raiser last night. A good turn-out, I'd say."

"Yes, it was."

Hal cleared his throat again. "Ah, I wondered if you might be free next weekend, Miss Jacobs."

She looked at him in complete surprise. It had been a long time since that particular question had been asked of her. Her experience with the opposite sex was all but unheard of these days. She'd received plenty of invitations the first couple of years of college. Class-mates. A professor or two. Several of whom had accused her of playing hard to get when she'd turned them down. Eventually her constant refusals took root, and men stopped asking. She now wondered if Hal's invitation stemmed from the fact that last night had been the first social gathering she'd attended in years, or if it had something to do with her being seen with Will Kincaid.

"I—I appreciate the offer, Mr. Downing, but—"

"Would some other time be better?" he asked un-certainly.

"Ah, not right now, I don't think." She looked down at her hands. "But thank you for asking."

Hal stood there, studying her for a moment before saying, "Let me know if you change your mind, Miss Jacobs."

And with that, he'd turned and left the library, leaving the book on the front desk.

Hannah pulled her coat tight against the late Feb-ruary chill, and set out for her car, coming to a halt when she noticed Will's Cherokee again parked be-side her.

He got out of the vehicle and headed toward her, the breeze ruffling his slightly wavy blond hair. Odd how wonderful a man could look in faded blue jeans and a worn leather jacket. She flushed at the realization of how glad she was to see him. Her voice quavered a little when she said, "Will, I—I didn't expect to see you here."

"I wanted to talk with you."

"I'm afraid I have to go." She tried to sidestep him, but he reached out for her arm and pulled her to a stop.

"Just a minute, Hannah." The request soft and cajoling. "I think it's something you'll be interested in."

She sighed. "I thought I'd made it clear last night that it would be best if we didn't see each other. I don't want everyone in town to think—"

"Who *cares* what everyone thinks?"

The question sounded so reasonable that she had trouble finding a reply. "You don't have to live here."

"Okay. But what if it's for a good cause?" he asked with an engaging grin.

She looked at him suspiciously. "What kind of good cause?"

He folded his arms and shivered. "It's cold out here. Let's go for a drive, and I'll tell you all about it."

The request sounded simple enough. And for anyone else, under any other circumstances, it might have been. But she still felt compelled to say, "If this is some kind of—"

"It's not a ploy just to get you to come with me."

"I wasn't going to say that," she said, feeling foolish.

"Yes, you were. So don't deny it."

With a sigh, she looked at him and smiled in spite of herself. Will Kincaid, with his lighthearted approach to life, was a difficult man to say no to. Certain she would live to regret the impulse, she said, "All right, I'll come."

A few minutes later, they were headed out of town, racing past the new pizza place and Tate's Gas & Go, past fields ready to be planted and construction signs announcing the development of soon-to-come subdivisions on the lake. Thus far, they had driven in silence.

Hannah searched for words. "Did you get your car fixed?"

"It's in the shop. Had it sent up to the city. But to be honest, I'd rather be driving this old thing." Will flipped on the radio, and a song she hadn't heard in years crooned through the speakers. "Afternoon Delight," by a group whose name she couldn't recall.

"Remember that one?" Will asked with a smile of nostalgia.

She nodded and said, "It seemed the height of rebellion when I sneaked into the Melody Shop and bought it. I was afraid Aunt Sarah would hear the lyrics and not let me play it."

He chuckled. "I guess by today's standards, it'd be considered pretty tame, huh?"

"Probably," she said. Nonetheless, the song had her shifting in her seat, glad when the DJ came on and announced that the weather would remain much the same over the next few days, brisk and sunny. She sat with her hands clasped in her lap, gazing out the window. What had Will been talking about? A part of her had responded to the excitement in his voice minutes earlier, while another part of her had wondered if this little outing was an attempt to save Hannah Jacobs from herself. The latter thought won out, and she found herself blurting, "Though it may not look that way, Will, I really don't need your help in filling my days. I'm—"

"Perfectly happy the way you are," he supplied, taking his eyes off the road long enough to level a look of disbelief at her. "Bull. You're about as happy as I am. It's pretty pathetic, you know. You at twenty-eight, me at twenty-nine and apparently all washed up."

She gave a small gasp. "I never said any such thing about myself."

"You didn't have to say it. I'm not blind."

She crossed her arms and stared out the window. "I don't have to listen to this. Just because you aren't happy with your life—"

"You're right. You don't have to listen to it. I've had my lecture today. The last thing I meant to do was give you one. I'm sorry. That's not why I wanted to see you."

She studied the mats on the floorboard. "Then why?"

He drove with one hand, resting the other on his injured knee, massaging it with his thumb. "The other night you mentioned the bookmobile was no longer operating."

"Yes."

"Well, I . . . I'd thought maybe I could help you get it into operation again."

Hannah turned to stare at him, momentarily speechless. "What?"

He cleared his throat and flexed his hand against the steering wheel. "I thought we could come up with some sort of fund-raising drive."

"You'd do that?"

He shrugged. "It was a good thing for kids. Shame to let it go that way."

"I thought so, too," she said with a hesitant nod. "But why would you..."

He made a pretense of brushing some stubborn speck of dirt from his jeans. "I'll be here a little longer. I might as well do something worthwhile with my time."

"I don't know what to say. It's a very generous offer."

He focused on the landscape flashing by his window. "Not really. I have the time right now."

"I'm sure there are other things you could be doing."

"If you're not interested..."

"No, of course I am. I just..."

He pinned her with his gaze. "You're surprised."

She tilted her head to one side. "Maybe a little."

"Then join the crowd. I might have just thrown myself a curve."

She tried to attribute the warm feeling of pleasure spreading through her to Will's generosity and nothing else. "What did...when did you want to start working on it?"

"Why not this afternoon? We could go down to Tarkington's Cove, order a pizza and throw around a few ideas. Sound okay?"

The offer was so unexpected she found herself responding without thought. "All right. That sounds fine." And with the warmth his responding smile sent through her, she forgot all about her vow to stay away from Will Kincaid.

WITHOUT A DOUBT, Tarkington's Cove qualified as Lake Perdue's crown jewel. From critics, the development had spawned such praise as "real vision... unsurpassed... nothing else like it on the east coast."

From the beginning, most said the developer had outdone himself and then some. Others said he'd overextended and was bound to go under. But regardless of what anybody said, the development was a masterpiece. No one could deny that. The road leading to the resort wound past fields of grazing cows and sloped gently up at just the right point so that when a car topped the knoll, the whole development came into view at once. And there was no better word than majestic to describe it.

Hannah took it all in now as the Cherokee made its way to the cobblestone entrance. An old brick house built in 1872 had been converted to a clubhouse, which sat by an Olympic-size swimming pool. Tennis courts had been laid out to accommodate professional tournaments. A marina housed sailboats and motorboats alike. Condominiums and town houses lined the shore of Lake Perdue, their presence unobtrusive in the winter sun.

"This is lovely," she said with awe.

"Been here before?"

She looked out her window in amazement. "Not since it was completed."

"Pretty spectacular, isn't it?"

"It's a shame for such a place to be on the verge of bankruptcy."

He frowned. "I didn't know that. That's too bad. Any idea why?"

"The developer overextended, according to the paper. Other than that, I don't know."

"That's a shame. I really like it here," he said as he parked the car, hopped out, then came around to assist Hannah. "I tried to pick up a few things before I left, but my house isn't exactly the neatest in the neighborhood."

She smiled and followed him to the door. He inserted the key and then stepped inside, motioning for her to follow. "See what I mean?"

The house looked lived-in, but she wouldn't have called it messy. She gazed about the room, taking in the oversize couch and chairs, the marble fireplace, the light oak floors and, best of all, the skylight, which allowed sunlight in the day and stars at night. "It's lovely, Will."

"A couple of hours ago, you might not have agreed. Have a seat. I'll get us a soda."

Hannah sank onto the sofa. How strange the paths life took. Here she sat in Will Kincaid's house. A month ago, she would have thought the idea preposterous.

Before she could further ponder the irony of it, Will returned with a Coke in each hand. He offered one to her and then went over to the stereo to drop in a CD.

She glanced up, surprise in her eyes. "Beethoven's 'Für Elise.' "

"I thought you'd know it," he said in a pleased voice.

"It's one of my favorites."

"I remember."

She looked away and then back again. "You decided to give it a try, then."

"I got to be real good friends with the manager at the record store off campus in college. Most of my friends think I'm crazy. I'm the only guy they know who works out to Mozart, instead of Bon Jovi. Guess I can thank you for that."

She smiled, not knowing what to think of the revelation.

He sat down on the opposite side of the sofa, his hand automatically going to his injured knee.

"How is it?" she asked, noticing the reflex.

"Better."

"Does it bother you?"

"Sometimes."

"More often than that, I'll bet."

He shrugged. "No use complaining about it. It's my own fault. Probably should have given up on it after the third round of surgery, but I was determined to keep playing. This last time was the final straw."

She frowned. "Can they do anything for the pain?"

"Keep me on drugs. I'd rather have the pain. It's not too bad."

An urge to reach out and smooth it away overwhelmed her. Hannah stared at her lap, disturbed by the feeling. This visit wasn't supposed to be personal. And it seemed to be heading in that direction. "Ah, what did you have in mind for the fund-raiser?" she asked.

Will set his glass on the coffee table and leaned forward, his expression enthusiastic. "Something for the kids, I think."

"Like what?"

"Clowns and dunking machines. Bobbing for apples and 'pin the tail on the donkey.'"

"A carnival, maybe?"

"Exactly."

"That sort of thing takes money up front," she said, skeptical. "I don't know if the board of supervisors would—"

"I'll take care of that. We'd charge admission, of course. And maybe I could see about getting a few local businesses to make a donation. People like Aaron and Betsy Tate. She's a teacher. She'll like the idea. I know they'll help out."

Hannah mulled over the suggestion. If anyone could convince the town merchants to make a contribution, it was Will Kincaid. She'd been sorry to see the bookmobile cut from the annual budget. It had been a real service to those children who lived out in the country and couldn't get to the library on a regular basis. She knew of a few who really loved to read and had been heartbroken when the bookmobile ceased operation. Realizing it had been their only way of getting books, Hannah made a trip out to their homes every couple of weeks or so to take them a fresh batch. She could just imagine their delight at learning the bookmobile was operating again. "Do you really think they'd go along with it?"

"I don't see why not. What have they got to lose?"

Will and Hannah sat there for an hour or so, tossing ideas back and forth, the excitement in their voices reminiscent of two children planning a school project. At some point, Will got up and ordered a pizza. When the doorbell rang a half hour later, they were both sorry for the interruption.

Hannah hadn't known this sort of anticipation in years. It had been a long time since she'd given herself a goal, apart from that of getting herself to work every day. This was something altogether different. It was "I'll look into this," and "You look into that." For a woman who had gone years without more than a nod to a member of the opposite sex, it was quite a shift. One she found surprisingly appealing.

"I'm not much of a cook, or I would have whipped something up for us," he said. "This is about the best I can do on short notice."

"I love pizza," she assured him, rearranging the books on the coffee table to make room for the box.

Hannah surreptitiously studied him as they munched, taking inventory of the changes the years had wrought. One, in particular, surprised her. "I never noticed that you were ambidextrous before."

He looked up. "Ambi-what?"

"You switch back and forth between your right and left hands."

"Oh, that. Yeah, pretty talented, huh? Comes in handy when one hand gets tired."

"Have you always done that?"

"Pretty much. Mostly when I eat." He grinned uncertainly. "Does that make me special?"

She smiled, a little embarrassed. Silence settled between them. She took another bite of pizza, dabbed at her mouth with her napkin, then said, "I don't know how to thank you, Will. I'm sorry if I seemed abrupt outside the library. The carnival is really a great idea."

He stared at her, his expression unreadable. "Believe it or not, Hannah, my reasons aren't entirely unselfish. I'm looking forward to doing something that'll fill my time for a few weeks. Something worthwhile, as my father would say."

She looked up in surprise. "He encouraged you to do this?"

"Not exactly," he said wryly. "His definition of worthwhile is a bit different from mine."

"Meaning?"

"He thinks I should accept some of the offers I've gotten since the Superbowl."

"I wondered about that. You must have received a few good ones."

"Financially, yes. But I'm not really interested in convincing the world to switch over to my brand of underwear. My dad doesn't seem to understand that."

A smile curved her lips as she reached for her Coke. "Surely there were others."

Will shrugged. "Nothing that interests me at the moment."

"Then what are you planning to do now that..."

"Now that my career is over? Good question."

She glanced away. "I'm sorry, I didn't mean to—"

"It's all right," he said on a gentle note. "I've spent the past few weeks pondering it myself. This fund-raiser is the first thing I've looked forward to doing in a while—haven't thought much beyond that. I'm glad we'll be working together on it."

She looked down at her hands and swallowed. A warning bell started clanging somewhere inside her. *Danger, danger.*

Before she could say a word, he set his plate on the coffee table and slid across the couch toward her, his movements remarkably graceful for a man his size.

She glanced up, startled to find him so close.

"Hold still. You have pizza sauce right—" he dabbed a napkin at the corner of her mouth "—there."

Hannah let her tongue dart out to find the spot he'd just touched. "Is it gone?"

"Yep."

But he didn't move back. He just sat there, very close, staring into her eyes. Hannah felt caught in the center of a circus spotlight, frozen, unable to move.

He didn't touch her. Not with his hands, anyway. But his gaze roamed over her face, searching, leaving a mark every bit as memorable as a touch.

Hannah's breathing quickened. She leaned back against the pillow behind her and looked up at him with eyes that questioned, wondered. Why had he sought her out? What could a man like him want from a woman like her? A man who'd become accustomed to big cities and glamorous companions. A woman better suited to small towns and books.

He leaned away, still silent.

Hannah put her plate on the table. She looked down at her lap and brushed away a few crumbs. "It's time I was getting back. If you could..."

He remained still a moment longer, then stood and reached for the pizza box. "I'll take you. Let me get my coat."

HANNAH AWOKE Sunday morning long before the sun peeked between her curtains. She'd tumbled from one side of the bed to the other most of the night, the events of the day before playing through her mind like scenes from a movie.

Will. The bookmobile.

The idea of working with him on the project sent shivers of anticipation through her as nothing had in a long, long while. But although the thought held its share of appeal, it also had her erecting all sorts of mental defenses.

At some point in the past decade, she'd realized that any feelings she once might have had for Will had been nothing more than girlish fantasies. And certainly, they had been.

But then how did she explain what had happened before he had taken her home yesterday? Why had his touch stirred her so? Made her want to put her arms around his neck, press herself against that strong, hard chest? Was it comfort she sought? The closeness of another human being? Or something more? How long had it been since she'd felt that way? Had she ever?

Yes, once. Once.

LATER THAT DAY Hannah drove to Meadow Spring to visit her Aunt Sarah. It was a visit she both looked forward to and dreaded at the same time. She never knew whether Sarah would recognize her or not. She checked in at the front desk and then made her way down the hallway filled with paintings of sunshine and ocean shores. A mop and bucket sat in the middle of the floor. The corridor smelled of disinfectant, and Hannah's stomach churned at the pungent odor.

She stopped in the doorway. Sarah lay on her side with her face to the window, staring out at the grounds where a few residents walked with visitors among the leafless trees. Hannah thought of the phone call she'd received from Sarah's doctor a couple of days before and his reassurance that the Alzheimer's symptoms did not seem to have progressed, for the moment, anyway.

She ached for what her aunt had already suffered, her losing touch with the things she held so dear, the things she had passed on to Hannah throughout her childhood: her passion for Chopin, her respect for Monet.

Hannah blinked and then forced the sadness from her expression before stepping inside. "Aunt Sarah?"

Sarah Jacobs turned, a smile transforming her pale, wrinkled face. "Hannah. You're here."

Hannah sighed, thankful to see that the eyes staring up at her were those of her aunt and not of some stranger. "And I'm so glad to see you. My, aren't you looking well today!"

A half smile crinkled the corners of the woman's mouth and brightened the tired eyes. "That's a matter of opinion, child."

"You look wonderful. I brought you some goodies. Apples and a couple of bananas."

"I appreciate it, dear. But you didn't have to do that."

Hannah sat down on the side of the bed and leaned over to give her aunt a hug, dismayed by the realization that Sarah seemed to be getting smaller with each passing week. Hannah pulled back to look down at her aunt intently. "How are you feeling?"

"Rather well, today. How are you, my dear?"

"I'm fine," she said, hoping the words were convincing.

Sarah reached up and ran a veined hand across her niece's hair. "You should wear it down, dear. Such lovely hair. You always had such lovely hair."

Hannah shrugged and made light of the remark. "It's just easier this way."

"Yes, I know," the old woman allowed with a pat on Hannah's hand. "But the young men like it down. Tell me, are you seeing anyone?"

Hannah looked away and told herself the white lie was for a good cause. If it made her aunt feel better, she would have no compunction about it. "Here and there. No one serious."

"You need a husband. Someone to give you children. When I think of what my life would have been like without you... You were a blessing to me. Whatever my brother's faults, I'll always be thankful to him for giving you to me." She patted her niece's hand again. "Tell me what you've done this week."

Hannah hesitated, debating whether to confide in Sarah about the events of the past few days. Needing to talk about it, Hannah said after a moment, "It's been rather unusual, really. An old acquaintance is back in Lake Perdue. He played professional football. Will Kincaid."

Sarah's eyes found Hannah's. "John Kincaid's boy?"

Hannah was surprised she'd remembered. "Uh-huh. Anyway, he wants to help raise some money for the library bookmobile. We're going to put on a carnival, if the board approves it."

"What a wonderful idea."

Hannah looked down at her hands to subdue her own excitement. "I'm looking forward to it."

Sarah studied her niece with quizzical eyes. "Is he married?"

Her cheeks warm, Hannah focused on the lawn beyond the window. "It's nothing like that. Will Kincaid is...famous. And he won't be in town for long."

There were days when Sarah Jacobs didn't remember the name of the state she lived in or where she had put her toothbrush. But this was a subject upon which the two of them had long been at loggerheads—Hannah's refusal to get out and join the living. Sarah's voice was unexpectedly strong when she said, "Now, what is that supposed to mean? I won't have you putting yourself down. You know I've been after you for years to fix yourself up a bit. You try far too hard to blend into the woodwork."

Hannah flinched. The words struck a little too close to the comment Will had made.

The old woman's voice broke as she added, shaking her head, "If it hadn't been for that business with Tom . . . I never should have let him get away with it."

Hannah blinked and said quickly, "Aunt Sarah—"

"No, no," she insisted with a raised hand, her words coming in rushed fragments. "He should have been punished. You've never gotten over it. It's all my fault—"

"Aunt Sarah, shh. Don't say that." She pressed a hand against her aunt's wrinkled cheek. "Please. Don't say that. My life's just fine. I have no complaints."

"It's not natural. You should be thinking about marriage. I know you never go out. You just say so to make me feel better." She took Hannah's hand in hers and clasped it tightly. "My dear, promise me you'll put the past behind you. You have a life to live. I couldn't die in peace knowing you'll never let yourself be happy."

Hannah swallowed. Her eyes grew moist. "Aunt Sarah, don't say such things."

"We both know I'm not going to be around forever, child," she said with the honesty she'd always insisted on in their relationship. She'd never kept anything from Hannah, not the fact that Paul and Katy Jacobs hadn't been ready for a child when they'd had her, or the fact that she felt responsible for Hannah's living a life that would lead to nothing but loneliness. "And if I don't take what chance I have to tell you how I feel, there may never be another. Put what's over and done with behind you. There are good men in this world. Give one of them a chance. That's all I ask."

Hannah leaned forward and took her aunt's frail body in her arms, holding on with all the love she felt for the dear woman, her throat too tight for words.

AFTER THE SUNDAY she'd spent with her aunt, Monday morning seemed gray. Hannah had been so glad to see that Sarah had been more her old self. But that lucidity always brought with it the questions that troubled the woman. What would Hannah do once she was gone? Would she never find anyone to share the rest of her life?

Sarah's distress always disturbed Hannah. But yesterday, her aunt had seemed particularly agitated. Hannah feared the worst—that her aunt had little time left. The doctors could give her no definite answers, only vague estimates that hung over her like a cloud threatening to burst.

Hannah wished she'd said nothing about Will Kincaid's presence in Lake Perdue. Sarah had latched onto the fact that they would be working together as if it meant a romance was sure to be in the making.

Hannah hadn't known how to tell her that nothing could be further from the truth. And so, she'd let the dear old woman think the possibility existed.

Now, as she stood before the bathroom mirror getting ready for work, Hannah yanked a brush through her hair, intent on punishing herself for her stupidity. How could she have done such a thing?

The bulb in the bathroom light fixture flickered, blinked off, then on again. She caught her expression in the oval mirror and felt as though she was looking at a stranger.

That face in the mirror. Sometimes, she didn't recognize it at all. It was a face she'd avoided scrutinizing for so long that it had become second nature. She never looked too closely for fear of what she might see. Now she leaned closer as if seeing herself for the first time in years.

Newly washed, her hair lay parted to one side. Left loose, it hung just past her shoulders, full with a slight natural curl. Not that the curl mattered, because she always wore her hair pulled straight back in a bun. It was easier that way. Wide hazel eyes stared back at her. If she had a best feature, they were it. She never enhanced them with eyeliner or mascara.

She thought about Will and wondered what he saw when he looked at her. Did he find her plain? Unappealing? She touched a finger to her face. How would she look with a touch of makeup? A dab of lipstick?

Had Aunt Sarah been right? Had she let herself become plain and detached from everyone and everything around her?

She dropped the brush, which landed with a clatter in the sink. She wheeled and headed for the bedroom where she yanked her navy wool jumper and a white blouse from the closet. She was who she was. There was no changing it.

SHE WAS WHO SHE WAS. But for the first time in years, Hannah had made one small change in her appearance on that brisk day in March. She stepped out the front door, turned the lock and set off down the walk with her hair full and heavy against her shoulders.

AS SOON AS SHE GOT to work, Hannah put in a call to Ralph Smithers at the supervisor's office. She explained Will's idea to him, relieved to find the man as enthusiastic about it as she was. "You mean Will's really willing to devote his time to the project?"

She affirmed that he was and hung up the phone with the assurance that they would have the board's full approval.

To Hannah's relief, twelve o'clock had come and gone before Jenny got a chance to corner her. They'd been busy that morning, but as soon as things tapered off, she looked up from her position at the front desk to find her friend bearing down on her with a look of determination.

Jenny leaned against the desk. "I thought I'd never get around to this."

"This?" Hannah asked innocently.

"You know very well what *this* is. You knew him," Jenny accused. "All that talking I did about him and you never said you knew him."

"It was nothing, Jen." She shrugged. "Really it wasn't. I knew him in high school. I didn't even think he'd remember me. In fact, he didn't. It was my car he rammed that day, and he didn't remember me until the next day. He only asked me to sit with him at the fundraiser to make up for that, I'm sure."

"And is that why he wanted to take you home?" the older woman asked with a raised brow.

Hannah looked down at the form she'd been filling out. "He was being courteous."

"And he thought you looked thirsty, so that's why he took you for coffee at the café," Jenny added.

Flustered, Hannah said, "It was nothing."

Jenny stepped back and gave her the once-over, uttering a suspicious "Hmm. Your hair looks really pretty that way. Haven't seen it down before."

Hannah cleared her throat and flipped through the papers before her. "I went to see Aunt Sarah yesterday. For some reason, it bothers her that I never wear it down. I thought I'd give it a try."

"How is Sarah?"

Hannah shook her head, sadness washing over her. "The doctor says she's no worse."

"That's good news." Jenny paused and then, in a kind voice, said, "Sarah's right, you know. You have nice features. Wonderful bone structure. I've always thought so. I'd love to do a makeover on you. Some blush and eye shadow... I see real possibilities."

"Thanks, Jen, but I—"

"It's hard to change when you're used to doing things a certain way. But you think about it. I agree with that dear aunt of yours. Just so you know, she cares about how you wear your hair because she wants you to catch a man. It's a start," she added with a sly smile.

Later that afternoon, Hannah looked up from her desk to find Will walking toward her.

His name came out on a breathless gasp. "Will. Wh-what are you doing here?"

He reached out to flick an end of her hair. "Now that's how I remember it. Looks nice."

Heat swam up in a wave from her toes. "Really," she managed lightly. "This town must be hurting for excitement. I fail to pull my hair back one day and it becomes the main attraction."

"I can see why."

The remark came out low and teasing, intended for Hannah's ears only. She pushed a lock of hair behind her ear and said in a shaky voice, "Did you need something?"

His eyes shone bright with amusement. "I told you I'd call. I was in the area so I thought I'd drop by, instead. Talked to the board yet?"

She cleared her throat and said, "As a matter of fact, yes. Mr. Smithers was very receptive to the idea."

"That's great." He slapped a hand on the desk and turned to Jenny, who'd just appeared at the front desk carrying a stack of books. He reached for them and said, "Afternoon, Miss Dudley. What do you think of the idea?"

Jenny stared up at Will and then appeared to melt. "Jenny. It's Jenny. What idea?"

"About the carnival."

"I hadn't mentioned it yet," Hannah explained.

"Oh. Sorry, I thought—" he began.

"Will has offered to help put on a carnival to raise money for the bookmobile," Hannah interrupted. "I just spoke to Mr. Smithers about it this morning."

"Why, what a marvelous idea!" Jenny clapped her hands together. "So nice of you to volunteer, Mr. Kincaid."

"It's Will. And I hope you'll be able to help out?"

"Why, of course. I'd be glad to."

The front door opened then, and they all glanced up to see Henry Lawson step through the entryway dressed in his customary overalls and bill cap. He promptly removed the hat.

Jenny picked up a few books and headed toward the shelves behind the table where Henry had taken a seat. "Just let me know what I can do," she added over her shoulder.

Will turned back to Hannah. Silence hung in the air as they stood there staring at one another. Will glanced over his shoulder at Henry. "Does he come in every day?"

"Just about."

"He must really love books."

"He does. About as much as anyone I know."

Will looked at the man sitting bent over a newspaper, one finger following the lines across the columns. He frowned and glanced back at Hannah. "Got any interest in throwing around a few ideas tonight?"

She ignored the way her heart jumped at the suggestion. How else, after all, would they get the project done if they didn't work on it together? "Tonight would be fine."

"Good." He backed away from the desk.

"What time?"

"About six. Come for dinner, okay?"

She nodded, her gaze following his as it swung once more to the table where Henry Lawson sat studying the daily paper as he usually did, one finger inching past each word. She watched in confusion as Will studied Henry for a moment, an uneasy look on his face. But before she could ask him what was wrong, he raised a hand, then wheeled around and headed out the door as if he'd just seen a ghost.

CHAPTER FIVE

HANNAH STOOD WAITING by the front window. She'd gotten home a little after five that evening and had jumped in the shower to freshen up. For reasons she refused to examine, she'd gone to her closet, rummaged through it and found a pair of blue jeans. Nothing else in her wardrobe seemed appropriate—the wool sweaters looked dowdy, the navy skirt and white blouse seemed schoolmarmish. She hadn't worn jeans in years, and this pair was faded and hugged her hips and thighs loosely.

But somehow, it felt good to put them on. She paired them with an oversize navy sweater and stood before the bathroom mirror surveying herself. Would Will notice? Would he think she was trying to change his impression of her? That thought had her yanking open a drawer and locating a rubber band. She pulled her hair back and wound it into a bun, then spent a couple of minutes fiddling with it, loosening the band to soften the severity of the style. But she left the jeans on; the change felt good.

She went back to the mirror and studied her image critically. What was she getting herself into? And who was she doing it for? Aunt Sarah? Or herself?

Both questions stung. For her own sake, it would pay to remember that Will Kincaid was not a permanent resident of Lake Perdue. He'd be gone soon.

And it wouldn't do to let herself begin to think otherwise.

ONLY A FEW BLOCKS away, Will whistled along with the song playing on the radio, trying not to let himself think too much about the evening ahead. He'd spent the afternoon out at Tate's, trading stories with Aaron and the boys. When one of them had brought up the subject of what was going on between him and Hannah Jacobs, he'd brushed it aside with just enough conviction to douse the fire beneath the gossip.

Now that he was alone, however, he wasn't at all sure he qualified as the upstanding philanthropist the town seemed to think him.

He'd meant every word about helping out with the bookmobile. But he wondered if his reasons for doing so had started out with needing a reason to see Hannah. During his years in California, he'd learned that no one ever did anything unless it would benefit them in some way. Taking that as a given, he again asked himself why he wanted to see Hannah. What did he stand to gain?

The answer to that question remained as elusive as the answer to what he planned to do with the rest of his life.

Maybe it had something to do with his father's disapproval. Or with the fact that he wanted to know what had sent Hannah's life in a different direction from what he would have expected. Or the realization that whatever had drawn him to her ten years ago might still be there.

He massaged his knee. Didn't matter, anyway. He and Hannah Jacobs still had about as much in common as a Baptist and a Buddhist.

And it wouldn't do to let himself begin to think otherwise.

WILL'S JEEP ROLLED to a stop at the curb in front of Hannah's just as the grandfather clock in the den chimed six.

Hannah let the curtain fall and ran to the center of the room. What was she doing peering out the window as if she hadn't had a visitor in ten years?

Her lips curved ironically. To her Aunt Sarah's dismay, it had been about that long since anyone of the male persuasion had come to pick her up at this house.

The doorbell sounded, making her jump.

She patted her hair before undoing the latch and pulling the door open. A hesitant smile touched her mouth as she said, "Evening, Will."

He stared down at her as if seeing her for the first time. "Hannah. You..." He cleared his throat. "You look nice."

She glanced away. "Pretty casual, I guess. I didn't think we'd be going out anywhere."

"It's..." His voice cracked again. "It's fine. You look fine."

"Well, all right, I'll get my coat, then. Be right back." She turned and walked toward the closet, berating herself on the way. This was not a date. And she'd do well to remember it.

His voice followed her to the closet. "You, ah, look great in those jeans."

She turned around and caught him jerking his gaze away from her posterior. Her face flooded with heat. "I...thanks. I'm ready," she said with an uncertain smile as she retraced her steps into the foyer and shrugged into her coat.

Will stepped forward. "Here, I'll help."

But he was too late, and his hand brushed her arm.

At that moment, she knew what those cattle prods she'd seen years ago out at the Bowmans' dairy farm must feel like. She almost ran to the door and stood waiting for him to follow her. He stepped forward, and they did a quick little dance trying to get out of one another's way.

She murmured an embarrassed "Um . . . sorry."

He shrugged and moved aside while she locked the door.

And with the silence surrounding them, they walked toward the Jeep, keeping a respectable amount of sidewalk between them.

To HANNAH'S SURPRISE, dinner was ready to be served when they got to the house.

She shrugged out of her coat and raised her eyebrows. "Don't tell me you did this yourself?"

"If I were smart, I'd probably lie and say yes," Will said, looking sheepish. "But the truth is, Aunt Fan, my father's housekeeper, came over and helped out this afternoon. She didn't think ordering pizza again was such a good idea."

"Oh. Yes, I know Fannie." Hannah nodded, unsettled by the notion that Will had thought the evening important enough to go to such trouble. "You shouldn't have done all this."

"Are you kidding? I was grateful for an excuse to get one of Aunt Fan's meals. Why don't we eat first? I'm hungry. You sit down. I'll have it on the table in a minute."

She took a seat at one end of the table, watching as Will crossed the room to turn on the stereo. Beethoven's "Ode to Joy" filled the room as Will returned to the kitchen and pulled dish after dish from the oven. There was something decidedly intimate about a man serving dinner to a woman. It wasn't something she'd ever experienced. Her cheeks grew warm at the thought. Trying to change her train of thought, she said, "Fannie must have thought you needed fattening up."

"Not me. You. Said you'd dwindled down to the size of a bird last time she saw you."

She flushed and looked away. "Hardly."

"I'd have to say I agree with her. Don't you ever eat?"

"I eat plenty. But I guess the last couple of years haven't been easy. Sarah, my aunt, has been in a nursing home for a good while now. She's diabetic. And she developed Alzheimer's some time ago. It's been difficult to accept." Her voice remained even until the last few words.

He watched her for a moment, then said, "I'm sorry to hear that. I remember Miss Jacobs well. From church."

She thought of the way Sarah had looked this past Sunday, intent, before she died, on seeing her niece happy. "It's not easy to watch someone you love...slip away. Especially not like this."

Once he'd laid all the dishes on the table, he sat down and sent her a look of sympathy. "I'm real sorry about that. I always thought a lot of her. If there's anything I can do..."

"Thanks. I appreciate that," she said, her voice faltering.

As if to break the awkwardness in the air, Will picked up a knife and began carving the baked chicken. "I think we've got enough here for ten."

"Maybe Fannie thought you'd invited a whole committee."

They both smiled then, passing dishes back and forth until both their plates were filled with chicken, mashed potatoes, green beans, broccoli, squash casserole and fresh biscuits.

"You like all these vegetables?" Hannah asked in surprise.

"I like anything green."

"I would have figured you for a steak-and-fries man."

He shot her an injured look. "You're looking at the number-one contender for best cholesterol level on my team."

She smiled. "You don't say?"

And so the conversation went, tidbits of anything and everything that added up to nothing in most cases, but served as pieces of the puzzle that together made the picture of who and what they had become over the past ten years.

He liked a bowl of fresh fruit before bed every night, but admitted to a love for Mallo Cups. She didn't have much of a sweet tooth, but professed a manic affinity for popcorn. He hated sitcoms but had been known to sit through the same movie three times in a row. She liked books, the longer and more complicated the better. He worked out up to three hours a day. She wilted at the mere thought.

"Three hours a day?" she repeated incredulously. They were in the living room now, and he had put on a pot of coffee. The aroma of some Irish blend scented the air.

He disappeared into the kitchen and returned a moment later with a tray bearing two cups of coffee and two candy bars. Mallo Cups, of course.

"No wonder you exercise so much," she said. "You really do have a fetish for those things, don't you?"

He grinned, an unsettling combination of boy and man. "Aaron Tate keeps them in stock for me. That and grape Nehi."

Hannah smiled, charmed. "I'll bet you still save the point cards inside."

Will looked up sheepishly. "Since I was about eight. One of my teammate's sons collects them. He made me promise when I left L.A. that I'd keep sending them to him."

She watched as he unwrapped the candy bar and proceeded to peel back the brown wrapping with the same respect one would pay Beluga caviar. "Don't you want yours?" he asked a moment later.

"Not if I expect to keep the seams of these jeans intact. It's a good thing I don't eat the way you do, since I'm not the athletic type."

"Why do you think you're not athletic?"

She shrugged. "I'm just not."

"Bet I could prove you wrong on that," he challenged.

"I don't think you'll get the chance. Unless it's a contest of bobbing for apples. I used to be very good at that."

From there, the conversation turned toward the carnival. Their excitement escalated as they moved from one plan to the next. Candied apples and popcorn balls—they were a must. So were clowns, a magician—kids love magic tricks—and pony rides. Hannah said she was sure Henry Lawson would help out. Volunteers, Will said. They'd need a lot of volunteers.

A good two hours had passed by the time they finished batting ideas back and forth.

She flipped through the pages of notes she'd jotted down. "Goodness. No one could accuse us of lacking inspiration."

"Looks like we'll need a whole army of volunteers. That won't be a problem. We'll call in a few favors. No big deal."

"I hope you have a few to call in, then. I don't. Do you think we can pull this off?" she asked, a note of doubt coloring her voice.

"I know we can." Will sat there holding his coffee mug, his expression warm and content. "It's nice to see you this excited about something. You look more like the way I remembered you."

"But you didn't remember me," she accused.

He looked down at his cup, then back again. "Hannah, I wasn't expecting to see you, and you were all wrapped up in that scarf and hat and—"

"—I didn't look the way I used to," she finished for him.

"No. You didn't," he said apologetically.

"You're right, of course," she said, thinking of the confrontation she'd had with the mirror that evening. It had been a long time since she'd given herself that kind of scrutinizing— really looked at the woman she had become. "I guess I hadn't realized how much I'd changed."

He stood up and moved to reach for her hand, pulling her up from the couch. "Let's go for a walk."

"A walk? It's March."

"And we have coats and gloves," he reasoned. "The cold air will do us good."

A few minutes later they were strolling along the shores of Lake Perdue. The night sky was clear overhead, with only a few stars winking in the distance. A half-moon sent a beam of light across the center of the lake.

She folded her arms across her chest. "It's beautiful here."

"It is, isn't it? The developer definitely picked the prettiest spot on the lake."

They stopped where the peninsula jutted out into the water. A small round gazebo sat there on the tip of the land. Will took her hand and led her up the steps to the wooden bench that looked out over the lake.

They sat down and he released her hand almost immediately. Hannah cleared her throat. They were sitting far too close for her peace of mind.

He stared out at the dark water. His voice rang out in the stillness when he said, "Hannah?"

She jumped. "Hmm?"

"What happened between you and Tom Dillon?"

Tension hung in the air.

"Wh-what do you mean?" she stammered finally.

"Something happened. What was it?"

She looked away. She'd have taken a dip in the still-freezing waters of Lake Perdue before she'd have told Will. "Nothing happened."

"You stopped going out."

"That happens to lots of people."

"You didn't date anyone else the rest of the year. Did you like him that much?"

She closed her eyes for a moment and then said, "My studies were more important than dating."

"It wasn't a broken heart, then?"

"No. It wasn't a broken heart." She swallowed the lump that had settled in her throat.

"Too bad I didn't work up the courage to ask you out before he did, then."

Her head jerked around. "Before he—"

"Yeah," he interrupted. "But you made it pretty clear that day at school that you didn't want anything to do with me."

She looked down at her lap. And then in a soft voice she said, "I'm sorry about that, Will."

He watched her for a moment, then asked, "Anything we could have talked about?"

"No," she said quickly. "No."

"We were pretty different, you and I. Still are, I guess," he said, crossing his arms. "You, the class valedictorian. Me, a dumb jock."

"I never thought of you that way."

"Even after that chemistry project we worked on together?"

She shook her head. "Of course not."

He let out a short laugh. "I felt like such a fake. I don't think I understood half of what was going on. You knew what all those signs and numbers meant...."

She sensed that although the words sounded light-hearted, the admission had not been an easy one. "You did your part. And besides, I never understood how you kept winning award after award for every sport Lake Perdue High had to offer."

Will clasped his fingers together and stretched his arms toward the lake. "That's not the same."

"Everyone has different strengths. But you're truly gifted, Will. Most people aren't so fortunate."

"I guess what it comes down to is that we always want what we don't have. I envied you all those academic scholarships."

"From what I heard you got more offers than I did."

"They weren't the same."

"A scholarship is a scholarship." In light of the conversation she'd had with Jenny just a few weeks ago, Hannah was surprised to find herself defending Will's chosen path in life. But then, it really never had been about football, had it? She had since come to realize that Will Kincaid had not grown into the man she'd imagined him to be. He was kind and surprisingly modest. Kind and modest, just as she'd thought so many years ago, before—

She interrupted her train of thought with a quick "You could have dated anyone in school. All the prettiest cheerleaders. They were crazy about you."

He turned to face her, raising one knee on the bench so that it pressed against her thigh. A smile pulled at one corner of his mouth. "Oh, you think so, do you?"

"It would've been hard to miss it."

His eyes found hers. One hand reached to tilt her chin toward him. Hannah's pulse started beating like a drum, while she marveled at how absolutely beautiful his smile was. She breathed in the scent of him, a hint of Irish coffee mixed with a trace of some cologne she instantly knew she would always associate with him.

"Hannah?" Will broke the silence.

"Hmm?" The response came out hoarse and uncertain.

"Would you mind very much if I kissed you?"

The question was not what she would have expected from a star athlete who'd dated his fair share of famous women. She found herself searching for a reply. "Kissed me?" she finally asked, the words barely audible.

He nodded slowly.

She looked away and began, "Will, I don't think—"

"That's right. Don't think." He lowered his head and one hand cupped her jaw, turning her mouth to his, while his lips gently grazed hers. The kiss had no more pressure than that of a butterfly alighting on a flower, but for all its delicacy, it sent a jolt of electricity through her like none she'd ever known. And then his mouth found hers once more, his lips firm and warm against hers this time, knowledgeable in their intent to evoke a response. The sensation was irresistible. It would have been impossible not to want more. And so she let herself sink a little closer against him. Gave herself over to the sweet, sweet sensation of being kissed by this man whom she'd never forgotten. And she remembered that long-ago day when the two of them had kissed just like this by the edge of the lake....

She jerked back and pressed her hand to her mouth, her eyes locked with his in the moonlight. She shivered. It had nothing to do with the crisp March air.

He again leaned forward and pulled her to him, encountering no resistance from her.

His mouth sought hers again, hesitant and questioning.

Her breath came out in a soft gasp. When he pulled away to look down at her, a multitude of questions bombarded her. *Why? How? What if?*

But the questions disappeared beneath the surface of her consciousness when Will reached around to the back of her head and pulled off the rubber band. He rubbed a lock of hair between his fingers. "Every bit as sweet as I remembered."

Hannah could only sit there, staring at him, certain that she'd imagined the words he'd just murmured so sincerely.

They remained that way for several moments while the gentle waves lapped at the shore.

Finally, somewhere in the distance, a dog barked. Will stood, his hand on her elbow as he pulled her up beside him. "I think we've given each other enough to think about for one night. Why don't I take you home?"

She could only blink and nod, not trusting herself to speak.

As HE REMEMBERED.

The words marched through Hannah's mind throughout the next day. Three simple words. Creating such complicated questions.

Had he thought of that long-ago afternoon by the lake as many times as she had? It seemed impossible.

And yet the thought tugged at her, even as she shelved books that morning, even as she turned out the light and locked the library door, even now as she wheeled her cart down the aisle of the grocery store.

It was amazing, really, how one could remember certain things, how the details and nuances of a time long ago stored away in one's memory could rush back so swiftly. Hannah reached for a roll of paper towels and dropped them into her basket, lost in her own thoughts. Ten years. Ten years and yet so clear.

HANNAH JACOBS had been aware of Will Kincaid's existence since the first day she set foot in Lake Perdue Elementary School at the age of seven. Will Kincaid was the boy everybody noticed. Parents beamed at him, boys vied to sit beside him, and girls simply gazed at him in silent wonder.

Hannah was no exception. From the moment she saw him, she knew he was something special. If such an adjective could be used to describe a boy, then she had thought Will Kincaid was beautiful. With a cap of dark blond, wavy hair, blue eyes that shone with mischief and a curiosity about what went on around him, he was beautiful, just like her father had been.

Everybody knew that Will had been held back a grade and was a year older than the other kids in the class. That made him all the more popular with his classmates. He'd experienced life's wonders a few steps ahead of the rest. The first to lose his front teeth, the first to get them back. The first to make the sandlot football league, the first to become captain of the softball team.

Aside from being the two smartest girls in their grade, Hannah and her best friend, Toby Cannaday, shared a secret fascination for Will Kincaid. Hannah was often in the same classroom as Will. But she admired him from within the confines of her own group, always a little surprised when he smiled at her or asked her a question about their homework assignment. By third grade, he'd established that academic subjects were not his strength. Athletics were. There he excelled. And despite his reluctance to focus on school-work, parents still beamed, boys still vied, girls still gazed at him in wonder.

With a football in his hands, Will Kincaid was gifted.

And so it went throughout their school years. Hannah won the spelling bees. Will was awarded first place at every sports banquet from fourth grade through twelfth. Their paths ran parallel but rarely crossed. Until one day during their senior year in high school. Mr. Wilks's chemistry class. Fifth period.

Most of the students in Mr. Wilks's class knew that Will Kincaid did not want to be there. For him, the class was a means to an end, necessary for admission to the college of his choice, even if he was going on a football scholarship. He only had to pass.

Forty percent of their grade would be determined by a project they were required to complete outside the classroom. On the day Mr. Wilks gave the assignment, Hannah had arrived late to class after meeting with her guidance counselor about a scholarship from the University of Virginia. The only seat left was in the front of the room. She slipped in and slid onto her stool just as Mr. Wilks said, "As you all know, your term projects will be due one week from tomorrow. Today, I'm going to divide you up into pairs, and that will be the person with whom you will spend much of your time over the next few days. To be fair, I'll go in alphabetical order." He began reading then. "Abrams, Beamer. Davis, Dillon. Fogerty, Hanover. Jacobs, Kincaid...."

Hannah's head jerked up. A wave of heat crept its way up her cheeks. She sat straighter on her stool, aware of the ribbing going on behind her.

"Way to go, Will. You get paired up with the class brain. The only one around to score over 1300 on her SATs."

The heat in Hannah's cheeks spread from limb to limb as she heard Will's whispered "Save it, Tom. I didn't have anything to do with that."

Tom's laugh held no amusement. "Yeah. Always the lucky son of a gun. Guess you won't have to do a thing."

Hannah sat there, her back ramrod straight until the class ended. When the bell rang, she scrambled off her stool and headed for the door, not waiting to consult with her partner as most of the others were doing.

Will caught her just as she rounded the corner of the hall. "Hey, Hannah! Hannah, wait!"

She stopped at the sound of his voice, hesitating a moment before turning to face him.

He stood there by a row of lockers reserved for the football team and cheerleaders, notebook tucked under his arm. "Aren't we supposed to get together on this project?"

She glanced down at the floor and attempted a nonchalant shrug. "Oh. I—I guess so. You know, if you'd like to get another partner, that would be fine."

Will looked away and then dug his toe into the floor. "Guess you heard Tom and his big mouth, huh?"

"It doesn't matter."

"It does. And I'm sorry about that. He didn't mean anything by it. Anyway, if it's all right with you ... I mean, I don't want another partner. Do you?"

Hannah looked up and met his eyes. "No. I guess not."

An uncertain smile touched his mouth and his eyes brightened. "Wanna get together tomorrow after school?"

She nodded, unsure she'd get a response past her lips.

His smile widened. "Great. I'll meet you at the library by the magazine rack around five."

She watched as he lifted a hand and then sprinted down the hall, his departing wave all but washing away the sting of Tom's taunting. And not for the first time in the past few months, Hannah wished her best friend, Toby, had not moved away. What a gab session they could have had about this. With no one to share it with, she hugged the pleasure to herself and set off for her next class.

The next day, Hannah arrived at the high-school library fifteen minutes early. She found a seat, then went to the rest room, fixed her hair and checked to make sure some stray particle of food hadn't gotten wedged between her front teeth. She then straightened the collar of her white blouse and brushed a few specks of lint from her red cardigan sweater.

Heading back to the table, she met up with Will.

"Hi," he said uneasily. His blond hair was tousled, and his hands were jammed in his pockets. "You were early."

She looked down and shrugged, trying to ignore the apprehension that had her heart pounding. "I got us a table already."

"Oh. Well, I guess we should get started, then."

She led the way, conscious of his eyes on her back.

The Quiet Room was empty today. It saw action mainly during exam period, and she'd figured no one would mind if their work required a little talking. She sat down at the table and opened her notebook. She cleared her throat and avoided Will's eyes as she explained her understanding of what it was they had to do.

"Does that sound all right to you?"

He smiled uncomfortably and said, "You obviously know what you're talking about. Chemistry's not my strength. I'm afraid you didn't get the most helpful of partners."

"You might end up liking it after this. Who knows?"

He shrugged and told her to go on, nodding here and there, but for the most part, remaining silent for the next hour or so. When she paused to riffle through the textbook to double-check an idea, he said, "I hope you aren't still bothered about what Tom said in class. Sometimes he can be a real jerk."

She glanced up. "You don't have to apologize for that."

"I wanted to. He gets a little out of hand sometimes."

"It's all right. Really."

"No. It wasn't. And, anyway," he added with a half shrug, "he was just jealous because he didn't get to work with you."

She fiddled with the neck of her blouse, unable to meet his gaze, searching for a way to change the subject. "Ah, what do you like to do aside from football?"

He propped his chin on one hand and stared out the window. For a moment, she thought he'd decided not to answer her. "Not much of anything, I guess," he finally said with a frown.

Hannah doodled in the margins of her notepaper, feeling his gaze on her, yet unable to look at him. "I didn't mean that the way it might have sounded. I'm sorry if—"

"No offense taken." He rolled his pencil between his palms and said, "What do you do outside of school?"

She considered the question, her pen ceasing its meandering. "I like to read. And I love classical music...."

He studied her for a moment and then slid lower in his chair, a look of interest on his face. "You know a lot about it?"

Certain she'd just made herself an even bigger square in Will's eyes, she blushed and stammered, "A...a little, I guess."

"Did your aunt teach you?"

"She's always loved it," she said, nodding. "She wanted me to know enough about the music to decide for myself whether I like it."

"Do you?"

She opted for honesty. "Yes."

"Who's your favorite?"

"Beethoven, I think. Maybe because he was such an amazing man. He started going deaf when he was twenty-eight years old. And a lot of people didn't like him because he became sort of bitter, I guess. But wouldn't your attitude change if suddenly one day you realized you might not be able to do the one thing for which you'd trained your whole life?"

"Did he give it up completely?"

"He kept playing and composing. Some people said that the deafness forced him to concentrate on composing rather than playing and that he might not have written his greatest pieces, otherwise. Aunt Sarah says that's ridiculous, though. She believes that such a man would have written those pieces regardless. His deafness couldn't prevent him from hearing the music in his head."

"It's sad though, isn't it? To devote your whole life to one thing and then realize you might lose your ability to do it."

"He didn't go totally deaf until the last years of his life. But to do such great things when there must have been days when he felt like not going on at all..."

Several moments of silence passed. "I can see why he's your favorite. He must have really loved music to have not given up."

"I don't think he could have lived for anything else. It was a part of him."

"You know, it's strange how the public develops a certain image of other people, especially famous ones, I guess, what they're like, how they live. I'll bet a lot of the time they're nothing like that at all."

"Maybe they think the public doesn't want to know who they really are. Maybe they think they wouldn't be accepted. I'm sure Beethoven must have thought no one would believe in his music if they thought he couldn't hear."

Will watched her, his blue eyes sharp and assessing.

Hannah held his gaze, and in those few seconds she felt as though they'd caught a glimpse of the other's soul. She glanced down at her notebook and said quickly, "I guess we should get busy."

He nodded slowly. "Yeah. I guess so."

They got back to work again after that and discussed nothing that didn't in some way relate to the project. Hannah lay awake that night thinking of their conversation and wondering why the Will Kincaid she'd spent those couple of hours with seemed so different from the one everyone seemed to know in school.

The next afternoon in the library, the conversation again strayed toward the personal and Hannah found herself asking, "Are you looking forward to going away to college, Will?"

He propped his elbows on the table and rested his chin on one hand. "Assuming I get there. I've been offered a full scholarship, but only if my grades are high enough. This class will make me or break me."

"Then we'd better make sure we get an *A*, huh?"

He stared at her for a moment, as if surprised by her response. "I could use it," he admitted. "After what Tom said in class the other day, I'd have thought you might hate me for needing a good grade out of this class."

She shrugged. "I'd like one, too. I don't see anything wrong with that."

He studied her, shaking his head. "You're not exactly what I'd expected, Hannah."

She smiled and turned her attention back to the book. "Neither are you, Will."

THEY FINISHED their work on the project that afternoon. Will asked, "You got a ride home?"

Hannah looked down at her books, uncertain what to say. "I can walk."

"Come on. I'll take you home," he insisted.

She nodded and tried to look as if it was no big deal, but her pulse set up a rhythm that said otherwise.

Outside, they climbed into Will's Wagoneer. "You thirsty?" he asked.

"A little."

He turned into Simpson's Ice Cream and pulled up to the drive-through, ordering them both a Coke and a banana split with two spoons. Once on their way again, he said, "There's a place I want to show you."

She sipped at her Coke, comfortable with the silence while he drove. That was the odd thing about the time they'd spent together. Whether they were talking or not, she felt at ease with Will, as if in him, she'd found a link missing in herself. She knew Aunt Sarah would be expecting her soon, but it wouldn't hurt to be late just this once. She couldn't bring herself to end their last day of working together yet.

He drove for ten minutes or so, then turned onto a dirt road that led to the lake. He parked on a knoll of land that looked out over the water. Reaching for the banana split, he said, "It's a little soupy now. But it ought to taste the same."

She smiled as he handed her a spoon, and they raced to see who would get the cherry. It was a tie, and they ended up dividing it in two just as the setting sun bowed across the lake, casting pink fingers of light across the water. "Wanna go for a walk?"

She nodded, and they climbed out of the vehicle and wandered toward the lake. She breathed in the scent of spring and wished this afternoon could go on forever. They sat down on a grassy spot near the shore. Nearby, a blackbird sang for its mate. Crickets chirped in barbershop-quartet harmony.

She gazed out at the lake where a fishing boat sat moored. "It's so pretty here."

"My father used to bring me fishing here when I was younger. Great place for bass. That was one of the few things we did together after my mother died."

"You aren't very close, then?"

He studied the grass beside him. "He's usually busy."

"Oh." She pulled a dandelion from the ground and blew the seeds into the wind.

"How about you and your aunt?"

"I love her very much."

"You're lucky."

The words were said with such raw honesty that Hannah ached for him. "I'm sure your father loves you, Will."

"As long as I follow the path he wants me to take."

"Which is?"

"Football. The right college."

"What about what you want?"

"Football's all I know."

"Is it what you want to do?"

"Never really thought about doing anything else."

She fiddled with the hem of her skirt. "I didn't mean to pry."

"You didn't," he said. "It's all right."

"I guess parents don't always handle things the way they should," she murmured, thinking of her own mother and father. They hadn't loved her enough to put up with the changes she brought to their life. And for the first time ever, she found herself admitting, "My parents left when I was small."

"Why?"

"I guess I was what you'd call an accident. They were young and not ready to be tied down by a baby."

His voice went soft with compassion as he said, "So what happened?"

"They decided to go away for a while. Sow some wild oats, Aunt Sarah said. They were killed in a car wreck just a few days after they left...." Her words trailed off, her throat too tight to allow her to go on. Her parents' faces were nothing but a blurred memory to her and yet the sadness still tugged at her.

He reached out and pressed his hand over hers. "I kind of know how you feel. Mama died when I was nine. And I still miss her." He looked away as though expecting ridicule at the admission. When he didn't get it, he said, "You know, you're awfully easy to talk to."

She looked away, trying to ignore the warmth creeping into her cheeks. "So are you, Will."

He reached down and pulled at a blade of grass. "What do you want to do when you get out of school?"

She considered the question at length, then said, "I've always wanted to teach. In a university somewhere. Maybe even write a book someday."

"You'd be a great teacher. I could testify to your patience," he said with a rueful grin. "What kind of book do you want to write?"

"Oh, I don't know. Something about the paths people take in life, how they get off track...." She suddenly realized she'd admitted more than she wanted to. "Anyway, that's enough about me."

He sent her a level look, his gaze intent. "I like talking about you. It's funny how a person can be so different from what you'd imagined. I wish we'd had a chance to get to know each other sooner."

"Me, too," she said with a shy smile.

"Guess I ought to get you home," he said after a moment. "Wouldn't want your aunt to worry."

She nodded. "I guess so."

But they remained there, both reluctant to leave, aware that after this, they had no reason to be together, that tomorrow they'd go back to school, two pegs perhaps wanting to fit into the same hole, but certain it was impossible.

"I'm glad we got to work together, Hannah. Even though I was a little intimidated at first."

Her eyes widened in surprise. "Intimidated? By me?"

"Well, yeah, with your being so smart and all."

"I'm glad, too, Will. Even though *I* was a little intimidated at first."

He chuckled and said, "Of me?"

"Of you. Star football player. All-round ladies' man."

Will's cheeks went red. "Oh, brother."

"It's true," she teased, enjoying his embarrassment.

They smiled at one another, and then he stood up, offering her a hand. Hannah took it, coming up a little too close to his chest. She gave a small gasp, pressing one palm against him to steady herself.

The fishing boat growled to life, then set off into the distance with a roar. And still they stood there, staring at one another for a long-drawn-out moment, before he looked out at the water, turned back to her with a boyish grin on his face and said, "Why don't we go for a swim?"

"A...a swim?"

"First one of the year," he said, and slapped a hand against his leg. "What do you say?"

She grappled for words, enthused by the idea and yet uncertain at the same time. "I don't have a suit and I—"

"I've got some shorts and a T-shirt in the back of the Wagoneer." He grabbed her hand and started for the vehicle. "It'll be great. Come on."

Hannah tripped along after him, too surprised to resist. "Will..."

But he'd already let down the back and had begun rummaging through a large duffel bag. With a triumphant "Aha!" he yanked out a navy T-shirt and a pair of red shorts. "These ought to do. You can change inside. I won't look," he promised.

She didn't know what convinced her—the excitement of spring in the air or the fact that Will Kincaid could talk a stone into walking if he had a mind to—but whatever the reason, she'd never done anything so impulsive in her life.

Caught up in his enthusiasm, she took the clothes and made for the front of the vehicle, climbing inside to change, and at the same time trying not to think about Will changing in the trees twenty feet behind the car.

She slid out of the Wagoneer five minutes later, pulling and tugging at the makeshift swimsuit.

Will came around front with a grin, surveying her where she stood with the waistband of the shorts bunched in one hand. "It'll work. Sorta."

"You know what's going to happen if I let go," she said.

"I wouldn't complain." He chuckled and slid into the vehicle, poking through the ashtray. A few moments later, he turned and announced, "Found it. One oversize safety pin oughtta do the trick. Come here. I'll fix it for you."

Hannah hesitated a moment, then taking the plunge, she stepped forward. "How do I know I can trust you not to stab me?"

He held up his hands and said with mock seriousness, "Steady as a sailor on a Saturday night."

"Oh," she choked out. "I feel much better."

He grasped the folds of the shorts in one hand, maneuvering the safety pin through the fabric with the other. She stared off into the distance, too unsettled by the expanse of his bare chest and the proximity of his blond head to her left breast to worry about the likelihood of his stabbing her.

"There!" he exclaimed a moment later, standing up to survey his handiwork. The shorts were hitched a little higher on the side he'd just fastened together, and the shirtsleeves reached to her elbows. "Well, it's not designer fashion, maybe, but under the circumstances . . ."

She glanced down at the ridiculous outfit and laughed, despite herself. There by the side of the lake, beneath an old oak tree, Hannah dropped whatever remnants of self-consciousness she might have been holding on to. It was spring. The first swim of the year. She and Will had more in common than she'd ever thought. She was wildly attracted to him, and it seemed pointless to deny it to herself.

"Ready?"

"If I can manage without losing one or more articles of clothing on the way."

"No problem. But we've gotta do it fast. No chickening out. Okay?"

She nodded confidently, determined to keep up with him.

"Then let's go." He took her hand, and they ran toward the shore, their bare feet tender against the twigs and pebbles disguised in the grass along the way. They hit the sand and then leapt into the water, two strides deep before taking the final plunge.

The water swallowed them. Within seconds, they came scrambling to the surface, Hannah shrieking, Will chuckling.

"Ahh," she screamed, her body in shock by the still-frigid water. She flapped her arms, then tried to hold on to her shorts, which threatened to come off despite the pin. "It's freeezing!"

"You're wearing more than I am," he hooted.

"You knew it would be this cold!" she accused, still sputtering and slapping a spray of water in his direction.

"Me?"

"Yes, you!" She aimed another at him, missed, then tried again and landed one smack in the center of his face.

"All right," he yelled. "Now you've asked for it! Time to go under!"

He came after her then, his powerful strokes eliminating the space between them, even as she set off in the opposite direction at a respectable pace. He grabbed for her foot, lost his hold, surged forward and hooked an arm around her waist, pulling her to him.

She fought him, determined he wouldn't dunk her. He merely reeled her in far enough that he could stand, then imprisoned her with both arms.

"Will Kincaid, if you don't—"

He yanked her beneath the surface, his arms still locked about her, and using the bottom of the lake as a springboard, he sent them both shooting out of the water like a cork out of a hundred-year-old champagne.

She sputtered and coughed, choking on her own laughter as she wiped the hair from her eyes.

He was laughing, too. "Know what they say about paybacks."

Uh-huh," she said with a grin, lunging forward and sending him sprawling backward under the water.

Since she couldn't touch bottom, she had precious little time for bravado. He was back at her again, tickling and threatening until she gave in and went under. So it continued, a game of jack-in-the-box, one up, one down, until they were breathless and giddy with laughter. Yelps and splashes echoed within the otherwise silent cove, the sounds of carefree youth, newly discovered attraction.

He towed her closer to shore, his chest rising and falling with the effort. He turned to face her, mischief still dancing in his eyes and water dripping off his chin.

Hannah could barely breath for the stitch in her side. A giggle slid past her lips and then died when she met his gaze.

The laughter faded from his face, as well. And he stood there, one arm around her waist, the desire in his eyes clear, the uncertainty just as plain.

She could only stare up at him, eyes wide, lips parted, while her body yearned for something she was reluctant to identify.

The water licked at the shore. The faint scent of newly bloomed honeysuckle perfumed the air. And they stood there, gazes locked as Will reached down and brushed the side of her neck with his fingers, his thumb rubbing across the fullness of her lower lip at the same time. His hand swept lower and brushed across the neck of her shirt, skimming the crest of her breasts, outlined by the wet fabric.

She tilted her head back, staring up into those compelling blue eyes, unable to move, unwilling to move, for fear the moment would end.

He continued to study her, his hand now caressing the curve of her jaw. A silent question enveloped them. *Do we go on, or do we stop here?*

Hannah's lips parted, in protest or surrender she couldn't have said. But once he touched the moistness there, the answer didn't matter. With a barely audible sigh, he leaned forward and kissed her, his lips gentle and soft, a sweet testing of the waters. He pulled back, his warm breath caressing the corner of her mouth, his eyes questioning.

In her own gaze, he must have seen the answer he sought. He pulled her close and lowered his mouth to hers in an explanation that held little of the gentleness of that first touch.

She wound her arms tightly about his neck, her breasts pressed flat against his slick bare chest. Will groaned and the kiss went wild, his mouth working feverishly against hers, teeth grazing, tongues hot and searching, breaths short and incomplete.

He reached down and swung her into his arms, making for the shore, water dripping from their limbs.

He knelt and placed her on the grass, following her down with something that sounded like "Oh, God, Hannah—"

"Will." Whether she'd murmured his name in protest or permission, she didn't know.

But it didn't matter as their mouths sought once more what they'd started there in the water. Hannah now felt as though a blue flame had licked its way up her body. Her hands were in his hair, on his shoulders, caressing, memorizing.

He held himself up on one elbow, leaving the other hand free to roam, pressing the throbbing pulse at the base of her neck, slipping up into her hair, then skimming down to hesitate at the bottom of her clinging shirt, before slipping inside to mold to the curve of her waist.

The kissing went from barely contained to out of control, hot, combustible. Will groaned and moved his hand to her breast, then to her back to undo the hook there.

He lifted his head long enough to look down at her, searching for some sign of denial or acquiescence. When she closed her eyes and shuddered softly, he shifted closer until his chest covered hers, his hand kneading the softness of her breast.

Surprise tripped through her, pleasure right on its heels. But just when they were about to reach a point when there would be no turning back, a fishing boat came around the bend, its engine shutting off as it came to a stop in the cove.

She struggled upright. Will groaned, looked over his shoulder, then sat up and moved to block her from view.

His voice sounded strangled when he said, "It's all right. It's that same boat." He hesitated, dropped his head back, drew a deep gulp of air. "Hannah, I'm sorry. I didn't mean to let things—"

"It's okay. I...we should go." Mortified now by her total loss of control, she jumped up and ran for the Wagoneer, her face redder than the still-dripping shorts. She grabbed her clothes from the front seat and headed for the trees that Will had previously used for cover.

With jerky motions, she fumbled into her skirt and blouse, wringing out the shirt and shorts before leaning over and forcing herself to breathe evenly. Straightening, she closed her eyes and then resolutely walked toward the vehicle.

He stood there waiting for her, an uncertain look on his face. "Hannah—"

"I should get home, Will," she said quickly. "Aunt Sarah will be wondering where I am."

"Can't we just talk—"

Too embarrassed by her behavior to even look at him, she interrupted. "Please, Will. Just take me home."

He stared at her a moment longer, then nodded and climbed into the Wagoneer.

A week passed, and Hannah didn't see Will. They'd turned in their project and both received an *A*. Will ducked out of class without so much as looking at her. In fact, he'd ignored her since the afternoon he'd taken her home.

Crushed and humiliated, she threw herself into her schoolwork in an effort to forget that afternoon and what had almost happened between them. She couldn't think of it without getting red in the face and hot all over. She could only imagine what he must think of her. She had almost convinced herself that he was probably used to girls responding so completely to his attentions.

Before that day by the lake, Hannah had only been kissed once. The boy had been Mark Sawyer, and there had been nothing about the dry furtive gesture that had inspired her to explore it further.

No, what had happened between her and Will could not have surprised her more. On her own part, at least, she knew it had been the result of accumulated years of infatuation. On the night he'd dropped her off, she'd closeted herself in her room praying that she hadn't imagined the message she'd seen in his eyes that afternoon.

But a week later she knew she had. And so she told herself it didn't matter, that she'd been foolish to think anything would come of it. The sooner she stopped thinking about him, the better off she'd be.

But the following afternoon, something happened that took her by surprise. She was sitting in the family room when the phone rang. Sarah answered it and called from the kitchen, "Hannah. It's for you, dear."

Pulse racing, she picked up the extension on the table beside her with a shaking hand.

"Hello."

"Hannah? It's Tom Dillon."

She remained silent for a moment, too surprised to speak.

"You there?" he asked.

"Ah, yes, I'm here." She flipped the book in her lap shut and frowned, curious.

"Yeah, well, the reason I was calling—there's a party next weekend out a Brad Manning's place. I was wondering if you'd go with me."

Again, she was too taken aback to respond. Taken aback and, if she admitted it, disappointed. Somewhere deep inside, she'd harbored the hope that Will might call. The thought now seemed ridiculous. "Thanks, Tom, but I don't think so."

"Oh, come on, Hannah," he cajoled. "I'm sorry about what I said in class last week. Guess I was a little jealous. Will's always so damned lucky. He got all the scholarships and he gets all the girls, too." He laughed uneasily, as if he hadn't meant to say the words out loud. "Anyway, everybody's got to have a little fun now and then. We won't stay late if you aren't having a good time. How's that for a compromise?"

She hesitated, at a loss for a reply. She'd had few opportunities to turn down dates. And certainly not from guys like Tom Dillon. Tom was popular with the girls, although not as popular as Will, but good-looking in an all-American-boy way and well liked as far as she knew. Hannah thought how unsophisticated she must have seemed to Will. He'd probably been embarrassed by the thought of admitting to his friends that he'd taken Hannah Jacobs to the lake. Maybe if he saw that Tom had asked her out, he'd see her in a different light.

Aware that all her reasons for accepting the date were unfair to Tom, she accepted, anyway, and without knowing it, set about changing her life forever.

CHAPTER SIX

HANNAH REACHED into the freezer for a box of broccoli and jumped as a hand clamped down on her shoulder, pulling her back from the past. She jerked around to find herself face-to-face with Tom Dillon. Just the two of them. Face-to-face for the first time in more than ten years.

"Didn't mean to scare you, Hannah." His face cracked in a smile that highlighted the wrinkles at the corners of his eyes. Dressed in the brown sheriff's uniform, he kept one hand on the holster at his side.

She took a step backward and pressed her fingers to her mouth. It was spooky to have the object of your thoughts materialize before you. She dropped the box of broccoli into her basket and said, "I have to go."

"Wait a minute, Hannah." His voice held a note of irritation as he reached for her arm and pulled her to a halt. "You've been avoiding me for years. Is that any way for two old friends to act?"

She gave him a level stare. "We were never friends, Tom."

"Now, I wouldn't say that," he insinuated.

She jerked her cart around and moved it quickly down the aisle. "Leave me alone," she said abruptly. "I don't have time for this."

"But then, you wouldn't have time for anything now that Will's back in town," he taunted, following her. "That's what you wanted all along, wasn't it, baby? A chance with Will."

Cold anger raced through her, turning the blood in her veins to ice. She came to an abrupt stop and wheeled on him, her eyes narrowed in fury. "You have some kind of nerve!" she snapped.

"To speak the truth? Everybody knows he's been hanging around your doorstep." Tom gave her the once-over. "Although I can't for the life of me imagine why. Not with all the hot babes he must have had over the past few years. A big star like him—"

She caught her breath and turned to bolt down the aisle. This couldn't be happening. "I don't have to listen to this."

Tom's shoes squeaked across the linoleum floor as he trailed after her, his tone casual. "No, you don't. Just one old friend trying to do another a favor. You settled for second best once. Maybe you'd like to try it again."

The implication behind the words rang clear. She swung around, staring at the glassy leer in his eyes. A fear she thought she'd buried years ago sprang to life within her. "Leave me alone, Tom," she said, hating the tremor in her voice.

"You're setting yourself up for a fall. You oughtta know that. Will Kincaid's got no use for somebody like you. But maybe you'd like to let him play with you for awhile before he goes back to L.A. and the women he's got waiting there."

Feeling the blood leave her face, she forced her voice to remain level as she said, "Get away from me. Get away and stay away. Or so help me, I'll march right down to that sheriff's office and give them reason to question your right to wear that uniform."

Tom stared at her for a long moment, the gleam in his eyes stating that he doubted her threat. After all, it had been ten years. Who'd believe her?

He backed off, anyway, his palms raised in surrender. The smile on his lips proved that he wasn't terribly worried.

Revulsion welled within her. She shoved the cart away from him, and almost ran down the aisle and around the corner, where she stopped and leaned her head on the handle.

The old familiar shame pulled at her, threatening to overwhelm her. *It was your fault. All your fault.*

Dear Lord, would it never go away? Would it never be over?

AFTER HIS EVENING with Hannah, Will spent most of the next morning on the phone with his agent, Dan Caulson. Dan couldn't understand what the devil was going through Will's head, and he told him so more bluntly than most people on a man's payroll would have dared.

"You've got umpteen offers for commercials and other campaigns, and all you want to do is hide out in some godforsaken little town in Virginia," he accused indignantly.

"I grew up in this godforsaken little town," Will reminded him wryly.

"No chance you're gonna give Grace another chance?"

"That's over, Dan."

Dan gave a snort of disapproval. "Only because you wanted it to be. You know how many guys would give their eyeteeth for a piece of that action—"

"Dan—"

"All right, all right," he said, letting up. So when are you coming back to L.A.?"

"I don't know."

"When do you think you might be able to provide me with that information?" Dan asked in exasperation.

Will leaned back in his chair. He could see Dan as clearly as if he were in the room with him, smoking one cigarette after another. "I haven't decided yet."

"The clock is ticking, Will. The notoriety you won from the Superbowl won't last forever. I've got offers from all the big names—"

"I know, I know, Dan. I just need a break, that's all."

"Take a break in six months. Get a few contracts under your belt, and then you can head down to the islands with a few bikini-clad lovelies in your suitcase. But right now, you've got work to do."

"I don't need the money, Dan," he declared reasonably.

"You know, that's your problem." Dan sighed into the phone. "You've always been able to draw the line at enough. I need clients who don't understand the meaning of the word."

Will chuckled. "I believe I've lined a few of those pockets in that fifteen-hundred-dollar suit you're no doubt wearing at this very minute. It's not my fault you've got so damn many of them."

Dan laughed. "Yeah, you try having a wife with charge accounts at every boutique on Rodeo Drive."

"I'll send you a pair of scissors, old boy. My treat."

Dan cleared his throat and said, "Just get yourself back out here to earthquake country. That's all I ask. You should've outgrown your hometown by now. You know, if I didn't know better, I'd say you got a little woman stashed away in those Virginia hills. There's sure as hell something keeping you there.''

"Give it up, Dan. I need a break, that's all. I'll be in touch." And with that, he put down the receiver, scowling.

Dan's words had touched a nerve. He leaned back in the kitchen chair, stretched his legs out in front of him and clasped his hands behind his head. Hell, he didn't even know why he was still here himself. It just . . . felt right.

And regardless of what Dan had said about his outgrowing the place, it was his home. Nothing could change that.

But Hannah had accused him of the same thing, hadn't she?

Hannah with her wide hazel eyes and soft voice.

Hannah. Something about last night had felt right, too. Like home. She had a way of putting those around her at ease, of making the simplest of moments important and memorable. Like sitting there on that bench with her, looking out at the lake. He couldn't remember the last time he'd felt so relaxed. He'd been at any number of Hollywood parties where the sight of big-screen faces was an everyday occurrence. He'd never enjoyed any of those moments as much as those quiet ones by the lake.

For the first time today, he let himself think about kissing her. What had made him do it? For the life of him, he didn't know. Except that he'd remembered being eighteen and wondering what it would be like to hold her in his arms. He also remembered what it had felt like when he finally had.

How many times after that long-ago afternoon by the lake had he tried to work up the courage to ask her out? How many times had he told himself that a smart girl like her wouldn't have a date's worth of topics to talk about with a dumb jock like him? And then to have to step back and watch her with Tom . . .

All Will had known last night was that he wanted to kiss her. And so he had.

Only he hadn't counted on the softness of that mouth beneath his. The little gasp of surprise when his lips had brushed hers. As if it was all new and startling. And, at the same time, achingly familiar. Over the years, he'd grown used to aggressive women, women who knew what they wanted and knew how to get it. Not women caught off guard by their own sexuality.

No, he hadn't counted on any of that. And he certainly hadn't anticipated the overwhelming feelings of resentment that had swamped him. Resentment of Tom. And Hannah, as well. Resentment of what might have been.

WILL HADN'T WANTED to go to Brad Manning's party that Saturday night. He'd wanted to drive over by Hannah's house and see if her bedroom light was on.

Since the afternoon he'd taken her home, he'd imagined all sorts of scenarios, trying to find an excuse to see her again—a flat tire a block from her house, accidentally running into her after she got off from work, anything to be with her again.

But none of those scenarios had come to pass. He told himself he was being ridiculous. Despite what had happened between them at the lake, they were very different people. What would the smartest girl in the class want to do with some jock who'd be lucky to graduate by the skin of his teeth? But he'd thought of little else since the day he'd let things get so out of hand. He lay in bed at night picturing the look on her face after he'd first kissed her, feeling her soft skin beneath his hands. Even his father had begun to wonder what was wrong with him.

"You got a girl on your mind, son?" he'd asked when Will had come down for supper that night.

Will's face had gone just red enough to belie his denial. "What makes you think that?"

"You've been moping around here for close to a week now. Can't think of what else it'd be." He passed Will a bowl of mashed potatoes and said, "No point in letting yourself get involved now. Fall will be here before you know it. Won't do to have anything but football on your mind then."

At that moment, football was the last thing on Will's mind. He couldn't think of anything but Hannah. He knew they had nothing in common. Well, almost nothing. He knew that once she got to know him, she'd see it, too. He'd held his breath the entire week they'd worked on that chemistry project, for fear she'd discover the truth—that he was a fraud—and end up hating him for it.

No. He and Hannah had nothing in common. And as much as he wished it could be otherwise, he didn't know how to change the fact,

He'd gotten to Brad's that night around eight-thirty. Since Brad's parents were away, the party promised to get out of hand.

Will stepped through the front door of the house, hands in his pockets. He met Brad just inside. "Hey, Brad."

"Will, glad you could make it, man. Come on in. Get you a beer. Tom's around here somewhere. And you won't believe—"

Brad broke off as another group of kids crowded through the door. Will moved toward the keg and poured himself a beer. He had no taste for it tonight, so he merely sipped at it, ducking his head into several rooms to look for Tom.

He found him out on the deck. Several other guys surrounded him, laughing and punching Tom on the arm.

Tom spotted Will and ducked through the circle. "Will. Thought you weren't gonna make it. Where you been?"

He shrugged. "Just being lazy. What's up?"

Tom hooked his thumbs inside his belt loops and smiled mysteriously. "Got a date tonight."

"Yeah? How much does she weigh?" Will threw him a half-hearted right hook.

Some of the guys standing nearby snickered.

Tom's forehead creased in a frown, and the smile slipped from his face. "When are you gonna stop thinking all the girls in school are crazy about you?" The words were light, but failed to disguise a note of bitterness. "And if I had to guess, I'd say about a hundred and five."

Will leaned against the deck railing. "Who..."

But before he'd finished the sentence, Hannah appeared by the sliding glass doors. Her eyes widened as she spotted Will beside Tom.

"Over here, Hannah," Tom called, a touch of bravado in his voice.

The two boys stared at one another silently. The surprise on Will's face was there for all to read, the

seeming nonchalance in Tom's was as easily inter-
preted.

Will stared at her as if she'd sprung from his imagination. When his mind made the connection between Hannah and Tom's "date," he blinked in
disbelief and cursed his own cowardice. Damn Tom.
How could he? Why had he asked her out? Had Tom
guessed he was interested in Hannah? But that was ridiculous. He hadn't given him a reason to think so.
Other than their working together in class. Maybe he
was getting paranoid. He and Tom had been friends
for years, ever since second grade.

His friend Tom now put an arm around Hannah's
shoulders as she edged her way into the group beside
them. She stiffened and tried to smile at Will.

"Hi, Will."

"Hey, Hannah. I—I didn't expect to see you here."

"She's kinda shy about this sort of thing," Tom
answered for her. "Doesn't like to come out by herself. Guess I took care of that, huh?" he said with a
wink.

"Will, I—" Hannah began, but Tom interrupted
her.

"I should've offered to bring her out sooner. Guess
I had to work up my courage."

Will and Hannah looked at each other. And Will
knew it wasn't just his imagination that Hannah
wished he had made the offer first.

Then why was she with Tom?

Did you ask her?

No, he hadn't. He'd been too much of a chicken.
He'd cared too much about what everyone would've
thought about a dumb jock dating the class brain.

He'd cared even more what Hannah would think if she ever discovered the truth about him.

The conversation went on, talks of the previous night's basketball game, the picnic at Louella's the next day, but Will's thoughts remained on Hannah. And with every chance he got, he let his gaze stray to her, noting the white cotton blouse tucked into slim-fitting blue jeans, and the way the shirt accentuated her breasts, the way the jeans molded her hips. Their eyes met once, and Will wondered if the silent messages between them were his imagination. He didn't think so.

Tom took Hannah's arm just after eleven and declared it time they left. The sly look he sent Will was accompanied by a low "Hadn't meant for this party to be the focus of the evening. Got better things in mind."

And Will knew one thing for certain. Paranoid or not, he hated Tom that night.

Monday morning after first period, Will's resentment grew. He'd spent the rest of the weekend stewing because he hadn't had the courage to ask Hannah out first. Because he'd spent a week of agonizing whether or not to pick up the phone and call her, he'd let Tom beat him to the punch. He had no one to blame but himself.

His mood didn't improve when Tom sauntered up to his locker and slapped him on the back. The bell rang, and students dashed down the hall for class.

"I know you're dying to hear all about it. And if I were a gentleman, I wouldn't tell you. But nobody ever accused me of that." Tom laughed.

Will turned around and looked at his friend, his eyes narrowed. "Tell me what?"

Tom leaned back against the locker and shot Will a conspiratorial look. "Everybody's got that Hannah figured wrong. Man, she's a firecracker."

"What?" He stared at Tom and hoped he'd imagined his friend's implication. "What the hell are you talking about?"

"Everybody thinks she's a cold fish, but I'm telling you it ain't so." Tom's shoulders puffed back like a banty rooster.

Will remained silent for a moment, then said in a quiet voice, "Are you saying you and Hannah—"

"Man, do I have to spell it out for you? *I scored.* Jeez, Will, what's wrong with you?"

Will swallowed and leaned back against his locker, feeling as though a wrecking ball had just landed him one in the gut. "You're a real hero, Dillon."

And with that, Will set off down the hall, determined to find Hannah and see if it was true. All he'd have to do is look in those big hazel eyes. And he would know.

But he didn't see her that day. Or for the rest of the week, either. Somebody said she had the flu.

THE TELEPHONE RANG, snapping Will back to the present. He ran a hand across his face and picked it up, his voice a little gruffer than usual.

"Will? You asleep or something?"

"Oh, hi, Aunt Fan. No, I'm not asleep. What's up?"

"Just wondered how last night went. Everything all right?"

"I'm sorry. I meant to call you. It was delicious. As usual. Hannah said to tell you so."

"I'm glad. You two have a good time?" The older woman's voice sounded a bit hopeful.

"Don't go getting any ideas, Aunt Fan. It wasn't a date."

"Who said anything about ideas?" she denied with an indignant squawk. "You must be the one with the ideas."

Will laughed. "It won't work, Aunt Fan. You're not tricking me into admitting anything. Not that there's anything to admit."

She chuckled on the other end of the line. "Suit yourself, boy. You get on out here and see us soon. You hear?"

"I will, Aunt Fan." He hung up and sat there staring at the wall.

He had a number of reasons for staying in Lake Perdue for a while. He had a few fences to mend with his father. And there was the carnival. Not to mention that he'd reached a point where he'd have to step back and admit his shortcomings now that the one skill at which he'd been competent no longer existed.

But none of it had anything to do with Hannah. Did it?

He shook his head. No.

No? Then why the hell had he kissed her last night? And why was he thinking about something that happened ten years ago, something that had nothing whatsoever to do with his future?

HANNAH DIDN'T HEAR from Will again until Thursday. And it was just as well. The incident with Tom in the grocery store on Monday night had shaken her. She spent the first part of the week trying to convince herself that the meeting had been accidental, refusing to dwell on Tom's taunt about the women in Will's life.

Jenny had noticed Hannah's quietness, but no amount of prodding pulled a confession from her. On Tuesday, Hannah barely said a word the entire day. On Wednesday, she smiled at one of Jenny's silly jokes. And by Thursday morning, she'd determined that she wouldn't let Tom Dillon throw her life off course again.

When Will called Thursday afternoon, she was finally more like herself. "I hadn't expected to hear from you," she said.

Will cleared his throat. "You busy?"

"Not really. Just finishing up a few things for the day."

"I've been doing some work on the carnival. Rounding up support from some of the local businessmen."

"Any luck?"

"Yeah. Actually got a few checks in hand."

"That's great. You *have* been busy."

"What do you think about two weeks from Saturday?"

"So soon?"

"I think we can get it all together by then. I called and checked on the armory. It's available that weekend."

"That sounds wonderful."

"Good. Then I'll call back and confirm it. You want to get together Saturday and make some calls?"

Hannah thought about what had happened on the bench by the lake. How impersonal this conversation seemed in light of that kiss. She touched a finger to her lips and wondered if he regretted the impulse. "After the library closes?"

"That'll be fine. I'll pick you up just after twelve."

"All right. See you then." She put down the phone and studied the wall of books in front of her.

She told herself she wasn't excited about seeing him again. Once the carnival was over, she'd have no reason to see him. No reason at all.

WILL SAT WAITING in the parking lot at five minutes past twelve on Saturday. He got out of the Cherokee and opened the passenger-side door, smiling at Hannah as he helped her inside.

The silence hung between them like a thundercloud. Hannah's hands clasped and unclasped. Will's thumb rapped a steady tattoo against the steering wheel.

Just as they whipped past Tate's Gas & Go, Will spoke, blurting out the words as though they'd been choking him for the past couple of days. "Look, Hannah, about the other night . . . I was out of line. I had no right to kiss you."

She looked at him. "You . . . There's no need to apologize."

"I just didn't want you to think . . ."

She pressed her hands in her lap and fixed her gaze on the road. "I didn't think anything, Will."

"Okay. Then we'll just forget it. All right?"

"Fine." She made sure her smile convinced him.

It almost convinced her, too.

DESPITE THE STRAINED relationship they'd established, those warm early days of April were the best Hannah could remember.

They worked late one Saturday afternoon and ordered a pizza for dinner. Hannah declared she'd soon gain twenty pounds if she kept hanging around him.

Will sent her an innocent look and said, "Work it off—that's the key."

"I probably couldn't run out to the car and back."

The next morning she discovered he'd decided to put her to the test. At just past seven, she found him pacing her front porch in gray sweatpants and a navy sweatshirt. She pulled open the door, and asked in surprise, "Will, what are you doing here at this hour?"

He shrugged, looking like a little boy with a secret in his back pocket. Except that he was a man, and his secret was a bike standing in the back of his Cherokee. A pair of spanking new running shoes dangled from his left hand. He held them up and said, "How about it?"

"You aren't serious?"

"As a heart attack. Which we're going to work on avoiding. I picked these beauties up last night," he said with a nod at the shoes. "Saleslady told me they're the latest in running wear."

She stared at him incredulously. "How did you know my size?"

"I peeked when you went to the bathroom last night. You left your shoes by the couch."

She continued to stare at him.

"Well?" he prodded her.

"I wouldn't make it past the Kinseys' house. And it's only a block away."

"You might surprise yourself. Come on."

She fumbled for an excuse. "How can you run with your knee—"

"The bike's for me. We'll go at whatever pace you want."

Unable to think of another excuse, Hannah waved him inside and went to change. When she came back wearing an old pair of red shorts and a white tank top, Will said, "You look like an old pro."

She laughed and gave him a skeptical look. "It won't take long to change your mind."

But despite her pessimism, she surprised herself when she made it past the Kinseys' with energy to spare. In fact, she followed Will all the way down Wilmington and halfway down Rutherford, admittedly at a slow pace, before her lungs gave out.

She stopped and leaned over, taking in great gulps of air. "Will?"

He turned around and pedaled back to her. "That was great! See? You surprised yourself."

"You're right," she gasped. "I'd forgotten what it was like not to be able to breathe."

He chuckled, pedaling circles around her. "Admit it. You liked it."

Catching her breath a little more easily now, she said, "I've...always...been one for self-inflicted torture."

"Just think of it this way. It can't get worse than this."

"Oh, thanks. I feel much better."

"Come on. Keep walking. And then we'll run a little more."

He took off, and she followed. Once her lungs stopped panicking, she did feel as though she could run a bit farther. She broke into a jog and set off after Will, who was a half a block ahead, doing figure eights in front of her. They headed off Rutherford onto Main. A couple of blocks down, Will circled back and said, "Okay, that's enough for today. Don't want you to be too sore tomorrow."

"What's tomorrow?"

"Day two of our program."

"Day two? Is this supposed to become a habit?"

"Yep. Come on, keep walking. I'll treat you to breakfast."

When Aaron Tate drove by blowing the horn of his old truck in greeting, Hannah nearly jumped into the bushes. By the time they reached the café, Hannah suspected her face had gone three shades of red. "Couldn't you have taken a side street?" she asked, puffing as she jogged up to Will where he stood leaning against the door.

"What? You embarrassed to be seen with me?"

"I feel a little foolish, running along behind you."

"Okay, next time I'll stay closer."

"Next time? Who says there'll be a next time?" She marched into the restaurant and headed for a back table, relieved to see that Louella wasn't working this morning. She didn't need the woman's questioning looks.

But despite all Hannah's objections, she felt better, and by her second cup of coffee, she admitted as much to Will.

He grinned. "So you did like it?"

"I didn't say that."

"You said you surprised yourself."

"Making it past my front hedge qualifies as surprise."

Will laughed and let his gaze lock with hers. In a soft voice he said, "You did just fine, Hannah."

She looked away, something warm and satisfying uncurling within her. "You're not too bad as a coach."

"Think not, hmm?"

"I think not."

They sat there looking at one another with smiles on their faces. She wondered at how comfortable she felt with him, when it had started, and most of all, how it would end.

HANNAH DROVE UP to see Sarah later that afternoon. Her aunt wasn't as lucid as she'd been the previous Sunday and was chatting about the man she'd almost married in 1956. But an hour or so after Hannah arrived, her aunt seemed to recognize her and began asking questions about the "young man" in her life. Hannah didn't know what to say. She leaned forward and took Sarah's hand, looking into the questioning eyes.

"Aunt Sarah, it's not what you—"

"Don't go telling me he's not anything special. There's a glow to you I haven't seen in years. And you're wearing your hair down. Is he responsible for that?"

Hannah touched her own cheek and tried to deny the warmth there. Did it show so much? Could Sarah really know that for the first time in years, she felt alive? And that Will was responsible?

"There's a bloom in your cheeks, my dear. Spring is here, isn't it? And the roses. I bet they're lovely. I do want you to be happy." The old woman stared at the wall as though wrestling with her next words. "Bring him with you next time."

Startled, Hannah said, "Aunt Sarah, I can't—"

"Please, Hannah. I want to meet him."

Hannah berated herself for letting this thing get started in the first place. How could she tell Sarah the truth? That there was nothing between her and Will? Admit she'd let her aunt believe something that hadn't been true. She couldn't. "I'll try, but I may not be able to get up here next Sunday. We've scheduled the carnival for two weeks from yesterday."

"Bring him next time, then. Please?"

"How about some juice?" Hannah offered brightly, trying to change the subject. "You must be thirsty. I'll be right back."

Hannah stepped out of the room and leaned against the wall, letting her head fall back. *What have I done?* There was only one way to fix it. By the time she came back in two weeks, she and Will would have to 'break up.'

THOSE TWO WEEKS passed in such a flurry of activity that Hannah all but forgot about Aunt Sarah's awkward request. There was so much to be done before the carnival. Signs to make. Food to order. Volunteers to recruit.

Will touched base by telephone several times a day, eager to get Hannah's opinion on some decision or another. He'd shown up on her doorstep at six-thirty on the Monday morning after she'd visited Sarah. Disregarding the protest put up by her sore muscles, Hannah had slipped on her sweats and they'd set off up Wilmington. But after the first few minutes, she began to enjoy herself—breathing in the crisp morning air, listening to the early-morning calls of the robins. In addition, she felt as though she was doing something good for herself, taking an interest in her well-being.

And so began for Hannah a new daily ritual. After a few days, she let Will off the hook, telling him he didn't have to drag her out of bed each morning at six-thirty. He could sleep later. She'd get up herself. Each day that she went a block or two farther, she shared her success with him, and he beamed his approval.

She looked forward to that praise and pushed herself that much harder. Running was even improving her outlook on life—and her sense of humor. One morning her neighbor came out for the paper just as Hannah was beginning her run.

"Why, Hannah dear, you're exercising," the woman remarked with wide-eyed disbelief.

Hannah chuckled. "Yes, Mrs. Tuttle. It surprised me, too."

CHAPTER SEVEN

LATE ON THE TUESDAY afternoon before the carnival, Will stopped by the library to drop off some extra poster board for some last minute sign-making. He appeared in the doorway of the children's room, where Hannah had recruited the help of a few regulars from the afternoon story hour.

She looked up to find him in the doorway, and her face broke into a smile. "Will. You're just in time to give us a hand."

A chorus of voices went up. "Wow, it's Will Kincaid!"

"Hi, Mr. Kincaid. You gonna help?"

"You ever gonna play football again, Will?"

He raised a hand and laughed as he made his way toward the round table where the group was hard at work making signs. "Whoa. How you doin', guys? I see you're doing some great work."

"Yeah," replied a little boy with red ink from a magic marker on one cheek. "Can you draw a donkey on my poster, Mr. Kincaid?"

"Good idea, John," Hannah said with a barely suppressed smile. "I bet Mr. Kincaid's very good with donkeys."

Will shot her a look and laughed. "I guess I can try." He squatted down beside the child and, taking the pen in his right hand, began to draw.

Hannah stood to the side, watching them. She realized she watched Will in much the same way the children did—almost in awe. Something about him drew others to him. Something warm and giving and yet needy at the same time. She took advantage of the moments he was busy and studied him intently. She thought about the way he'd kissed her that night, and she felt a sudden yearning for that moment again—to run her fingers through his thick golden hair and feel for herself those strong, wide shoulders.

Just then, he looked up at her and smiled. And to Hannah, the whole world held promise.

ONCE THE SIGNS were finished, Hannah and Will thanked the children and then waved goodbye when their mothers picked them up. She went to wash her hands, leaving Will standing at the front desk. Jenny had gone out on an errand, so he'd agreed to watch the desk for her. He tapped his fingers on the wooden top, taking in the room that made up Hannah's world from eight to five.

He envied her in a way. Being surrounded by books each day. To him, it was like having access to all the knowledge in the world. What a privilege to have the freedom to pick up a book, any book, and sit down and read.

His gaze fell on a nearby table where Henry Lawson sat flipping through one now. With a glance at the front door, Will headed toward the table. "Hey, Henry. How's it going?"

Henry looked up at Will. "Just passing a little time. How 'bout you?"

"Been working on the carnival. Appreciate your volunteering. We can use all the help we can get."

"Glad to do it. My granddaughter's awfully excited about bringing her pony over for the pony rides."

Will smiled. "Good. What're you reading there?"

The older man looked down at the book and then shrugged, giving Will a startled glance. "Nothing, really. Just looking."

Will studied Henry, noticing the sudden spots of color in the man's cheeks. He thought about the day he'd noticed Henry following the lines of the page with his finger. Then it hit him. Henry Lawson couldn't read.

Will swallowed the lump in his throat, backed away and raised a hand. "I'll be seeing you, Henry. And thanks again for the help."

"Sure thing, Will," Henry said with a nod. "Sure thing."

THAT AFTERNOON when Hannah got home, she unfurled the garden hose and went to work on her rosebushes.

She loved this time of year, when everything unfolded with new life. The maples in the front yard were covered with leaves and the tulips by the mailbox were in full bloom. But the rosebushes were the real miracle—how they appeared to die with the winter, only to return in full majesty with the rebirth of the season.

For the first fifteen minutes, she forced herself to concentrate on her work, refusing to wonder about Will and his reasons for leaving the library without saying goodbye. But as had been the case for the past couple of weeks, her resolve weakened, and her thoughts drifted to his face, his smile.

She hummed a little tune as she smoothed the soil at the base of the bushes, picturing the two of them cavorting down Main Street, he on his bike, she determined to keep up. Strange to think of herself that way. It had been so long since she'd done anything carefree.

The phone rang just as she reached to pull a few dead leaves from the bush. A thorn pierced the center of her palm. Grimacing, she headed into the house.

When she reached for the receiver, she was breathless. "Hello."

"Catch you in the middle of something?"

"No. I just . . . I was outside with the roses."

"Oh." He hesitated. "I wanted to apologize for running out on you today. I'd forgotten about something I needed to do."

"That's all right," she said uncertainly.

"I'm sorry, Hannah. I should have waited." He paused and then quickly changed the subject. "I guess we're ready for Saturday."

"I think so." She tried to sound casual. She'd been silly to worry. It hadn't been her place to be concerned about him.

"Good, then. I'll see you early Saturday morning."

"Sure. See you then." She replaced the receiver and dropped her forehead onto her palm.

She'd gotten carried away over the past few days. Had she let herself begin to believe the white lie she'd told Sarah? That the laughter and companionship she'd shared with Will was something more than just two people working together on a project?

Well, it wasn't. She recalled Tom Dillon's words with a clarity that set her head to pounding. *You're setting yourself up for a fall. . . . Will Kincaid's got no use for someone like you.*

THE DAY OF THE CARNIVAL dawned crisp and sunny. Hannah drove to the armory, her mind racing from one potential crisis to the next. She pulled into the parking lot at just after six-thirty. Wheeling in behind her, Will waved as he stepped onto the pavement.

"Morning," she greeted, shoving her hands in her pockets. She'd spent most of the evening before telling herself that now was the time to remember exactly what her position in his life was. Temporary. Just temporary.

Will pulled a fifty-pound sack from the back of the Jeep. "Apples. Thought we might need a few more."

She watched him heft the bag over his shoulder. It might as well have been a sack of feathers for all the effort he expended. "Are you planning to participate?"

He shot her a surprised look. "You bet. You're looking at the 4-H fair apple-bobbing champion three years in a row."

She pressed a hand to her cheek. "My, I had no idea."

He raised an eyebrow. "Well, don't tell anybody. Wouldn't want to scare off the competition."

She laughed and followed him into the building. She'd wanted to be indifferent to him this morning. All business. Tacking up signs. Lugging in sacks of apples. But how could anyone be indifferent to Will Kincaid?

He flicked on a panel of lights near the door, then jogged back outside and soon reappeared with two cups of coffee. "Thought you might like one."

"Thanks." Her eyes met his. Seeing her own excitement reflected there, she resolved to put aside whatever reservations she might have had about being with him. Today was a special day. And she wanted to enjoy it. "Let's get busy. There's work to be done."

Will smiled and snapped her a salute. He set about pouring the apples into tin buckets. Hannah began tacking up signs for "pin the tail on the donkey." And every ten minutes or so, one of them would creep over to the other with a question about this or a comment about that.

She had no idea when her reliance on his opinion had begun, or his on hers. But it was there.

At one point, she tapped him on the shoulder, holding up the donkey tail for inspection. "Do you think the kids will like this?"

He looked up, a nail sticking from the corner of his mouth, and gave her a crooked smile. "Sure they will."

"I don't know," she said skeptically. "Kids today seem so much older than when we were young. Now there's Nintendo and Donkey Kong."

He chuckled. "Yeah, but deep down they're just the same."

"You think so?"

"Yep. They like banana splits and hot chocolate with marshmallows and football on Sunday afternoons..."

"Figured you'd get that in," she teased.

He stared at her for a long moment, then reached out and traced the curve of her jaw. "It's true though."

Gooseflesh danced up her arms. She drew a quick breath. "I—I expect it is."

"There was something I wanted to tell you." His voice dropped a few decibels.

She looked down at the ground, unable to meet his eyes. "What's that?"

"I've really enjoyed working on this with you. I mean it. It's the first thing I've done in a long time that seemed to have some worth."

Surprised, Hannah looked up and said, "I'm sure you must have done charity work."

"A lot, actually. But it wasn't the same. It didn't seem personal. This does."

"I'm glad you suggested it. It's something I should have done a long time ago."

"But then we wouldn't have been able to do it together, so I'm glad you didn't."

She held his gaze, and the silence hung between them. Awareness sizzled in the air, and she wished more than anything that he would kiss her.

A door opened behind them, breaking the spell.

Hannah cleared her throat and made an immediate study of the ceiling. "So... do you think it's too dark in here?"

"Oh. Yes. The bulb. You're absolutely right. Maybe I should get some extra bulbs," he said quickly, then shot a look of wide-eyed innocence at the kitchen doorway. "Well, look who's here. Hello, Jenny."

Jenny ambled toward them, a faint knowing smile tugging at the corners of her mouth. "Good morning. Since you two seem to have the light-bulb situation under control, I'll start with the chairs."

THE CARNIVAL WAS scheduled to begin at ten. The few hours before passed far too swiftly. At one point, Will stepped aside long enough to watch Hannah as she darted here and there, making suggestions.

He suspected that had she been standing on the perimeter of things looking in, she wouldn't have recognized herself. Today, Hannah Jacobs was a woman of confidence, whirling from one project to the next, a compact, efficient tornado of activity. The closer ten o'clock came, the faster she went. This was the Hannah he had expected her to become.

Not for the first time he wondered what had changed all that. Why hadn't she gone away to school as planned? Why had she never left this town, even for a couple of years, as most of the young people did?

What difference did it make to him, though?

It wasn't as if he'd be around long enough for it to matter one way or the other. After the carnival, he'd have no excuse to see her. He'd get on with his own life and let her get on with hers.

He frowned and drank the last of his Coke, before dropping the cup in a trash can and setting out to make himself useful.

IF SOMEONE HAD asked her around eight-thirty that morning, Hannah would have sworn they'd never get it all done. But somehow, by ten o'clock, everything was in place. And when the first ticket holders began coming in, she surveyed their handiwork with a sigh of pleasure. She spotted Will on the other side of the room and smiled when he gave her a thumbs-up.

Difficult as it was to believe, they had pulled it off. Hannah surveyed the room, pride etched on her face. A bevy of smells permeated the air: freshly perked coffee, popcorn drenched in butter, oil from a doughnut-making machine. And if that didn't give the occasion the feel of an old-fashioned carnival, other things did. A dunking booth where Mayor Nichols now sat looking skeptically at the water below him; church-group booths set up offering goodies like apple spice cake and homemade ice cream; cotton-candy stands; apple cider from a nearby orchard.

Perfect. She wrapped her arms around her waist and surveyed the carnival with satisfaction. And she owed it all to Will.

Her gaze fell across the laughing faces of the children now attempting to dunk the town mayor.

A wave of regret swept over her. How long had she kept herself removed from all this? Being involved with other people. Sharing in their laughter, being a part of something. For years, she'd kept herself locked up as though she was the one who'd done something wrong....

If the morning went off without a hitch, the afternoon was even better. There was a fresh crowd of folks and the armory was so full at times there was hardly room to stand.

Sometime just around one, Will tracked Hannah down and put his arm around her shoulder. "A success, you think?"

She turned to him, aware that she was grinning with happiness. "A success, I would say."

He patted her on the back and then turned for treatment of the same kind.

She obliged and said, "I'd say we deserve it."

He munched on the popcorn ball in his hand and then said, "You won't get any arguments from me on that score."

She pointed to the apple barrel. "Have you done it yet?"

He backed away and appeared to be looking for an escape route. "Actually, no, I—"

She grabbed his shirtsleeve and tugged. "What about all that bragging I heard this morning?"

The people around them overheard and began chanting, "Yeah, Will. Come on, Will. Take a turn."

He sent Hannah a glare, but she only smiled at him. He handed her his partially destroyed popcorn ball and, taking a mock bow, stepped forward, reaching for a towel to drape over his shoulders. "Okay, if you want me to show the rest of you up."

"We'll see, we'll see," she teased.

He lowered himself on his good knee and ducked his face into the water.

Hannah stifled a laugh with her hand as she watched him stalking the apples with his mouth. The children standing around the barrel shouted, "Go, Will! Go, Will!"

Will's head dipped again and again, and sure enough, within twenty seconds he jerked out of the water, an apple held prisoner between two rows of white teeth. He turned to Hannah and lifted both palms in the air in an "I told you so" gesture.

She bowed to his obvious apple-bobbing prowess, and then shrieked when he came to a halt in front of her, shaking the water from his hair like a shaggy dog.

"Will!"

He leaned forward and offered her the apple with his mouth. The children were laughing and cheering him on. She had no choice but to take it.

Will lifted his head and gloated, his hands on his hips. "So what's my reward?"

She let the apple drop into her hand and, grinning up at him, reached for one of the blue construction-paper ribbons they'd designed for the winners.

"I made that one, Mr. Kincaid," Janie Clemens piped up from the circle around them.

Hannah patted the ribbon against Will's chest and then, punching the words with her finger, declared with a grin, "Extra Ordinary Apple Bobber."

He looked down at the honorary insignia and grinned. "Well, I think...I'd say that's quite an honor. Extra ordinary, huh? Thank you, honey." He reached down and gave the little girl a hug, careful not to get her wet.

Janie Clemens all but melted. And looking up at the big, good-natured man before her, Hannah knew exactly how she felt.

For Hannah the day would have been perfect had Tom Dillon not decided to put in an appearance. The thought that he might show up had flitted through her mind a time or two, but she'd pushed it away, determined not to let anything mar the day.

But about half an hour after the apple bobbing, she looked up from where she and Will stood talking to the mayor. Her knees nearly buckled at the sight of the deputy making his way toward them.

"Ah, excuse me," she said, interrupting Mayor Nichols who had been congratulating them on a job well done. "I need to check on the—"

But she didn't get a chance to finish before Tom slapped Will on the back and said, "Don't rush off, Hannah. Wanted to let you know what an impressive show the two of you put on here."

Still wet from his dips in the dunking machine, the mayor excused himself, and Will nodded to him before saying, "Thanks, Tom."

"Lot of hard work must've gone into this little production, huh, Hannah?"

She raised her head defiantly. "You could say that."

"Lotta late nights, I bet." There was no denying the implication behind his words.

Will sent Tom a strange look, then glanced at Hannah. She tried not to let on that the other man's presence bothered her.

"That's why you haven't made it out to Clarence's yet, Will. I knew it wasn't because you didn't want to see your old friends."

Will's gaze narrowed. "Yeah, I've been meaning to get out there. But it's been one thing after another."

"Know what you mean. Now that you won't have Hannah to keep you busy, you come on out, you hear?"

Will watched curiously as Tom locked eyes with Hannah and then turned on his heel and left. He remained silent for a long moment before saying, "What is it with you two?"

Hannah balled up the napkin in her hand and said, "I don't know what you mean."

"Yes, you do."

"No. I don't."

"Then why did you freeze when you saw him?"

"I didn't."

"Hannah, I've got eyes. I can see. What is it about him that makes you so jittery? Seems like more than just a case of nerves about an old boyfriend."

"He was never my boyfriend," she shot back, cheeks flushed.

Will's features were etched in disbelief. "Did the two of you date or not?"

"One date," she said softly.

"One?"

"One."

"Come on. You went out for weeks. We didn't see Tom for at least six Saturday nights in a row. From what I understood, you were pretty involved."

She stared up at him, her arms folded protectively across her chest. "And just where did you get that information?"

"From Tom. Where else?"

She bit her lip and forced her voice to remain even. "And I guess you'd believe everything he said."

"Did I have a reason not to?"

"I don't know, did you?"

"Why would he have lied?"

She glanced away and then said, "Maybe you didn't know your best friend as well as you thought."

He looked down at her in exasperation. "Hannah, what the hell are you—"

"Next time, maybe you'd better check out your sources a little better." And with that, she stomped off, her shoulders stiff with anger.

The scene with Will left a black mark on the day, but Hannah forced it to the back of her mind and pretended it didn't matter. It didn't matter that Will believed the lies Tom had told him. It didn't matter. It didn't.

By five o'clock that afternoon she had almost managed to convince herself. The carnival was scheduled to last until nine. And it looked as though the crowd might just hold up until then. She made her way outside, where a line of children stood waiting their turn at the pony rides.

Here, the air smelled of a combination of hay and oats, manure and saddle leather. On the grass just outside the makeshift ring Henry Lawson had set up for the day, a group of children darted back and forth in a game of tag, their shrieks and laughter ringing out beneath the blue spring sky. Henry raised the bill of his hat as Hannah approached and said, "Looks like you're gonna have enough money for that new book-mobile."

"It sure does," she agreed. "Everyone's been so supportive. I appreciate all your help, Henry."

Henry helped a little boy off one of the Shetland ponies and boosted up a small girl with long blond braids in his place. His granddaughter set off leading the child around the ring. "Guess you caught up with Will the other day? Ever figure out why he took off like that?"

She shook her head. "He said he had some things to do."

"Oh." The older man looked down at the ground and scuffed his boot toe in the dirt. "Thought I might've had something to do with it."

"Why would you think that?" she asked, frowning.

Henry stared out at his granddaughter, now laughing as she tugged the reluctant pony along. "I never told you this, Miss Jacobs, but I, ah... Heck, might as well say it. I can't read. All those books I look at every afternoon, that's all I'm doing. Just looking. I think Will might've figured that out and, well, I thought he might've been a little disgusted." The words came out in a rush.

Hannah stared up at the older man and swallowed to keep the emotion from rising within her throat. She knew what the admission must have cost him. She touched his shoulder. "Why didn't you ever let us know, Henry?"

He looked down at the ground. "Too ashamed, I guess. That little granddaughter of mine can read better than me."

"That's because she's had a chance to learn," Hannah said in a compassionate voice. "Did you?"

He shrugged. "Don't reckon I did. Dropped out in the third grade to work on the farm. I missed so many days before then I never really caught on."

Hannah listened to the story with sympathy. Many of the kids from Henry Lawson's generation had never finished school. In rural communities, working on the farm and helping out with the family had often been more important. "Do you want to learn?"

Henry Lawson's lined face appeared torn between the desire to say yes and the certainty he'd never accomplish it. "I suppose it's a bit late now."

"It's never too late. Never. And if you want to learn to read, Henry Lawson, I'll see to it that you do. Even if I have to teach you myself."

Jenny sauntered over then. A smile lit her face as she looked up at Henry. "Why so serious? Aren't you all having fun out here?"

Henry nodded. "Fine time, Miss Dudley. Just fine."

Jenny proceeded to go on about the success of the carnival and how Hannah deserved most of the credit.

"It was Will's idea," Hannah asserted.

"Both of you deserve a pat on the back in my opinion. Don't you agree, Mr. Lawson?" Jenny prodded.

Henry nodded again and traced a pattern in the dirt with his boot toe. "Sure do. My granddaughter's already wonderin' when the bookmobile will be getting out our way."

Hannah stayed and chatted for a few more minutes, then turned and headed back into the armory, her mind already working on how she could go about seeing that Henry Lawson learned to read. She'd have a talk with Jenny on Monday. Between the two of them, they could use the time he came in each afternoon to teach him. Jenny would help. Hannah knew she would.

But something Mr. Lawson had said nagged at the back of her mind. Why would Will have left the man with the impression that his inability to read bothered him? That didn't sound at all like Will. Maybe Henry was just extrasensitive about it.

Something tugged at her heart at the thought of a grown man going through his whole life trying to hide such a secret from the rest of the world. She couldn't imagine Will feeling disgusted with a man for that. It had been Henry's imagination. Born of years of being ashamed. Nothing else, she was sure.

BY NINE THAT NIGHT, Hannah's limbs ached with exhaustion. But it was a wonderful fatigue, the kind that let you know you'd worked hard and earned something for the effort.

It had been an extraordinary day. And by last count, they'd taken in enough to make a significant contribution to the purchase of a new bookmobile. The realization had Hannah smiling and shaking her head in disbelief.

"You look like the cat who ate the canary," Will teased as he approached the front table.

The last of the crowd had dwindled out, leaving the two of them standing alone in the foyer. Jenny had disappeared somewhere in the back to help clean up the kitchen. Forgetting about the words they'd had that afternoon, she looked up at him, unable to hide her happiness. "This is unbelievable to raise so much money in one day. I still can't get over it."

He nodded. "Most folks believe in a good cause."

She kept her gaze even with his. "A lot of them came to see you, you know."

He looked down at one running shoe. "Nah."

"They did. I never heard so many oohs and aahs from fourteen-year-olds," she said, enjoying his embarrassment.

He looked up with a half smile. "What about the town matrons?"

"You had a few of them in a tither, as well."

With a directness that took her off guard, he asked, "And just what would it take to get you in a tither, Hannah?"

She glanced away. "I'm a little past tithering."

He chuckled and said, "Twenty-eight is over the hill, huh?"

Looking away, she fumbled with the cash box and ignored the comment. "I—I don't know how to thank you for all this."

"There's no need to."

"There is. This will mean so much to so many children."

"I'm glad."

Silence.

She looked up at him and knew a sudden sorrow that they would no longer have a reason to spend time together.

When they spoke, their voices collided in midair.

"Hannah, I'm sorry if I upset you earlier—"

"About this afternoon, Will—"

They broke off at the same time.

She made a pretense of brushing dust off the lid of the box. "I'd just rather not talk about Tom."

"Why?"

"It doesn't matter why."

"Then why do I get the feeling it does matter?"

She shrugged. "Let's just forget it."

A fluorescent light above them flickered. Somewhere in the back of the building pots and pans rattled.

"What are you doing tomorrow?" he asked quietly.

"Cleaning up here in the morning, I suppose."

"I'll come over and help." He hesitated, then said quickly, "What would you think of going for a picnic somewhere after that?"

Pleasure skipped through her, followed by a wave of disappointment. "I have to visit Aunt Sarah. I didn't go last week. She'll be expecting me."

"Why don't I go with you? You said she's up at Meadow Spring, right? It's a pretty drive. What do you say?"

She tried for nonchalance, while inside she felt like bursting with sudden happiness. "Are you sure you want—"

"Yes. I'm sure."

Just then Jenny shuffled out of the kitchen, heading toward them. "Terrific day, you two," she said with a wave. "See you in the morning."

"You need a ride, Jenny?" Hannah offered.

"No. Actually, Mr. Lawson's dropping me off."

Hannah raised an eyebrow. "I thought he left earlier to take the ponies back."

"He did. But he was coming back, so..."

"So," Hannah said with a knowing look.

Jenny blushed and hustled out the front door, bidding them good-night over her shoulder.

"Do I smell romance in the air?" Will asked as Jenny shut the door behind her.

"Maybe. Mr. Lawson's an awfully nice man."

"Widower, isn't he?"

"Yes." She hesitated and then said, "He told me something today that I'm ashamed to say I hadn't picked up on."

He glanced toward the door and said, "Oh?"

"He can't read. All those years of coming into the library and I never guessed."

Will shifted from one foot to the other, but remained silent.

She met his eyes. "You knew, didn't you?"

He looked away. "I picked up on it the other day."

"He mentioned that. He seemed to think you might have been . . . bothered by his not being able to read."

Will frowned. "Why on earth would he think that?"

She lifted her shoulders. "Maybe he's self-conscious about it."

He ran a hand through his hair. "There's a hell of a lot more to a man than whether he can read or not. Henry Lawson's a damn fine one."

"He wants to learn."

"Good. I'm glad for him," he said, his expression blank.

"I'm going to try to teach him. I plan to talk to Jenny on Monday about helping."

"That's nice, Hannah." With jerky movements, Will began folding up chairs and standing them against the wall. "I'll start cleaning up now. I've got too much energy to go home yet."

She folded her arms across her chest and watched as he set about stacking tables and putting away chairs with surprising zeal, considering the fatigue he'd admitted to minutes earlier. She studied him a moment longer before reaching for a chair and helping.

CHAPTER EIGHT

AS IT TURNED OUT, Hannah's own energy level picked up enough that she stayed on until she and Will had put the place back in order. The only thing left was the sweeping and mopping, and the armory had agreed to have a janitorial service do that.

The courthouse clock had long since struck midnight by the time they locked the doors and headed for their cars. Will walked Hannah to hers, stopping to lean against the front of the "green boat," as he now referred to it.

The moon rode high in the sky and the crisp night air felt brisk on her cheeks. Somewhere in the distance a trash can fell over, and a cat let out a yowl.

"I'll see you tomorrow?" He shoved his hands into his pockets and looked at her for the first time since they'd begun cleaning.

"I'd planned to leave around noon."

"I'll come by and get you."

"All right." She fumbled for her keys and turned to open the car door.

She could feel his eyes on her back. And then, as if the words were beyond his power to hold back, he said in a voice so low she thought she might have imagined it, "Hannah, come here, please."

She froze. "I—I really should go, Will. It's late."

"Come here, Hannah."

Three such simple words. A choice. Go to him. Or leave. So simple for some. But a turning point for Hannah. Her pulse throbbed. Her palms grew moist. She glanced over at him, releasing the door handle but remaining where she stood.

He moved to stand in front of her, saying nothing, allowing his eyes to speak. With his back to the car, he spread his legs and hooked an arm around her waist, pulling her to him.

Hannah's breath caught in her throat. She could not take her eyes off him. She was frightened and yet warm with a startling anticipation. She placed her hands on his chest, wanting to lean into him, wanting to push away.

Before she could do either, Will's head dipped low, blocking out the moon behind him, and his mouth brushed hers, tentative, testing, tender in a way that sent her inhibitions scattering.

A small gasp of surprise escaped her. But rather than push away, she found that she wanted nothing more than to slip her arms around his neck and wind her fingers into his hair.

And so she did. Uncertainly. Hesitantly. A whisper of longing rose from somewhere deep inside her.

The pace of the kiss accelerated, like a roller coaster, having crept its way to the top, then plummeting down the other side. The rush of feeling overwhelmed her, terrified her, and yet at the same time, thrilled and tantalized her.

He pulled back a moment later, his breathing uneven. He looked down and met her eyes.

She remembered how this had felt.

But had she ever forgotten?

No.

He pulled her to him with a low groan and covered her mouth with his once more. Time fell away. And suddenly they were back at the lake on that long-ago afternoon. The magic had not changed.

He pulled back again, her face still cupped in his hands. "Mmm, you taste good. Like candied apples and popcorn."

Letting her head drop back, she looked up at him, her voice teasing. "And you taste like...Beeman's gum?"

Will's laughter rang softly in the night. "Had a hell of a time finding the stuff in L.A."

Hannah smiled, enchanted by this endearing combination of boy and man.

And suddenly he was pulling her closer one more time, his hands slipping inside her coat.

Reason set a bell clanging inside her, and she twisted her head aside, reaching for a last cobweb of sanity. "Will..."

The word sounded like a plea for release and a desperate cry for more.

But he only groaned and stepped around to switch places with her, then lifted her and sat her on the edge of the car's hood. He wedged his body between her legs, leaning over to let his mouth find hers once again. There was nothing gentle about the kiss. This was about physical want. The need of a man for a woman. She recognized that need because it echoed inside her.

His hands shimmied down her arms, past the curve of her breasts, along her waist, then to her hips, where he fit himself closer inside the grip of her thighs. And all the while, he continued to kiss her. He kept one hand on her thigh, then let the other find its way to the back of her neck, holding her in place while his tongue plunged into her mouth. She instinctively arched toward him, certain only that she did not want him to stop.

There was nothing threatening about the way he held her. This was desire between a man and a woman as it should be. Hannah's arms wound around his neck, and she pressed herself closer to him, unable to think of anything but the hunger building inside her. He kissed the tip of her chin, then grazed her jaw with his teeth, skimming along her neck to her ear. She splayed her hands across his back. He pulled her hair to one side, undid the top button of her blouse and kissed her shoulder.

She tilted her head back, her eyes closed, her need for him pounding in every pulse point of her body.

She all but forgot that it was almost twelve-thirty in the morning, that they were in the middle of the Lake Perdue Armory parking lot. Nothing mattered but this closeness. And that getting closer seemed inevitable.

A car rolled past on a nearby street. A horn sounded in the distance. The sudden noise had them pulling apart like two teenagers caught in the glare of the front porch light. Will stepped back and brushed a hand across his mouth.

They stared at one another, their chests rising and falling, their lips slightly parted.

She touched a hand to her mouth. With the physical separation came a tidal wave of common sense, flattening her with its force. "I—I'd better go."

He reached out a hand and smoothed a lock of her hair between his fingers. "I think you'd better, too."

Hannah slid off the hood, trying to right her clothes about her. She fumbled for the door handle, then stopped and risked one last glance at him.

He stood there watching her. The look in his eyes told her she was asking for something she might not be ready for if she stayed.

And so she went.

WILL'S CHEROKEE ROLLED to a stop in front of Hannah's house just before noon the next day. From her front window, she watched him stride up the sidewalk. How would she act? What would he say? Would they ignore what had happened? Pretend it hadn't?

She looked down at the denim skirt and meloncolored cotton sweater she wore. Would he think she'd tried too hard? Not enough?

She forced herself to cross the room and pull open the door. She gave Will what she hoped was a casual smile.

"Morning, Hannah." He stood there in her doorway, his face expressionless. Obviously he was going to act as if nothing out of the ordinary had passed between them the evening before.

Taking her cue from him, she was determined to appear similarly unaffected. She stepped back and said, "Let me grab my coat and I'll be ready."

She turned and headed for the closet, returning a moment later with a fixed smile. Will helped her on with her coat, and when his fingers brushed her arm, she stepped quickly away from him.

He shot her a puzzled look and then waved her ahead of him out the door. Silence seemed to be the topic of choice for the first fifteen minutes of the drive. They had passed the Bowmans' dairy farm a few miles outside town when Will finally broke it. "You're thinking about what happened last night."

"Let's just forget—"

"To be honest," he went on as though she hadn't spoken, "I've thought of little else since you pulled out of that parking lot. It took us both by surprise. But a few kisses last night that probably shouldn't have happened don't have to ruin today." He waved a hand at the passing scenery, silos and fields of dead winter grass finally turning green again. "The weather's beautiful. Let's just enjoy it."

When she turned to look at him, her eyes mirrored none of the confusion tumbling around inside her. He was right. It was silly to let it come between them now. Maybe what had happened was only natural. They'd spent so much time together. And the day had been a success. There was no reason to think it would ever happen again. She knew Will would easily dismiss the incident. But for Hannah, who'd been overwhelmed by the unexpected feelings he'd tapped in her, it would not be so easily forgotten.

And so, having made the admission, she was determined to put it into perspective as he had done. She pointed out the window at the signs announcing a new lakeside development and said, "I hear they're starting construction at Pyle's Point. The land there is beautiful. But I don't see how it could compare to Tarkington's Cove." Chatter. Meaningless fill-in-the-blanks conversation.

Will glanced at her and said, "Yeah, it'd be hard to."

And so the ride went. They talked about the success of the carnival and what a good time everyone seemed to have had. They discussed the possibility of a budding romance between Jenny and Henry Lawson and rejoiced in the fact that so many more children would get a chance to use the library now. They talked about everything except what had happened between them. That was taboo.

"When do you think they'll order the new bookmobile?" Will asked.

"Ralph Smithers assured me first thing Monday morning, assuming we raised enough money."

"Can't say we didn't do that. But instead of waiting for it to come in, why don't you rent an RV and stock it with some books so you can start right away?"

She looked at him in surprise. "What a good idea. It'll be weeks before we see the real thing. But where..."

"I saw an ad for a place in Roanoke that sells them. Maybe they'll rent us one. I'll give them a call and look into it."

"You'd do that?"

He shrugged. "Why not?"

"Because maybe you have a life you'd like to get back to."

"I will. When I'm ready," he allowed. "For now, I'm content."

The look in his eyes brought back far too vivid memories of his mouth on hers, his hands on her skin.

The temperature in the vehicle was suddenly uncomfortable. Her hands clasped in her lap, she stared straight ahead and steered the conversation clear of anything personal with the same adeptness with which Will avoided potholes.

Fifteen minutes later they turned into the driveway of Meadow Spring nursing home. As always, Hannah's gaze flitted over the building and grounds, looking for some sign that the place might not be fitting for her aunt, a reason to insist that Sarah come home with her. But as usual the place was immaculate, the sidewalks tidy and well-kept, and she'd never been able to find fault with the staff who took care of her aunt.

Will reached across and squeezed her hand. "You hate leaving her here, don't you?"

She looked at him sadly. "More than anything. Every time I come I wish I could take her home with me."

Will rubbed his fingers back and forth across her wrist. "This is what she wanted, right?"

Hannah nodded. "She didn't want to burden me."

"Someday we might have to make the same choices, and I'll bet we'd feel the same way."

Knowing he was right, she pressed her lips together to stem the emotion in her throat. After a moment she said, "Let's go in. She's probably wondering where I am."

Hannah had packed a basket of leftovers from the carnival—some popcorn, a soft pretzel, a few pieces of fruit. She reached for it now as they climbed out of the Jeep and headed for the entrance. Inside, she checked in at the front desk. As they made their way to the private room, she prayed that Sarah would be well today.

But the moment they stepped inside the doorway, Hannah knew she wasn't. The dear and familiar eyes that stared at them from the bed were those of a stranger, a woman who knew no one outside the world in her mind.

Hannah pressed a hand to her mouth and turned to set the basket on the windowsill. Will touched her shoulder, giving her the strength to step forward. "Aunt Sarah?"

The woman turned to stare blankly at her. "Who are you? What day is this?"

"It's Hannah. Your niece. And today is Sunday."

"Where are we?"

Hannah pressed her lips together and reached down to give her aunt a hug, but there was no response. When she spoke again, her voice trembled. "I've brought someone with me today."

Will stepped up from behind her. "Hello, Miss Jacobs. I'm Will Kincaid. We went to church together a few years back."

The woman darted a glance at him and then looked away with total disinterest. "My brother is coming today."

"Aunt Sarah, you know Daddy's..." Hannah left the sentence unfinished, then said, "Have you had your lunch?"

Sarah shook her head.

"I'll go check on it. Will, would you mind waiting here?"

"Not at all." He pulled up a chair and sat down beside Sarah's bed. The second Hannah cleared the doorway, Will said, "That's some niece you have there, Miss Jacobs."

Sarah looked up at him and frowned, as though something in his face had struck a chord. "You look like my brother."

"Hannah's father?"

The woman ignored the question and went on, as though she'd just slipped off to another world. "He wouldn't forgive me. My brother would never forgive me."

"Forgive you? For what?"

"Letting it happen. That awful Dillon boy. I never should've let him get away with it."

Will's gaze narrowed and he leaned forward. "What's that, Miss Jacobs? Get away with what?"

"I never should've—"

Hannah reappeared in the doorway then, looking from her aunt to Will. "Aunt Sarah, what are you filling Will's head with?" she chastised gently, crossing the room to press the woman's hand affectionately. "The nurse said you weren't hungry earlier, but she's going to bring a tray down in just a minute."

Hannah pulled up another chair, then leaned over to smooth her aunt's hair.

"All right," Sarah said. "Mama said if I eat all my lunch, we'll go shopping this afternoon."

Hannah squeezed her eyes shut and then flashed her aunt a bright smile. "That sounds wonderful."

Will watched Hannah, noting the love in her eyes, the gentle way she held the old woman's hand. Sarah's rambling still puzzled him. But he supposed it had been exactly that. Rambling. He knew how hard it must be for Hannah to see her that way. And in that moment, he had never admired anyone as much in his life.

THEY STAYED for almost two hours. By the time they left, Will thought Hannah looked ready to shatter. They walked mechanically down the white halls and out the front door. But once they reached the Cherokee she seemed to wilt.

"Hannah? Are you all right?" He put a hand on her shoulder and turned her to face him.

She nodded.

But he knew otherwise, and he opened the door and helped her in before going around and climbing in himself. He put the key in the ignition and then drove slowly out of the parking lot, away from Meadow Spring.

He drove for twenty minutes, letting the silence hang between them because he couldn't think of a single comforting thing to say. *It'll be all right?* No. Because it wouldn't. *Don't worry about her?* How could she help it?

He turned onto an old dirt road off the highway. Hannah didn't even seem to notice the change in routes. She just stared out the window, lost in her unhappy thoughts.

Will followed the road until it reached a point where it looked out over the waters of Lake Perdue, the same spot he'd taken her all those years ago. How much simpler things had been then. For both of them, it seemed.

Her gaze found his then, and tears welled up in her eyes.

He asked himself what right he had to offer her comfort when he had no idea how long he'd be around to give it to her. But seeing her anguish, he wished for nothing more than to be able to make it go away. "Hannah. Come here."

He reached for her, pulling her across the seat and wrapping his arms around her. Knowing that words weren't what she needed, he just held her, fitting her head against his shoulder, stroking her back with his hand.

She remained that way for a long time, until finally her shoulders began to shake and the pain rose within her, pouring out in a wail of mournful sorrow.

Will's heart clenched in grief and helplessness. He wanted to tell her it would be okay, but he couldn't give her false promises. "I know, sweetheart. It hurts like hell, doesn't it?"

He held her more closely, stroking her back, having no more to offer her than the comfort of his presence. "Just let it out, honey. You've been carrying this around for too long. It's okay to let go."

The soft words pulled forth the sobs, and Will did what he thought she needed most. He held her and let her cry.

Some time later, Hannah pulled back and, with a tear-streaked face, risked a look at Will. "I'm sorry. I shouldn't have put you through this."

"Hey—" he pushed a strand of hair back from her face "—there's nothing to be sorry about. You have a right to your grief. Maybe this has been a long time coming."

"But I shouldn't have—"

He touched a finger to her lips. "Shh. It's all right to let somebody else be there for you now and then. I don't know how you've done it alone."

She pulled back and settled into her own seat, searching through her purse for a tissue. She didn't know what had come over her. It wasn't as though she'd never seen her aunt that way. But somehow having Will there to witness it, made the reality of the situation hit her like never before. "It's not always that bad. Sometimes she's the same person I've always known. And then sometimes, like today, she's in another world."

"I don't know much about Alzheimer's, but I guess that's what makes it so awful."

Hannah nodded and dropped her head back against the seat, murmuring, "The loss of dignity. That's what breaks my heart the most. She was always so strong. I'd give anything to be able to make her better."

He covered her hand with his. "I know. But sometimes things just aren't in our control. How long has she been sick?"

"It started a few years ago, maybe before then. It seemed so innocent at first, forgetting names, dialing the wrong telephone number, misplacing her keys. But it just got worse from there. One time she was missing for four days. That happened just before she went to Meadow Spring."

He looked at her with solemn eyes. "It's been a lot for you to shoulder, hasn't it?"

"I'd do it all over again for her," she said, sniffing. "She's all I have."

"That's not true. If you need me, I'm here. All you have to do is ask."

In that moment, Hannah realized her own weakness. Logic demanded she pull away, insist he take her home. But what chance did logic stand when the heart got in the way? She looked out at the sun sinking in the west. "It looks the same, doesn't it?"

"I wondered if you'd remember," he said softly.

"I never forgot."

He reached for her, pulling her close against him. And she stayed there. In his arms. Just as she'd wanted to the last time they'd come here. Ten years ago.

WHEN WILL DROPPED Hannah off at her house, he sat there at the curb for a couple of minutes, taking note of the lights popping on in the living room and then a few seconds later, in a room upstairs.

He propped his forearms on the steering wheel and leaned forward, gazing at the dark street ahead, debating whether to go to her door and make sure she was okay. It had been a difficult day for her. But as soon as the thought registered, he dismissed it. Bad move. The last thing he needed was to be alone with Hannah. For the first time in his life, he didn't trust himself. He'd offered her comfort today. But when he'd held her in his arms, he'd known the stirrings of something that had nothing to do with consolation.

He'd made every effort to put last night's incident in the back of his mind. But now the memory of it came flooding back. He drew in a rush of air as he recalled the way she'd felt in his arms. Passionate and needy.

Playing with fire. That's what he was doing. Maybe he could afford to get singed once or twice. But Hannah couldn't. His time in Lake Perdue was limited.

He knew as sure as he was sitting there that the best thing he could do for her was to get away from this house and leave her alone.

Hadn't she had enough to deal with?

He thought about Sarah Jacobs and the obvious fact that she wouldn't be there for Hannah. Sadness gripped him. He thought again about the woman's ramblings and recalled with sudden clarity her mentioning "that Dillon boy."

Tom Dillon? And what had she meant by not letting him get away with it? Get away with what? And why would Tom have lied all those years ago about going out with Hannah?

He sat up and looked again at Hannah's house.
Something didn't add up. Maybe he'd drive out to
Clarence's and see if he could figure out what it was.

OVER THE YEARS, Clarence's had garnered a reputation as the local redneck hangout. Will and Tom had
never frequented the place in high school, but Tom
had apparently changed his opinion of it.

Not that it looked any different.

It was still a joint. Little more than a dilapidated
cement-block shack. It sat on the outskirts of town,
and judging from the number of cars parked outside,
its popularity had increased over the years.

A few moments later Will stepped through the front
door and squinted into the dimness. A jukebox sat to
one side of the room. Clint Black complained through
the speakers of a love gone bad. Cigarette smoke hung
in the bar like L.A. smog, trapped with nowhere to go.

Moving across the room, Will caught the bartend-
er's eye and asked for a beer, then nodded to a couple
of men as he leaned on one elbow and propped a heel
on the rail at the foot of the bar. "Tom Dillon been
out this way tonight?"

A man in a black Caterpillar hat said, "Ain't he always? He's back there." He pointed to a side room.
"Playing pool."

Will picked up his beer and headed in that direction, not quite sure what he wanted to know. He
stopped in the doorway, leaning his shoulder against
the frame.

He watched as Tom lined up the cue ball for a victory stroke, then sent it scooting across the table,
slapping the last ball into the corner pocket. Tom let

out a whoop and threw a fist into the air. Then he noticed Will leaning against the doorframe.

"Will," he said in surprise. "Hey, buddy. Don't just stand there. Come on over and join us."

Will raised a reluctant hand. "Don't think I'm up to the competition."

"Oh, come on, come on. I'll go easy on you, won't I, boys?" He'd directed the question to the two men standing behind him. Like a couple of puppets, they nodded and then stepped aside to make room for Will at the table.

"Had the devil of a time getting you here," Tom said.

"Yeah. Never figured you for hanging out at Clarence's."

Tom rubbed chalk on the end of his cue stick. "Things change, you know."

"Few practice shots?" Will suggested.

"Not unless you want them." When Will shook his head, Tom said, "Then go to it."

He stood back and watched as Will racked up the balls and proceeded to break them, using the pool stick in his left hand. "You're still as good with your left as your right, I see."

Will shrugged and said, "Doesn't seem to make much difference. Whatever feels good at the time."

Tom's laugh was a little forced when he said, "Been keeping yourself busy, I hear."

Will aimed at the red and sent it whizzing into the pocket. "Oh, yeah?"

"Hanging out with Hannah Jacobs."

He lined up another shot. "Is that what they're saying?"

Tom chewed on his lower lip. "Hannah's changed since school. Never would've figured she'd hold your interest. Not with all those starlets you must have had." The pause that followed held a good measure of drama. "Word around town is that you've been seeing her."

Something told Will he'd never get anything out of Tom if the man thought the rumors held an ounce of truth. He chalked his stick and kept his eyes on the table. "Then word has it wrong."

"Yeah?" The question held a note of disbelief.

"I don't think my friend in L.A. would care too much for the idea."

The deputy drew one eyebrow up and said, "Wouldn't, huh? So who is she? Model? Movie star?"

"Nobody you'd know."

Tom's smile didn't reach his eyes. "Yeah, reckon not. She pretty hot?"

"Pretty hot," Will said as he lined the upper half of his body with the cue.

"Didn't figure there was anything to those rumors about you and Hannah. I tell you, that woman's strange."

"She's strange all right. She ever go out?"

"Hell, no. Not that anyone's asked," Tom scoffed.

"Why's that, do you think?"

"All those signals she sends off, I guess."

"Seemed friendly enough when you were going out with her."

Tom sent Will a man-to-man smile. "Pretty friendly."

"I remember you gloating about it."

Tom laughed. "Looking back, it wasn't worth gloating over. Guess I just enjoyed proving she wasn't the goody two-shoes everyone thought she was."

Will looked up at his old friend. Tom held his gaze as though daring him to question the truth of the statement. "Why'd you lie about going out with her after that?"

Tom went still, his eyes narrowed. "What do you mean, lie?"

"Hannah says the two of you just went out once. So why'd you make the rest of us think you were dating her?"

Tom rested his cue on the floor. "Man, I don't know what the hell she's—"

"Cut it out, Tom. She's got no reason to lie."

"Like I do?" he said indignantly.

"I don't know. Do you?"

"Women," he said with a snort.

They stood there for almost a minute before Tom finally said, "So we only went out once. Big deal."

"Why'd you lie?"

"Aw, hell," Tom said on a sigh of disgust. "What'd she have to bring this up for? It's not like it happened yesterday, you know." He hesitated. When Will remained silent, he said, "I figured the rest of you would've given me a hard time if you knew we didn't go out more than once."

"You sure that was it, Tom?"

"What else would it have been?"

Will refocused and sent the cue ball heading for the last ball on the table. It hit the pocket with a thunk.

Tom placed his cue on the rack behind the wall. The "good ol' boy" grin had returned when he swung around and said, "Always were the superior sportsman, weren't you? Come on out and let me buy you a beer."

But Will shook his head and reached for his jacket, no longer able to keep up the conversation with Tom. The need to defend Hannah was too strong. He couldn't yet ask himself why. And he sure didn't want to lay it out for Tom's scrutiny. "Gotta get home. Early day tomorrow. See you around, Tom."

As Will drove home that night, he called himself a fool for going out to Clarence's at all. So what if Tom had lied? It wasn't a criminal offense. After hearing what Sarah Jacobs had said that afternoon, he'd thought that maybe, just maybe, Tom had been somehow connected to the life Hannah had led the past ten years.

The very idea was ridiculous. Tom could not have influenced her life so drastically. There was obviously nothing between them. And there hadn't been since high school.

But the thought of Tom's bragging about what had taken place between Hannah and him tied a knot in Will's gut. He'd wanted to punch his old friend in the mouth. Hannah deserved better. But then, how was he any different? Hanging around. Comforting her. Offering to be there for her as if he'd be in Lake Perdue indefinitely.

Rounding the curve just past Tate's Gas & Go, Will gunned the Cherokee and shot off down the two-lane road, trying to leave the questions behind. But it didn't work. So he slowed down and forced them into perspective.

He'd been acting like a fool lately. He didn't know what he was going do with the rest of his life. If he was honest, he'd admit that just beneath the surface of their friendship lay the desire to be more than friends. Just as it had ten years ago. That hadn't changed.

But neither had the fact that Hannah wouldn't have anything to do with him if she ever learned the truth about him.

HANNAH STEPPED OUT of her house the next morning just before six-thirty. The screen door slammed behind her, the only sound in the early-morning stillness. She hugged herself, shivering in the cool morning air, then set off down the sidewalk at a moderate jog, determined that today would be the day she went two miles without stopping. Admittedly, her pace was slow, but placing one foot in front of the other, she'd do it.

One foot in front of the other. A philosophy at which she ought to be an expert. Trudging along, one day to the next. Week after week. Month after month. Until the years had passed and she found herself here in Lake Perdue, living the life of a nun. At twenty-eight.

She picked up the pace, her shoes pounding the sidewalk.

She'd never minded before. Before?

Before Will Kincaid came back to Lake Perdue.

How many times had she told herself it wouldn't do to get close to him? How many times had she done so, anyway?

She thought about yesterday and the way he'd held her in his arms, letting her vent her grief. She'd needed him then. How she'd needed him. He'd known it, and he'd been there for her.

She reached the one-mile point and, making the turn to head back, jogged on, breathing harder now.

Already, he'd wrought such changes in her life, lassoing her into working on the carnival, bullying her into taking up jogging. Both for which she was grateful.

Her thoughts went again to the concern he'd shown her. Who would have imagined such tenderness in someone like him? A man whose life-style suggested fast women and fast cars. Love 'em and leave 'em. Tenderness? Will Kincaid was kind and gentle. Far different from the image she'd painted of him in her mind over the past ten years.

Would he be leaving Lake Perdue as he'd planned? Or would he stay on?

She completed the two miles with a smile of satisfaction. And she realized that she'd also crossed a line from which there was no turning back.

She had begun to hope.

BUT THE NEXT WEEK crept by and Hannah didn't hear from Will. Pride prevented her from calling him. She forced her mind to other things, tending her roses with gloves now since she had no desire to be pricked again. But she welcomed their blossoming buds with less enthusiasm than she had in years past.

On Monday, she'd taken Jenny aside and explained what Henry Lawson had confided to her on Saturday.

Jenny's astonishment had equaled Hannah's. "Henry—I mean, Mr. Lawson—can't read?"

"It's hard to believe we didn't pick up on it, isn't it?"

Jenny had nodded, still too stunned to speak.

"He wants to learn though, Jenny," Hannah had said. "And I'm going to start teaching him. Would you be willing to help?"

"Well, of course, I will."

"I thought we could take turns for an hour each afternoon when he comes in. The other one can cover the front desk."

"Of course we can."

They'd begun that afternoon. Hannah had collected some primary books from the children's room, and she'd started Mr. Lawson out with the basics. He'd said he felt foolish at first, but she'd reassured him, "We all have to start somewhere. There's no shame in starting at the beginning."

And by the end of the lesson, Henry hadn't been able to hide the pleasure on his face when Hannah praised him for his efforts and the progress he'd made. This kind man, well into his fifties, deprived of the education he'd secretly yearned for over the years was learning to read with an enthusiasm most people couldn't muster for anything.

The project meant a lot to Hannah. She both welcomed and needed it. For that one hour during the day, her thoughts did not stray to Will.

That only left twenty-three others with which to contend.

CHAPTER NINE

THE WEEK WAS ONE Will didn't care to repeat. He avoided the telephone and resisted the urge to drive by Hannah's house. He'd made a decision to back out of her life, for her and himself. Knowing the uncertainty of his own future, he had no business letting her think he might have something to offer her. And he made every effort to follow through on the resolution.

On Monday afternoon, he went out to his father's for a visit, hoping that they'd be able to have a conversation that didn't lead to what he planned to do with his life. The hope had been in vain.

He let himself in through the back door, surprising Aunt Fan with a bear hug from behind. "It's about time you got out here to see your aunt Fan, boy. Where you been hiding?" She turned to glare at him, then she swatted him with the dish towel and fussed until he agreed to sample her apple cobbler.

John Kincaid appeared in the doorway, frowning at Will, who stood by the stove with his arm around Fannie. "Thought you'd forgotten where I lived," he said, crossing the room to pour himself a cup of coffee.

The laughter left Will's face. "Aw, Dad, don't start."

"You come home for the first time in years and spend more time with strangers than you do with your own father."

Fannie pushed Will toward a chair and set a plate of apple cobbler in front of him, topping it off with a scoop of ice cream.

Before he could respond, his father went on, "I'm surprised that agent of yours is letting you get away with this. All those contracts..."

Will dug into the cobbler. "In case you forgot how it works, Dad, Dan works for me. Not the other way around."

John Kincaid snorted and took a swallow of his coffee. "Your not working is money out of his pocket, too, isn't it?"

"I guess it is."

"Well, then—"

"I didn't come out here to argue with you, Dad."

As if recognizing the threat in his son's voice, the elder Kincaid remained quiet for a moment and surveyed Will over the rim of his cup. "You're still seeing that Jacobs girl, I take it?"

Will glared at his father before answering. "I think that's my business. I can see this conversation's not going to improve." He pushed back from his chair and went to give Fannie another hug. "Thanks for the dessert," he whispered, just before he slipped out the back door.

The rest of the week didn't get any better. He resisted the urge to drive to the library and see the rented bookmobile at least a hundred times. On Wednesday he gave in to the need to hear her voice, picked up the phone and dialed the library number. When she answered, he held the receiver until she hung up, and wondered at the wave of loneliness that washed over him.

On Thursday afternoon, Will let himself into the house, dripping sweat from the thirty-mile bike ride he'd just completed. He'd pushed himself to the limit the last ten miles or so and still felt the strain in his lungs. For some reason, the self-abuse felt good. The phone was ringing as he unlocked the door. He sprinted across the room and picked it up.

A woman's voice asked, "Mr. Kincaid?"

"Yes?" he managed, still breathing hard.

"This is Anna Jones, at Meadow Spring nursing home. I've had a request from one of our patients. Sarah Jacobs?"

"Yes, what is it?" he asked, alarmed.

"Your name and number weren't listed in our files, but she was adamant about seeing you, so I called information and got it."

"That's okay, but what's—"

"She's been asking for someone to call you since she woke up this morning. She'd like to see you. Today, if possible."

Will sank into a kitchen chair and rested his forehead against his knuckles. "Do you know why?"

"I don't know any more than that, Mr. Kincaid. May I tell her you'll be here?"

He closed his eyes and wondered if his going up to Meadow Spring would weave him more tightly into the fabric of Hannah's life when his sole aim this week had been to extricate himself. He didn't let himself answer the question, but sighed and said, "I'll be there as soon as I can."

An hour and a half later Will made his way down the hall of the nursing home, stopping just short of

Sarah Jacobs's room to draw a deep breath and run a hand through his hair. Outside, the first storm clouds of the season hung low in the sky. Thunder rumbled in the distance. He took another breath, knocked on the door and stepped inside.

He'd stopped off at a florist and picked up an arrangement of tulips. He now felt awkward standing there with the basket in his hands. She probably wouldn't even remember him. "Miss Jacobs, I'm Will Kincaid. How are you today?"

She looked up and managed to smile at him. "What lovely flowers. Are those for me?"

Will came closer and stopped just short of her bed, uncertain what to do or say now that he was here. "I thought you might enjoy them."

"They'll look pretty there on the windowsill."

He nodded and set them by the window, then returned to stand by the bed. "You wanted to see me, ma'am?"

She sighed, then leaned back against the pillows. "Since Hannah wouldn't bring you, I called you myself."

Will's heart clenched as he realized the old woman did not remember his being here before. He opened his mouth to speak, but Sarah went on.

"I can't tell you how glad I was to learn that Hannah had made a friend. A gentleman friend."

Unsure what direction the conversation was taking, he said, "Hannah's very special."

"She is," the old woman allowed, shaking her head. "Very special. And to think of all the years she's wasted . . ."

Will thought of how he'd accused Hannah of as much, but still found himself saying, "I don't think she considers her life wasted, Miss Jacobs."

Sarah ignored the remark and said, "So many things she could have done. All those colleges trying to recruit her. One incident, one misfortune, can set a person off on such a different path." She reached across the bed to take his hand in hers, gripping it with a strength surprising in someone so frail. "But you're here for her now."

He shook his head in confusion. "I'm sorry, Miss Jacobs, I don't quite follow—"

The older woman turned her gaze toward the window, still gripping his hand. "All my fault, you see. She came in that night, clothes torn, face scratched. She said they'd been in an accident. That Tom had run into a ditch. But I should have known. I should have known." The words rang out in the still room.

Will stared at her as if he'd misheard. He felt as though a rack of weights had been dropped on his chest. He struggled to keep his breathing steady.

In his mind, pieces of the puzzle began to fall into place. *That Dillon boy... clothes torn, face scratched....*

Will's lungs expanded with air, which then whooshed out in a rush of realization. That son of a bitch. He'd lied. The whole thing had been a lie. And the picture of what must have happened that night after Brad Manning's party was as clear as if someone had opened a window to the past and allowed him to look inside.

He sat there, too stunned to move while Sarah Jacobs stared out the window. When anger began to wash away the shock, he scooted his chair back and leaned over to give the old woman a gentle kiss on the forehead. "I have to go now, Miss Jacobs. Thank you for calling me," he said, gently disentangling his hand from hers.

Sarah turned to stare at him with eyes that no longer recognized him.

Despite the downpour, Will made the hour-long drive back to Lake Perdue in forty minutes.

Anger ate at him, so hot and out of control he thought he might explode. His hands clenched the steering wheel. One question hammered in his head like the rain on the windshield. *Why?*

He wished he had no idea what the answer was. But he did. He had a very good idea.

Barreling past the town-limits sign, he applied the brake. He didn't want to get stopped for speeding and delay his mission.

That mission was to find Tom Dillon.

He drove by the sheriff's office. Tom's car wasn't there. He drove by the café, then wheeled out to Clarence's. Still no sign of Tom's car. Beginning to despair that he wouldn't find him, Will circled back by the sheriff's office. When he spotted Tom getting out of his brown county vehicle, he gunned the Cherokee into the parking lot.

He slammed on the brakes and slid to a halt just behind the other car, spewing gravel in his wake. He flung open the door and with every ounce of the fury raging inside him, charged at the man he'd once considered his friend.

The deputy glanced up in surprise, his mouth opening to utter a stunned "Will, what the hell are you—"

Tom Dillon never stood a chance.

He'd gone pudgy over the years. Will had not.

If anything it was raining harder now, and Tom slid on the wet pavement as Will grabbed him by the shirt collar and flung him against the county car.

Tom grunted and then stared up at Will with wild eyes. "What the—"

Will slammed a punch into his gut, oblivious to the other man's cries of outrage and moans of pain. All he could see was Tom's face the day he'd stood there by his high-school locker, gloating about having "scored" with Hannah Jacobs.

Shouts and sirens wailed from behind them, and in seconds two deputies were rushing toward them, struggling to pull Will off Tom.

Will shook the two deputies off. Chest heaving, he grabbed Tom by the shoulders and forced him to look at him. "You son of a bitch," he snarled. "You *raped* her, didn't you?"

Tom's head lolled back, and when he didn't answer, Will's demand became a shout. "Didn't you? Admit it, you bastard! You knew I was interested in her. That's why you did it, wasn't it? Was it because of football? Because you didn't get the scholarship you wanted, and I did? Was that it? You thought you could get back at me that way?"

After hearing Will's accusations, the two deputies looked at one another, dropped their hands to their sides and stepped back. One went to radio for an ambulance.

Will shook Tom again, demanding, "Answer me, damn you!"

Tom finally looked up at him, his expression dazed. A smile touched the corners of his mouth, turning into an obscene grimace as blood trickled from between his lips.

Will released him as if he were a bag of week-old garbage. Tom collapsed to the ground.

"Not that anyone would ask her," Will rasped. "You did that to her, you bastard! You did that to her."

He backed away, stumbling as he wiped at his mouth. He swung around and dropped his head back, the rain pelting his face as he limped back to his vehicle, climbed inside and drove home.

NEWS OF THE FIGHT spread through Lake Perdue like a match thrown to kerosene-soaked hay. Word reached Hannah's ears just before she left the library that afternoon. Kay Lynn Gillespie, Jenny's friend, had dropped off some books after work, obviously bursting to share the news with someone.

Jenny and Hannah were both at the front desk when the woman came through the door.

"Well, hello, Kay Lynn," Jenny said.

"Jenny, Hannah." The woman dropped the books on the desk and shook her head from side to side as though a heavy secret were weighing on her soul. "Bet it's been pretty quiet around here this afternoon, compared to what it's been over at the sheriff's office."

"Pretty quiet here. What's going on over there?" Jenny asked.

Kay Lynn allowed herself a dramatic pause, then said, "Will Kincaid beat the tar out of Tom Dillon, that's what."

Hannah's head jerked up from the cards she'd been sorting. "What?"

"Beat him within an inch of his life, they said," Kay Lynn said with a nod.

"Why?" Hannah and Jenny said together.

The woman leaned forward, her voice dropping several decibels lower. "Rumor had it Will said something about Tom raping somebody. Can you believe that?"

Hannah stepped back, the blood draining from her face. "Wh-who?" The word pushed past her lips, barely audible.

Kay Lynn shrugged. "Nobody seemed to know. Tom says it's a lie, but the funny thing is, he refused to press charges against Will. Pretty strange, don't you think? Except, I guess, that they used to be such good buddies."

Noticing Hannah's expression, Jenny put a hand on her shoulder. "You all right? You've gone white as a sheet."

"F-fine. I'm fine. I think I'll go ahead and leave, though." She slid off her stool and bent over, reaching with mechanical movements for the drawer that held her purse. "Can you lock up, Jen?"

Jenny eyed her strangely. "Of course I can. You sure you're okay, though?"

Hannah headed for the door without answering.

She got in her car and drove. The car might as well have been on automatic pilot. She had no control over the direction it took.

Her mind could register only one thing. She had to see Will.

She kept her thoughts blank as the car nosed around the curves and over the hills leading to Tarkington's Cove. She wouldn't think. She had to see him first.

Heading into the development, Hannah ran the stop sign in front of the marina, wheeling the old Cadillac into the parking lot beside Will's Cherokee. She shot out of the car, leaving the door open.

Her heels echoed on the wood entryway. She banged on the door with a fist. "Will?" Not giving him time to answer, she continued to pound.

Seconds later, the door swung open, and he stood looking down at her with regretful eyes. "Oh, Lord, Hannah, I'm sorry."

She stared up at him, her voice barely more than a whisper. "Say it isn't true."

"Hannah..." The way he said her name told her more than she wanted to know.

"How could you?" The question was torn from her.

Will shook his head, his expression a mixture of pain, regret and sympathy.

"Now everyone will know. They'll all know." She spoke slowly now, precisely, as though this moment had been inevitable.

"Hannah, sweetheart, I'm sorry." His look was helpless. "It's okay. It'll be all right."

But she just shook her head, certain nothing would ever be all right again.

He reached to push a strand of hair from her face. She flinched and stepped back. His hand dropped to his side. "Hannah, I shouldn't have let it out that way. It was wrong. I realize that now. I was just so consumed with anger I didn't think about—"

"How did you find out?"

"Sarah was asking to see me. I went there today. She didn't tell me anything outright. But I put two and two together. And all I wanted to do was kill the bastard."

"Why didn't you come see me first?"

"Had I been sane enough I would have. I just...
Hannah, honey, I still want to kill him for what he did
to you. He's why you've stayed here all these years,
isn't he? He's why you've locked yourself away, convinced yourself you had nothing to offer anyone."

Hannah's glance skitted away. She couldn't meet his
eyes. She didn't want to see the truth reflected there.
Admitting it to him would be admitting it to herself.

"Why didn't you tell someone after it happened?"

She bit her lower lip at the compassion in his voice.
"I—I was too ashamed."

He groaned and hauled her against him, overcom-
ing her protests. His lips were close to her ear, his voice
low. "I should have known something was wrong. I
should have known he lied about it, should have
known better than to believe him. I couldn't understand why you had—after what had happened between us at the lake. He was my best friend. I had no
reason not to believe him. If I had thought for one
second that he forced you—"

She held up a hand and said, "Will, don't."

"Oh, God, Hannah. Hannah."

She collapsed against him, wilted and defeated.

They stood like that, her head on his shoulder, his
hand stroking her back. Long minutes passed. How
many, she did not know. For the moment, she needed
his strength, his protection. For the moment, nothing
else mattered.

When she finally raised her head, she felt embarrassed by her display of vulnerability. She looked away
and slipped out of his arms.

He let her go, watching as she went to stand by the
window and gaze out at the lake. "I didn't think to ask
if you were all right," she said.

"I'm fine."

She turned to pin him with her gaze. "Are you sure?"

"Don't even think about me." He came to stand beside her. "What are you going to do about this?"

"About what?"

"The rape," he said softly.

Hannah flinched. How ugly the word was. How odd that she'd never said it aloud before. "It's been ten years, Will."

"I called my attorney just before you got here. There's no statute of limitations for criminal charges of rape in Virginia. It could be thirty years, and it wouldn't matter. You still have the right to press charges."

"No. Nobody would believe me now."

He reached out and tilted her chin toward him. "I believe you."

What would she have given ten years ago to confide in him, to know that he would have believed her? She pulled away and turned toward the lake once again. "I could never go through that now, Will," she said. "I realized a long time ago that I should have gone to the police that night. But I didn't. I couldn't. That's the last thing I want now."

"He should have to pay for what he did to you."

"It's over, Will. I've put it behind me. I don't want to dredge it all up again. And after today..."

"But that's just it. You haven't put it behind you. You live it every day of your life. You let that bastard convince you that you'd done something wrong—though I know there's part of you that knows that isn't true."

"No, I—"

"Damn it, Hannah, can you deny that you've buried yourself in that house of yours, hardly coming out except to go to work, attend church or visit your aunt?" The words were quick and angry. "You're twenty-eight years old. You've got a life to live."

She stared at him, overwhelmed by a need for time to think. "That's right. And I don't need you to tell me how to do it," she said before bolting for the door.

Will stood there at his living-room window long after Hannah's car had roared out of the driveway. He rubbed the back of his neck with one hand and let out a weary sigh. He'd let her go for now. But they weren't finished. Not by a long shot.

HANNAH ARRIVED HOME some fifteen minutes later. She raced up the sidewalk on shaky legs, stepping over the Madam Butterfly rose that had fallen from the bush by the porch. She didn't bother to pick it up. She slammed the door behind her and leaned up against it as if by doing so, she might somehow hold the world at bay. Shut out the nightmare that had been resurrected.

She closed her eyes and drew a deep breath. How had this happened? Why couldn't things have remained as they were? Now everyone would know.

The thought launched her up the stairs. She turned on the shower and stripped off her clothes before stepping under the hot steaming water, letting it pound against her, burning her skin, cleansing her as it had cleansed her that night ten years ago. How long she stood there she couldn't have said. Finally, leaning her head against the wall, she turned off the faucet and stepped out onto the bath mat, wrapping a white fleece robe around her.

She went to the kitchen and put on the tea kettle. Just to busy herself while the water boiled, she washed the dishes in the sink. Her mind was blank. Her hands worked automatically. Wash, rinse. Wash, rinse. Wash, rinse.

The whistle sounded. She jumped, then reached for a bag of Earl Grey and dropped it into a cup before adding the water.

She shut off all the downstairs lights, climbed the stairs to her bedroom, slipped into her nightgown and slid under the covers, and lay there, sipping at her tea.

Apprehension tugged at her, fears both old and new, yet equally frightening in their reality. What would everyone think? How would she face them? Would they believe that she hadn't wanted it to happen? That Tom was lying when he'd said she'd wanted it?

With fumbling hands, she reached for the book on the nightstand beside the bed. Flipping it open to the bookmark, she forced her eyes to follow the words across the page. She needed to escape. To step into someone else's world . . .

But the effort was wasted. The world between the covers of that book held no magic for her this night. She was not a part of it. And for the first time ever, she admitted to herself that the people in those pages weren't real. *This* was real. Here and now. The weight of the changes in her own world lay heavy on her heart.

She flung the book aside and lay there staring at the ceiling, a solitary tear streaking down her face. Had Will been right? Was she punishing herself? Had she really put it behind her?

She closed her eyes and saw Tom's face as he had looked that night when they'd left the party. So gentle. So admiring. She relived anew the shiver of unease that had passed over her when Tom had announced to the others that they were leaving.

Why had she dismissed that unease? If only she'd asked someone else to take her home. If only. If only.

Snapshots of what followed flipped through her mind like pages of an old photo album. The dark dirt road he'd turned onto about five miles outside town. The smile on his face as he'd reached for her across the seat of the car, pulling her to him with no effort at all. The way she'd tried to make light of his advances at first. Tried to resist him. Afraid. Terrified. Fear building. Escalating within her until she thought she might choke with it. The sounds of fabric ripping. The feel of his wet mouth on her breast. The obscene scraping sound of her jeans zipper. Her hands fighting him until ...

Her eyes flew open. She stared at the ceiling, her heart thudding unevenly in her ears. How many times had she walked down the street and wondered if passersby could just look at her and *know?* How many times had she wanted to stop and cry, "I was raped! Maybe it was my fault. Maybe I could have fought harder. I could have ..."

She reached across the bed and pulled open the drawer of the nightstand, shuffling beneath a stack of papers for the book of Beethoven's letters Sarah had given her for her eighteenth birthday.

She flipped it open to the letter the young composer had written to his brothers as an explanation for the way he was living his life. The letter had struck a familiar chord within Hannah's young heart when she'd read it ten years ago. It still did.

> Oh! ye who think or declare me to be hostile, morose, and misanthropical, how unjust you are, and how little you know the secret cause of what appears thus to you!

She closed her eyes and let the book rest against her chest. Will was right, she realized with a sickening rush of clarity. It wasn't over. It had never been over. In a way, it had just begun.

CHAPTER TEN

HANNAH WAS OUT OF BED the next morning well before the sun rose. At first light she went for a run, then showered and went to work as though nothing was wrong. Jenny stood waiting for her at the front desk when she arrived.

"Are you all right?" the older woman asked, her forehead wrinkled with concern.

Hannah shrugged off her coat and tried to smile. "Fine."

"After the way you took off yesterday afternoon, I was beginning to wonder—"

"Everything's fine."

"Did you see Will?"

Hannah nodded and attempted a light "He seems to be none the worse for wear."

Jenny crossed her arms and eyed Hannah shrewdly. "Did that fight, by any chance, have something to do with you?"

Hannah shook her head. Then she went still, and the wall of composure she'd erected around herself crumbled. She'd forced herself not to think about anything this morning—the rape, Will and Tom's fight, the town's knowing—running until her lungs screamed for relief, pounding herself with the shower's cold spray to force the tormenting thoughts from her head. But now, for the first time, she didn't think she could face this alone. "Oh, Jenny, I don't know what to do!"

Jenny took her by the arm and led her into the back room. "You come and sit down," she said, pressing a gentle hand against her shoulder. "What is it, Hannah? You can tell me. It can't be that awful."

"It is," she said. "It is."

"Why don't you let me be the judge of that?"

And so, Hannah told her, letting the whole awful story spill forth, ending with Will's beating Tom to a pulp.

"Well, good for him," Jenny said with a slap of her hand on the desk. "Oh, my dear, what you must have been through because of that lowlife!"

"But don't you see, Jenny? It was over. I'd put it behind me. And now..."

"It's back again. Hannah, dear, you must realize that you'd never really put it behind you. I never would have guessed this. Though I always knew there was something in your life not quite the way it should have been. It's not natural for someone as bright and gifted and attractive as you to lock herself away at such a young age. This was why. Am I right? You've been punishing yourself for something you had no power to prevent."

"But don't you see? I could have—"

"Could have what?" Jenny interrupted in a gentle voice. "What could you possibly have done?"

Hannah dropped her chin and stared at her hands. "Not gone out with him in the first place."

"Oh, Hannah. You were so young. You couldn't have known."

"I always felt that it was my fault, that I some-how... asked for it." She looked up and let her gaze meet Jenny's. "I had a crush on Will then. When Tom called to ask me out, I thought—" her voice fell "—I thought Will might notice me as something other than the class brain if I had a date with one of the other football players. I got all fixed up, hoping I'd see Will that night. And somehow, Tom knew that I didn't really want to go out with him. So you see..."

"Oh, Hannah," Jenny said compassionately, "what I see is something any young girl might have done. Why, when I was eighteen, I borrowed my father's car and ran it out of gas circling the Weiner King looking for Herman Dancey."

"But, Jenny—"

"But nothing. You weren't to blame for what Tom did. That was a crime. He was the criminal. Not you. I don't know what you plan to do about it now, but there's no point blaming yourself. The past is done. Your concern should be with the future. And it seems to me that Will Kincaid has been making every effort to be a part of it."

"No. It's not like that."

"You think just any man would beat the tar out of somebody like Tom Dillon?"

"Will was just doing what he felt was right."

"What he felt compelled to do, no doubt. And I have a feeling there's more to that compulsion than either of you are willing to admit."

WILL HAD BARELY SLEPT that night, and when his doorbell rang at seven the next morning, he welcomed the diversion from the thoughts that tormented him. He pulled open the door to find Aaron Tate standing on his doorstep.

Will attempted to stretch, then flinched when his muscles protested. "What're you doing out so early, Aaron?"

"Came to see if you were still alive."

Will waved him inside and smiled for the first time in twelve hours. "Still in one piece. I see you have as much faith in me as ever."

Aaron looked around and let out a soft whistle. "Quite a place you got here."

"Yeah, well, it's home for a while, anyway."

Aaron gnawed the inside of his lower lip, then said, "I don't reckon there's any point in me not being blunt about it. What the hell were you thinkin' about last night, boy?"

Will rubbed the back of his neck and sighed heavily. "Don't you start in on me, Aaron. I know I jumped the gun, but damn it, you don't know the whole story."

Aaron shook his head. "I know more than you think. I reckon you're aware you opened up a whole can of worms for that young woman."

Will looked away with a trace of the anguish that had eaten at him since Hannah had raced out the door the evening before. "I plan to make it up to her."

"And just how're you gonna go about that? She's probably spent the last ten years trying to forget it ever happened. And then you come along and—"

"Somebody had to make him pay," Will said with a surge of the anger that had sent him after Tom Dillon the afternoon before.

Aaron reached for his tobacco pouch, filled his pipe, then without lighting it, rested it on his lower lip and gave the assertion some thought. "That Hannah, she's not your standard young woman. Almost ran over her one day, a few weeks before you got back to town. We'd just had a little rain, and I came up over a knoll there just before you get to Clarence's. And there she was, scrambling to pick up a terrapin and get him across the road before someone came along and made him into turtle stew. She looked kind of embarrassed when I slowed down to see if she needed any help. Got the feelin' it wasn't the first time she'd helped out one of those devils. I don't know about you, boy, but I always was kind of partial to terrapins, myself."

Will looked away and swallowed.

"So, yeah, I'd agree, boy, that somebody needed to make Tom Dillon pay. But now that girl has to live in the same town with that big mouth who's gonna be defending himself at every raised eyebrow by telling them how she *asked* for it."

Will swallowed a protest. He knew Aaron was right.

"I reckon you know that boy's green with envy at what you've done with your life. There's a lot of years of resentment behind whatever punch he might get lucky enough to throw your way."

Will's lips pressed together in a tight line. He recalled with perfect clarity Tom's verbal darts. Got all the scholarships and all the girls.... Leave it to you to get paired up with the class brain.... He knew then that Tom's anger hadn't been directed at Hannah. It had been directed at him. "Guess I'll go have a talk with him," he said slowly, realizing what it felt like to be hated.

"Seems to me it might be a good idea to suggest he find another town to live in. Rumor has it Tom's got himself a little business on the side at his daddy's old farm. If it was me, I'd collect a little evidence of that and see if I couldn't do some persuading. That is, if you think you could use your mouth and not your fists to do the convincing."

Had the words come from anyone else, Will might have bristled with the need to defend himself. But not with Aaron. He was right, after all. Will had started this. It was up to him to finish it.

HE FOUND TOM out at Clarence's later that day. When Tom looked up to see him standing in the doorway of the pool room, his jaw went slack, and the cue he'd been holding fell to the floor, its loud clatter causing the two men with him to look up with startled expressions.

"I want to talk to you, Dillon," Will said in a low voice, barely able to conceal the anger that still boiled inside him when he thought of what Tom had done. Aaron had been right, though. Using his fists this time would probably land him in jail. And he had no intention of handing Tom that particular victory.

Tom glared at him through his one good eye, the other swollen shut. "Who the hell do you think you are, Kincaid? You're no longer God's gift to football, you know. You're lucky I didn't have you arrested yesterday."

"You're lucky I didn't kill you." The words made the man standing next to Tom give a nervous cough. The other stepped back and put his cue in the rack on the wall. "Ask your friends to leave, unless you want your dirty laundry aired in front of them."

Tom gave a short, uneasy laugh, then looked at his buddies and said, "The man wants some privacy."

Once the two had left, Will closed the door that separated the pool room from the bar area. "Went out to your daddy's old farm this afternoon. Got me some video coverage of that little cash crop you've got growing out there. Bet the sheriff would be interested in a matinee out at my house." He paused and let the words sink in. "I'm going to say this once. I want you out of this town. By the end of the week. And if I find out you're still here, I'll spend every nickel I've ever made to put you behind bars."

The look on Tom's face was a blend of fury and hatred. He was trapped and he knew it. "Don't tell me you've gone to all this trouble for that bitch—"

"You even say her name, and I'll make what I gave you yesterday seem like a picnic."

Tom slammed a fist against the wall. "Man, we were friends. How can you—"

Will cut him off. "We stopped being friends a long time ago. If I ever hear that you've been anywhere near Hannah Jacobs, I'll make sure you regret it." He turned and opened the door, adding over his shoulder, "I'll expect you to be gone within a few days. If not, I'll be giving the sheriff a call."

FOR THE TEMPORARY bookmobile's maiden voyage, the plan was that Hannah would take it out. Concerned that she might not be up to it, Jenny offered to go in her place, but Hannah wanted to go, needing to escape the confining walls of the library.

Making her way to the back of the building, she stopped short at the sight of Will leaning against the side of the vehicle.

She averted her eyes, unable to meet his unwavering gaze. "I'm not up to this, Will."

He stood with his arms folded across his chest, looking as though he'd expected that response. "We need to talk."

"Not now," she said quickly, unlocking the door and rushing up the steps to the driver's seat. "I'm late getting started."

He put one hand on the door handle. "Then I'll go with you."

"No, you can't—"

But he was inside the vehicle and sitting on the passenger seat before she could finish. She climbed in and said, "This is crazy." She let her head fall forward on the steering wheel, then looked over at him. "You can't go."

"But I promise to be good."

She stared at him for a moment and then sighed in defeat. She didn't have the energy to argue. She turned the key, slipped the bookmobile into gear and rolled out of the parking lot.

"You all right?" he asked in a concerned voice.

She blinked and nodded, not trusting herself to speak.

"Hannah, I want you to know I'm sorry about some of the things I said last night."

"You have nothing to be sorry about."

"I had no right to tell you how to deal with all this. You've lived with it for ten years. I'm sure you've come to terms with what's best for you. I was just so damn angry...."

She sighed and, eyes still on the road, let her head fall back against the seat. Her hands clenched the wheel until her knuckles whitened. "I'd be lying if I said I didn't appreciate knowing Tom Dillon got the fool beat out of him. But I wanted to leave the whole thing dead and buried.''

Will reached out a hand to touch her shoulder. "And I made that impossible." He hesitated, searching for words. "Aaron came to see me this morning. He made me realize something I'd never let myself admit before. Tom's always resented what he considers my successes. He still does. We grew up together. We were pretty inseparable for a lot of years. But then things started changing and he... I guess he resented it."

His eyes were laden with regret when he turned and said, "What Tom did to you was because of his anger at me. I guess he'd suspected there was something between us and I wanted it to be more. And before I could get up the courage to do anything about it..."

Her pain almost tangible, Hannah said, "Oh, Will..."

"If I could do anything to go back and change all that for you, Hannah, I would."

"Don't, Will." Her voice broke. "I just want to forget it."

He stared down at his hands. "If that was what you really wanted, then I'm sorry for what I did. I really am. But I don't think he'll be bothering you anymore."

She glanced at him, suddenly afraid he had put himself at risk. Who knew what Tom might do if he were backed into a corner? "Will, what did you—"

He lifted his head and said quietly, "It doesn't matter."

She heard the determination in his voice and knew that whatever he'd done had been for her. She didn't need to know what. They'd reached the bookmobile's first stop by then, and she negotiated the turn-off with an overwhelming feeling of relief.

An old blue-and-white Ford sat waiting for them in the gravel lot of the Presbyterian church. The children were out and standing at the side panel door of the bookmobile before Hannah had turned off the ignition. She opened the door and smiled down at them. "Hello, Heather, Michael. Come on in. We have a visitor with us today. This is Mr. Kincaid."

"Will," he said with a nod at the eager children.

"Wow, you're Will Kincaid!" the little boy said with an awestruck expression.

The children's mother stuck her head in and waved hello to Hannah, then blinked in surprise at the sight of Will. "I'll be in the car. Let me know if the kids drive you crazy. Ever since we saw the notice in the paper about the bookmobile, it's all they've talked about."

Hannah smiled. "That's what we'd hoped for. Don't worry. They'll be fine."

Will followed the two children to the back where they began sifting through Nancy Drew mysteries. They sought Will's approval on each selection. Hannah warmed at the sound of their eager voices. She wouldn't think about her own problems for now. She wouldn't.

THE STOPS WERE a huge success, and by the time they reached the last one, Hannah admitted to Will, "I'm glad you came along. The children really seem to like you."

"Kids like anyone who'll show them a little attention."

"Especially famous football players."

"And pretty young women," he said with a half smile, his voice light, his eyes dead serious.

She forced herself to ignore the comment as she backed the vehicle into place. This time only one child waited, seven-year-old Rebecca. As with the others, the little girl immediately took to Will.

Before long, they'd picked out a handful of books, running the gamut from Babar the elephant to Beezus and Ramona. Rebecca's mother had run down to the store a mile or so away, and once the little girl had finished checking out the books, she went over and climbed onto Will's lap.

"Read one to me, Mr. Kincaid. Please?"

Will's mouth opened in surprise. "Ah, Rebecca, your mom will be back any minute. Wouldn't you rather she read to you when you get home?"

"Uh-uh. I want you to. So I can tell all my friends."

Will glanced at Hannah, his right hand clenched. Something about the look in his eyes made her think of a lion she'd seen in a zoo years ago. Trapped. Pacing the cage with angry pride.

He looked down at the book and then back at Hannah.

That same angry pride. She'd seen it in one other face. Henry Lawson's.

"Please, Will?" the little girl cajoled.

He jerked out of the seat and set the child on the stool across from him. "Why don't you ask Miss Jacobs to start it for you, honey? I need to get some air."

Hannah watched as he disappeared down the steps and around the back end. Frowning, she went to sit by Rebecca, opening the book and beginning to read.

Some ten minutes later, the little girl's mother returned. Hannah promised to see them again next week. Once Rebecca and her mother had pulled onto the road, she climbed into the driver's seat just as Will reappeared, his expression sheepish.

"Bet you think I'm a real brute, huh?" He climbed in and sank into his seat.

"No," she said softly. "I don't think you're a brute."

"Guess I acted a little foolish."

She stared at this man who had turned her life upside down in the last few weeks. Maybe it was the revelation of her own problems that had opened her eyes to Will's. Or maybe it was just something she'd subconsciously known long ago in school when they'd worked on that chemistry project together. Whatever the reason, Hannah knew she was right when she said, "You don't read very well, do you, Will?"

The question was so direct that he bolted upright in his seat, a look of surprise on his features. "I don't know what you're—"

"It makes sense now. The way you acted when you learned Henry Lawson couldn't read. And I'd have to be blind not to have realized it just now."

He lifted his head and stared at her with a shamed expression. "Pretty damn sad, isn't it?"

She studied him, her throat tight. "Only because of the way it makes you feel."

"Like an idiot, most of the time."

"Oh, Will, it shouldn't," she said quickly, the words raw with compassion. "It's nothing to be ashamed of."

"Don't say that, Hannah. Because it is, and I know it."

She resisted the urge to reach out and press her palm to his cheek. "What happened that you didn't learn in school?"

He shrugged and looked away. "I did learn up to a point. But around the fifth or sixth grade, it seemed like everybody else started reading really fast, and I couldn't keep up. So I just quit trying."

"But the school system, how could they—"

"As long as I could catch a football, nobody seemed to care whether I could read worth a damn or not," he interrupted in a rough voice.

"And college?"

"I only stayed three years before I was drafted. As unusual as that was, I was grateful to get out. It was getting too easy to get by. There were always other students willing to write a paper for the right price. And the coaches 'suggested' I take certain classes, the sort hand-picked for guys like me. That kind of thing was done all the time. But I hated myself for going along with it." He looked down at his hands. "It's not something I'm proud of."

"What about the contracts you had to sign? How—"

"One of the benefits of having money. I hired the best lawyers the stuff could buy. As you might imagine, illiteracy doesn't go over too well with the fans. You can buy a lot of silence for the right amount of cash. Pretty pathetic, huh?"

This time it was Hannah who reached across the seat for his hand, holding it for a moment before giving it a gentle squeeze. His problem could be fixed. Unlike her own. Odd that only a matter of hours ago, he'd been the one offering consolation. Now she was.

Both of them admitting to thorns that had stabbed at them from beneath the surface for so many years.

"Oh, Will, no. No, it isn't. You're no different from Henry or anyone else who never got the attention they might have needed. There's no reason you can't still learn."

He shook his head, weary acceptance etched in his drawn features. "It's too late for that, Hannah. Some things you just can't go back and redo."

She turned to him and pressed a hand to his arm. "How can you say that? Henry Lawson is in his fifties. He's learning. Every day he makes progress. You're young. And you have your whole life ahead of you."

"I've had my whole life to accept what I am. Somehow I convinced myself it was all right. I had football, and I threw myself into learning about classical music once I got to college. Because of you, I guess. I thought that was one area in which I could be educated, too. At least, that was one class where I did well. The professor let me take oral exams."

"Why?" she asked softly.

"Maybe he suspected. Maybe he didn't want to buck the system. Maybe he knew how much it meant to me, I don't know." He hesitated, then said, "After my football days were over, I realized what a trap I'd built for myself."

She watched him, her heart aching for him.

He leaned against the door. "I've dreamed of what it would feel like to tell someone. Someone other than a person I had to pay to keep quiet. You don't know how many times I've wondered what you would think if you knew. School always came so easy to you. I always envied you that."

"You envied me?" she asked in disbelief.

"You intimidated the hell out of me."

Hannah stared at him. The thought was ludicrous. "Why?"

"Because you were so bright. I hated Tom for having the nerve to ask you out. You don't know how much I wanted to after that day at the lake. It was all I could think about, but I didn't think you'd... I didn't see any way you could stay interested in a guy that..."

She continued to stare at him, thinking how different things might have been if he had had the nerve to ask her out.

At last she said, "Will, you just didn't get the attention you needed. That's all."

"I don't think so." He gave a deprecating shrug. "I've tried on my own. Self-teaching courses. Whatever I could do without anyone having to find out. Nothing seemed to work."

She remained silent for a moment, debating the wisdom of what she was about to suggest. But something told her it was right. "Let me teach you, Will. Jenny and I have had such success with Mr. Lawson, I know we could—"

He held up a hand. "Hannah, I tried. I really tried. And it just seemed to get harder to keep up. I couldn't do that again. No. It's not the same as it is with Henry."

"Why not?"

"It just isn't."

Filled with a determination she could not explain, she said, "*Anything* is possible, if you'll put your pride aside long enough for me to show you I might be right. All I ask is a chance. If you don't think it's working, we'll stop."

His face mirrored a mixture of desire and uncertainty. "Do you really think it would work?"

She nodded and put a hand on his shoulder. "Yes. I do."

He blinked and then stared at the floor. "You sure you want to take this on?"

She nodded with more conviction than she'd ever had about anything in her life.

A full minute passed before he said, "All right, then, Hannah. I'll give it a try."

And for the moment, she pushed her own problems to the back of her mind, focusing, instead, on someone else's, a tactic she'd perfected over the last ten years.

AND SO BEGAN a daily ritual for Hannah and Will. With his permission, she'd confided in Jenny, who'd agreed to take over Henry's lessons completely, allowing Hannah time to work with Will.

She set about her goal with a determination born to help Will, but also to get her own mind off the recent events that had brought the nightmare of Tom Dillon back into her life.

Knowing that Will had been harboring this secret for so many years made her own secret that much easier to turn away from. She realized she wasn't the only person in the world with a cross to bear. Every rose garden came with its share of thorns. Even a garden as abundant as Will's.

Of course, she worried about whether anyone knew who Tom Dillon's victim had been. Through Jenny, who was firmly tapped into the town grapevine, Hannah learned that for a while the gossip floated from one mouth to another. But a week after the fight between Tom and Will, the gossip mill turned to other things, and Hannah was able to put the whole thing at the back of her mind. It had been ten years, after all. She refused to let herself become consumed by it all over again.

Instead, she concentrated on Will and on her desire to help him. She could not explain the satisfaction that came from knowing she might have something to give him. So many things had become clear since the day he'd admitted to not being able to read. His uncertainty about what to do with the rest of his life. His refusal to do commercials.

She wanted to help him overcome that. Give him back something to compensate for what he'd given her. But she was disappointed by their lack of progress after the first few days of lessons.

On the fourth day Will strolled into the library with a pleased look on his face. She watched him stride through the door, her pulse leaping at the sight of him. Crossing the carpeted floor, he leaned across the counter and said, "I've got some news for you."

"Are you going to keep me in suspense?"

"Tom Dillon left Lake Perdue yesterday."

The words hit her ears, a bomb detonating. She went silent. When she finally spoke her voice cracked. "He's really gone?"

"He's really gone."

"Oh, Will..."

He skirted around the desk then, and right there in front of anyone who cared to look, he folded her into his arms and held her close. "You can put this behind you now. Think you'll be able to do that?"

She pulled back to look up at him gratefully. "I don't know. But I'm going to try."

IT WAS A MIRACLE, really, how Tom's departure seemed to change Hannah's life. Since the day Will had confronted Tom, Hannah had been holding her breath, certain that at any moment, the truth would come out. Maybe now she could truly put the past behind her.

The next few days were some of the happiest she'd known in years. She went for a run each morning, pushing herself a little harder each day, caring about the progress she'd made. And Jenny, pleased to see Hannah looking lighthearted for the first time since she'd known her, claimed she was a new woman.

The only unsettling aspect of Hannah's life was the lack of progress she seemed to be making with Will. With each passing day, she could see his frustration mounting.

One Thursday afternoon, he propped his elbows on the table and rested his forehead on his palm. "It's no use, Hannah. We're both wasting our time."

She leaned back in her chair and sighed. "We are not wasting our time. Stop talking nonsense."

"Are you saying I've gotten anywhere at all these past few days?"

She frowned and said, "Try this line again."

Will did, but it sounded as though he were inverting certain letters or maybe even reading them backward. Another thought occurred to her. One that had been tugging at the back of her mind for the past couple of days. She recalled the way he sometimes ate with his left hand, then switched to his right, without even being aware of it. The notion that she might be onto something sent anticipation racing through her.

She put a hand on his arm and said, "That's all right. I have an idea. We'll stop for today, but promise me you won't give up yet. Please."

He looked as though the entire endeavor were pointless. But with a shake of his head, he finally nodded and said, "Okay."

Once Will left the library, Hannah got on the phone and made a few calls. She tried the county's adult-education program first, and after a few specific questions, they referred her to an educational psychologist who specialized in the type of problem she had described. He was located in Washington, D.C., three hours away.

With a shaking hand, she dialed the number, hoping that Will would understand her taking such a step without his permission. There was no point in getting his hopes up. Her hunch could be wrong.

Luckily enough, the doctor was between appointments. She remained on hold until he came on the line with a harried "Jim Edwards. Can I help you?"

She explained then how she had been trying to help a young man improve his reading skills. She described their lack of progress, along with some of the problems he seemed to be having. She then gave him examples to support her suspicions as to the cause.

Dr. Edwards agreed that it did, indeed, sound as though she might be correct. "But I'd have to see him to be certain. There are tests we administer for such cases."

She tried to keep her voice even. "When could he come in?"

There was silence, followed by the sound of paper shuffling in the background. "Let's see . . . I have a cancellation tomorrow afternoon. Three o'clock. Could he make that?"

She closed her eyes and prayed she was doing the right thing. "I think so. Yes, I'll make sure of it. We'll see you then, Dr. Edwards. Thank you so much."

She replaced the receiver with a mixture of apprehension and joy. If she was right . . .

There would be time to think about that later.

Now she had to convince Will to keep the appointment.

CHAPTER ELEVEN

AFTER WORK she drove to Tarkington's Cove, hoping Will would be at home. She knocked on the door of the house and stood there waiting, fighting a sudden surge of self-doubt. *What if I've done the wrong thing? What if he hates me for it?*

He opened the door a moment later, giving her a weary smile as he mopped the sweat from his face with a small towel.

"Oh," she said, taking a step back as her eyes swept the expanse of his bare chest. Heat flooded through her. "I—I'm sorry to barge in like this. I should have called first."

"That's all right. I was just lifting a few weights. Trying to burn off a little frustration." He waved her inside, refusing to meet her eyes. The last couple of days had been difficult for them both, with Hannah realizing he needed help she couldn't give him, and Will certain he was incapable of learning. She could see now that he was ready to give up. "Come on in. Let me get a shirt."

When he returned to the living room, she said, "I won't stay long. I just wanted to...." She reached for a note of composure, then launched into her speech before she lost her nerve. "I know how difficult these last few days have been for you, Will. I have to admit I was getting frustrated myself. But the other afternoon, I remembered something from an article I'd read a couple of years ago. So I called a doctor in Washington and told him what we've been doing."

"What kind of doctor?" he asked with a frown.

"He specializes in learning problems. He's an educational psychologist," she said carefully.

He scowled and said, "Hannah, look, I appreciate what you're trying to do, but—"

"I think he can help. He'd like to do some tests on you. I made an appointment for tomorrow afternoon."

Will shook his head. "It'd be nothing but a waste of time."

"I don't think so. Please. Let's just give it a try."

He rubbed a hand across the back of his neck. "Look, I went along with this knowing it wouldn't work. I've tried before. I thought... It's just that you were so excited about it that..." His words trailed away.

Hannah was startled. He had done this for her, certain all along of impending failure, yet self-sacrificing enough to realize he could offer her a way to focus on something other than Tom. When she finally spoke, her voice shook. "You mean you did this for me?"

He shrugged and looked away. "I thought it would get your mind off things. And it has. But it seems foolish to keep—"

"You're right. It did help me. You gave me something other than my own problems to think about. And I'm grateful for that." She looked down at her hands and then raised her eyes to his, a new determination coursing through her. She was right about this. She just knew it. And she wasn't going to give up now. "But I won't be satisfied until I've helped you, too,

Will. So I'm asking you one more favor. And if you won't do it for yourself, then do it for me. I'll go with you. If I'm wrong, I'll never bring up the subject again. How's that for a deal?''

He paced the floor in front of the bay window. When he stopped, he pinned her with his gaze and said, ''Anybody ever mentioned you drive a hard bargain?''

''As a matter of fact, no.'' Her smile widened. She reached for his hand and squeezed it gently. ''But I kind of like the way that sounds.''

THE WASHINGTON STREETS wheezed and hummed with pre-rush hour traffic. On every corner sat a food vendor, offering everything from gigantic pretzels to ice-cream cones. Dr. Edwards's office was on the top floor of a renovated old building just off Pennsylvania Avenue. Hannah and Will arrived a good fifteen minutes early for the appointment. They took their seats in the cheerful waiting room where glass end tables were scattered with copies of *Esquire, Sports Illustrated* and *People.* They were both nervous and anxious, each trying to outdo the other in proving otherwise. Will sat with a wrist draped over the side of the chair, his thumb beating out a nervous tattoo. Hannah sat with her legs crossed, one foot bobbing back and forth.

When the receptionist finally called Will's name, they both jumped.

The woman had been casting glances at Will ever since they'd entered the office. She looked at him now with admiring eyes. ''Dr. Edwards is ready for you, Mr. Kincaid.''

Hannah watched as he gave the woman the disarming smile he was famous for. Part boy, part man. At first glance brimming with confidence, at the second hinting at uncertainty. He looked back at Hannah and said, "Should you come, too?"

She smiled reassuringly. "You go ahead. I'll be here when you get back. If it's all right with the doctor, I'll come in after he's finished testing you."

He gave her a skeptical look, then nodded and followed the receptionist down the hall.

Hannah sat there in the waiting room for the next hour and a half, intermittently pacing the floor and checking her watch. She prayed that her hunch had been right.

At just after five-thirty, the receptionist peeked around the corner and said, "You can go in now, Miss Jacobs."

Hannah grabbed her purse and hurried down the hall, taking a deep breath before she stepped into the doctor's office.

Will sat in a wing chair to the side of the desk. The doctor stood and offered her his hand. "I'm Jim Edwards. Will tells me you've been working with him recently."

She nodded, her anxious gaze skirting from Will, whose expression gave away nothing, and back to Jim Edwards. "Did you find out anything?"

The doctor smiled. "We made a good start, I believe. Your suspicions seem to have been correct, Miss Jacobs. Will does indeed exhibit some of the classic symptoms of dyslexia."

She let out a sigh of relief. "He does? That's wonderful!"

Both the doctor and Will laughed. In any other situation, it would have been an absurd response.

"I mean, I had hoped—"

"That it was something that could be dealt with?" Will interrupted, beaming.

Hannah beamed back at him, overwhelmed by the relief she saw on his face.

"Hold on a minute now," Dr. Edwards said, looking at Will. "While dyslexia can be addressed so you can learn to read on a level you might never have expected before, it'll take hard work and continued education. Nothing about it will be easy. You'll have to learn a whole new way of looking at things."

Will nodded. "I understand that."

"As I mentioned, I'll need to do some further testing to determine the extent of your problem and exactly what direction to take with your program. I'd like to start on that as soon as possible." He leaned forward. "No one ever suspected this, Will?"

"If so, it was never mentioned to me."

"You grew up in a small town?"

Will nodded.

"I can't imagine this getting through the safety nets of a bigger school system, but in the smaller ones, sometimes it still happens. Sometimes kids develop what we call coping skills that allow them to sneak by. They might learn to recognize key words that help them get by on tests, or they might have very good comprehension skills."

Dr. Edwards sat back again, making a steeple with his fingers. "And I suspect you know that a lot of times things are ignored in the interest of making sure certain school sports get priority. No offense intended, but—"

"None taken, Dr. Edwards," Will said with an ironic smile. "There were a lot of times when I deserved to be taken off the team for grades. They were overlooked. Bad thing was, as far as I know, no one ever looked to see why I was doing so poorly. I guess, like me, they thought I wasn't smart enough."

Jim Edwards shook his head. "That wasn't it, Will. Your IQ is higher than ninety percent of the population. That's often the case with people who have dyslexia. That's why their academic failures are so frustrating to them. They've always felt they could do the work and then some, but fail to come through on tests."

"I know exactly what that's like," Will said.

"Dyslexia is three times more common in boys than in girls. It's nothing to be ashamed about. Some very famous, very successful people have been dyslexic. Thomas Edison, Albert Einstein."

"You think you can help me, then, doctor?"

"I believe you'll be surprised at your progress now that we know what we're dealing with." He stood up and offered Will his hand. "I'm awfully proud to meet you. Been a fan for years. And I'm even more of one now. It took a lot of courage for you to confront this. It must have been hell keeping a secret like this for so long."

Will shook the doctor's hand. "I would never have come if it weren't for Hannah. You're right, though. And I guess now that I've been handed the ball, it's up to me to run with it."

A few minutes later Hannah and Will left the building. They'd remained silent in the elevator. But no sooner had they cleared the building's revolving doors than Will grabbed her by the waist and proceeded to swing her in a circle, shouting, "I'm dyslexic! I'm dyslexic!"

She threw back her head and laughed. "People will think we're crazy!"

"Not crazy. Just happy. Can you imagine somebody being *happy* to learn he's dyslexic? But I am so relieved, Hannah. I can't tell you how much. All that stuff he said, it was like he looked inside me and told me exactly what I've been feeling all these years."

His expression became serious. "It's like having a door opened and being able to look inside and see what I thought should have been there all along. I can't tell you how it feels to know that I'm not stupid. I always felt like I had what it took to do as well as anyone else. But then every time I tried to take a test..."

He reached down and pulled her up against him, hugging her fiercely. "I owe it all to you. If you hadn't called this doctor, I might never have known."

"That's not important," she said gently. "What matters is that you can start taking the necessary steps to correct it."

"And I have hope. I can't tell you how that makes me feel."

Her heart was full. "You'll do it. I know you will."

"We can't go home tonight. There's too much to celebrate." He stepped back and, keeping her hand in his, started toward the Cherokee.

"Will, wait!" she protested, pulling him to a stop. "We didn't bring any clothes—"

"I'd hoped we might end up staying," he admitted. "I brought a few things just in case. We'll buy you whatever you need."

Common sense told her to object. But she hesitated, the desire to stay with him overruling all doubt.

He took advantage of that hesitation. "Come on, Hannah. We're going to do this town right."

"Right" began with valet parking at the Willard Hotel on Pennsylvania Avenue. Hannah protested as he led her through the front doors to the lobby. "We can't stay here. It's too expen—"

She broke off as he marched toward the registration desk and asked for the best suite available. The clerk recognized him immediately and set out to make sure that whatever Mr. Kincaid wanted, Mr. Kincaid would get.

"Ah, yes, sir, we have a wonderful suite available for you. Two adjoining rooms with en suite bathrooms and a nice parlor in between."

"Will—"

But Will nodded and took the key from the clerk. "Sounds perfect."

"Glad to have you with us, Mr. Kincaid. Take care of that knee, huh?" he added as Will and Hannah headed toward the elevators.

"Will, this is far too extravagant!" She was still searching for a good reason why they shouldn't be here when he stuck the key in the lock and opened the door. But as soon as she saw the room, arguing was the last thing on her mind. "Oh, Will. Look at this!" She stood back in awe and let herself take in the opulent surroundings. A sitting room served as the focal point of the suite, complete with a wet bar and two comfortable-looking couches. Straight ahead, a window allowed for a magnificent view of the city. And to either side of the room lay a bedroom, one for each of them.

"No more protesting, all right, Hannah? Let me spend a little of the money I otherwise have very little use for. I'm taking you out tonight." He picked up the phone and asked the concierge to recommend somewhere exceptional for dinner. He then asked where they might go shopping. He listened for a moment, then hung up the phone and, grabbing Hannah's hand, headed for the door.

Before she could catch her breath, they were back on the elevator, then heading through the lobby and out the doors to hop into one of the taxis lined up outside the hotel.

"Union Station," Will told the driver.

"Sure thing." The driver tipped his hat and started out into the traffic.

"Hey, aren't you . . ." The driver peered at them through the rearview mirror, rubbed his chin and said, "You're Will Kincaid. Hey, you guys beat the hell out of my hometown team this year."

Will's face crinkled in a smile. "Yeah, we did, didn't we?"

The driver laughed and slapped his hand on the front seat. "Mario won't believe this. My son's a big fan of yours. Wants to play football someday. Got time for an autograph?"

"Got a pen?" Will asked.

"Sure thing." The driver handed him the pen and a piece of paper, simultaneously honking his horn and whipping around a slower-moving car.

Will signed his name and handed the paper back to him. Soon they came to a stop in front of Union Station. He opened the back door and slid out after Hannah, leaning back in to say, "Tell Mario to get an education first. The rest will come."

A monstrosity of a building, Union Station had been renovated to serve not only as a train station but a shopping mall, as well. Swinging through the front door, Will set off for the escalators with Hannah in tow.

The first store he pulled her into was one she would never have gone into alone. Most of the shop consisted of wall space rather than clothes. It followed, according to Hannah's speculation, that the prices of everything would be astronomical. She didn't have to look at the tags to know she was right.

"Why don't we look somewhere else, Will?"

"This looks just right." Seeing her reluctance, he said, "Let me do this for you, Hannah. I want to. Look what you did for me today. Please. Just let me do this."

Still, she hesitated, but he took her hand and led her inside where he immediately pulled a dress off the rack, holding it up to judge for size. "Six. Sound about right?"

She nodded reluctantly.

"Here's another," he said, sounding like a little boy on his first expedition through a candy store. "This would look great on you."

She frowned. "It's red. I don't usually wear red."

His look dared her to try it. "You were the one who said there's a first time for everything. You'd look great in red."

By the time the salesclerk led Hannah to a dressing room, she had at least eight dresses draped over her arm. The clerk hung them up and sent Hannah a look of envy as she said, "Let me know if you need anything."

Hannah tried the red one first, and stealing a glance in the mirror, had to admit she looked like a different person in it. A little puffed at the top, the sleeves hit just above her elbow. The neckline scooped low in front, just covering the tops of her breasts. The waist-line curved in and then rounded out to fall in a straight line from hip to knee.

"Come on out, Hannah," Will called. "I want to see."

She peeped around the corner and, seeing no one else in sight, stepped out. The salesclerk had provided her with a pair of black heels, and Hannah teetered a little as she walked across the rug.

He stared at her for a moment before saying, "Wow."

"Will, this isn't really me," she protested. "I don't think—"

"Whoever it is, I'm taking her to dinner tonight. You look incredible."

When she saw the admiration shining in his eyes, she *wanted* to look like the kind of woman Will Kincaid would take to dinner.

"Go try on the rest," he ordered in an oddly tender voice.

Hannah obeyed and Will's reaction to each was similarly flattering. But he liked the red dress best of all, and before she could protest further, he instructed the clerk to ring it up along with the shoes, three sets of lingerie, a pair of cuffed black pants and a tailored white blouse, just in case she needed them.

"That was much too extravagant," she chastised him as they headed out of the store and down the escalator.

"It'll be worth every penny to see you in that dress."
He took her hand and descended the escalator steps at
a brisk pace. "Let's get going. We've got a full evening ahead of us."

WILL HAD MADE the dinner reservation for nine
o'clock. Hannah took a shower and fussed with her
hair, pulling it back, then letting it down again. There
were hairpins strewn across the dresser while she stood
in front of the mirror, glaring at herself in frustration.

On this, of all nights, she wanted to look beautiful.
For this one special evening, a single slice of time out
of sync with what constituted their normal lives, she
would have what she'd only dreamed about. Will
would be leaving Lake Perdue soon. Today's outcome with Dr. Edwards had made that a certainty. She
closed her eyes and wrapped her arms about herself.
It would not last forever. But she wanted this night.
How very much she wanted this night.

In the end, when Hannah slipped into the red dress,
her hair fell to her shoulders, shiny and full. The dress
fitted perfectly, and the sheer black stockings were
smooth against her calves. She stepped before the
mirror and blinked, not recognizing herself.

Red. Imagine that. On a woman who'd existed in
navy and forest green for the last ten years.

Would he think her beautiful? The answer mattered far too much for her own good.

She stared at herself and marveled at how far she
had come in the months since Will Kincaid had returned to Lake Perdue. So much had changed. A year
ago, she never would have imagined herself wearing
such a dress.

Will had made her care. Made her want to impress him. He'd awakened anew all those feelings she had thought long since gone.

But they were back. With an intensity that frightened her. Anticipation tumbled through her. It had been a magical day. What would the evening bring? What did she hope for it?

On that question, she turned away from the anxious face in the mirror, as if in her own eyes she might find the answer.

A few minutes later she stepped into the sitting room, her hands clasping and unclasping as she took in the sight of Will standing before the window.

Her eyes lingered on the back of his head, the tousled dark blond hair, the strong athlete's shoulders. His legs were long and firm beneath charcoal-gray suit pants. He was, without a doubt, the most handsome man she'd ever seen.

He swung around, caught sight of her, opened his mouth to speak and then went silent. His voice cracked when he finally said, "I knew you'd look like that."

The words were soft, sincere. Heat flooded Hannah's veins as she raised her eyes to his. "I—I feel conspicuous somehow."

He moved forward and tilted her chin up with one finger. "You should. You're conspicuously lovely."

To Hannah's surprise, he leaned forward and brushed her lips with his, a feather-soft caress, unexpected, yet no less devastating in its effect. Her eyes closed. Her breath made a funny little noise in her throat. She savored the crisp, clean tang of his aftershave. Slowly, she opened her eyes, feeling like a butterfly slipping loose of its caterpillar shell. The smile on his face made her weak with an emotion that was altogether unsettling.

The tone of the evening was set. On this April night, Hannah Jacobs felt special in a way she had never felt before, and she marveled at being the center of this wonderful man's attention. His gifts touched her, the red dress, the beautiful hotel room. But what pleased her most of all was the intent behind them and the pleasure he took in giving them.

A black limo sat waiting outside the hotel for them. In Lake Perdue, climbing into such a car to go to dinner would have seemed ridiculous. But in this city, it felt appropriate. And she felt a thrill as Will helped her into it, like Cinderella climbing into the magic coach. He slid in beside her and gave the driver instructions before raising the glass partition between them.

Hannah glanced at her surroundings, a little awed by the opulence. "You shouldn't have done all this."

"I wanted to." He popped the cork from a bottle of champagne, and then passed the crystal glasses for her to hold while he poured. He set the bottle down in the ice bucket and raised his glass to hers. "A toast. To our evening together. A special evening."

Hannah clinked her glass against his, then raised it to her mouth, giving the champagne its due, letting it caress her tongue and glide down her throat. Proper. Appropriately appreciative. But then she took another sip and the bubbles tickled her nose. Watching her, Will began to laugh, and she soon joined him.

They drained their glasses, eyes still locked in mirth. Will pushed a button, and a panel in the roof slid back. He stood up and reached for her hand, pulling her up beside him.

"Will! What are we doing?"

"Seeing the city."

They stood there, heads and shoulders sticking out the opening, laughing and teasing as the night wind blew at their hair. The car swung right at a light and hit a pothole, jostling them into one another. They collapsed back into the seat, weak with laughter.

When their laughter abated, they leaned back, each with a shoulder in his or her own corner, staring at one another, a face-off of sorts. It was one of those moments when words were unnecessary.

She met his eyes, acknowledging in that moment that the attraction she felt for him was mutual. She saw it in the way he looked at her, the way the pulse at the side of his neck raced at a faster rate than his fit body would have demanded. Desire surged through her, giving her a high much greater than the champagne could.

Will reached for her, pulling her across the seat until she sat still as a statue before him. She was aware that it would take no more than the smallest of gestures for her to sink into his arms.

"You missed a drop," he said, lowering his head and letting his tongue flick across her lips, "right there."

Hannah's breath expelled softly, and she closed her eyes. His touch was a little like jumping into the lake on a hot summer day. The body yearned for it, yet somehow feared the submersion at the same time. Even when the outcome was so satisfying.

"Hannah?"

Her eyelids fluttered open. "Hmm?"

"You know where this is headed, don't you?"

She looked past him, focusing for a moment on the city lights slipping past outside the limousine window. Then she met his questioning gaze with eyes that acknowledged—and acquiesced.

"I want us to have a good time tonight," he said in a low caressing voice. "To enjoy each other. But this isn't casual. Never, ever think this is casual."

She glanced down at her hands, shaking her head as she said, "No. It could never be that."

He trailed a finger along the line of her jaw and then let it come to rest on the fullness of her lower lip. "Just wanted to make sure we had that straight."

The limousine braked to a stop in front of Michael's, the restaurant where Will had made the reservation. He helped her out of the car, then leaned back in to tell the driver that he would call him when they were finished.

Hannah took Will's arm as he led her into the darkened foyer where the wonderful aroma of fresh bread and simmering sauces filled the air. She blinked once as if to bank the emotions swirling with such intensity inside her. The last thing on her mind was food. She felt as though she'd been shot full of some nerve-sensitizing drug, and every pulse, every heartbeat, had become magnified.

They took the waiter's suggestion and ordered the special. But dinner was only a prelude. She sensed Will knew that as well as she did and suffered through it as one might an appetizer when the entrée has been announced as filet mignon.

Hannah dropped her fork three times. Will spilled first his water, then his red wine.

By the end of the meal, her nerves were shot. And when they were surrounded at the doorway by autograph-seeking sports fans on their way out of the restaurant, Will displayed less than his usual graciousness.

They both remained silent in the car on the way back. Will had left the divider glass down, almost as if he didn't trust himself to raise it. The driver looked at them curiously, as if aware of the change in his passengers.

At the hotel, Will helped her out of the car, then removed his hand from her arm and kept a good two feet between them as they walked through the lobby. In the elevator she assaulted herself with a dozen arrow-sharp questions, all aimed inward. *What am I doing here? Did I really think clothes and makeup would make me into the woman Will desires?*

As soon as he inserted the key in the lock and swung open the door, she headed straight for her bedroom. When he said her name, she stopped.

She closed her eyes and hesitated before turning to face him.

"Come here, Hannah."

She focused on the wall behind his right shoulder. "I think I should go to bed now."

"I don't think so."

She blinked and took a step back.

He crossed the room and took her arm, tilting her chin up with one finger. "What's wrong, Hannah?"

She studied his face, cherishing the high cheekbones, the somehow vulnerable hollow just below, the strong jaw now clenched. "Ah, you've been so quiet. I thought—"

He didn't let her finish the sentence. Instead, he let out a low groan and pulled her to him, burying his face in her soft hair. "Hannah, I'm sorry. I just...I was afraid if I looked at you one more time in that damned car, I wouldn't be able to keep my hands off you."

Her head flew up.

"It's true," he said in a low husky voice. "You're ... you're so beautiful. I wanted this to be a special night. And I haven't been able to think of anything other than getting you back to the hotel. I'm sorry if I ruined everything."

She smiled at him, astonished that she could have had that effect on him. It would be one night. No promises. No thoughts of what tomorrow or the next day would bring. His own words echoed in her mind. *You're twenty-eight years old, Hannah. You've got a life to live.* "You mean that? About not being able to think of anything—"

"Yes," he interrupted with an indulgent grin. "I really mean it. Why don't you let me prove it to you?"

The question was a rhetorical one, and she didn't bother to answer him as he swung her up in his arms and carried her to her bedroom. The maid had been in to turn down the covers of the bed and flick on the lamp beside it, bathing the room in soft light.

Still holding her in his arms, Will dipped his face into her neck and said, "You smell good. Like springtime and flowers."

How could a woman resist such words, offered with utter sincerity by a man who gazed down at her in admiration? This woman could not.

He lowered her legs and, still holding her by the waist, let her slide down the length of him. Then, resting both hands on her shoulders, he eased her onto the bed, dropping to one knee before her, raising the inside of her wrist to his lips for a soft heartfelt kiss.

He raised his head and forced her to meet his eyes. "I wish I could have prevented what he did to you. If I could go back and change it—"

She pressed a finger to his lips. "Will, I don't want to think about the past tonight."

There in the quiet haven of the elegant hotel room, he kissed the tip of that finger, then leaned forward and pressed his lips to the skin above the neck of her dress. "Then we won't," he said in a husky voice.

She sighed and cupped the back of his neck with her other hand. Whatever fears she'd had in the past about what this moment might be like melted away. How many times had she wondered if she would ever want to be with a man, the way a normal woman wanted to be with a man? How many times had she told herself she would never think of this simple act between a man and woman with anything other than revulsion?

But now, past and future disappeared. There was only the present.

"Do you know how many times I've wondered about this?" Will asked. "Wondered what would have happened that day at the lake if we hadn't stopped?"

"As many times as I have?" she said softly.

"Are you sure this is what you want, sweetheart?"

A multitude of questions lay behind those words. Hannah somehow knew there was only one answer. She wanted this man. It was no simpler, no more complicated, than that.

She nodded. One night. Hers. His. Theirs.

He brushed the back of his hand across her throat, letting a finger trail down her arm. He leaned forward, and her eyes closed just as his mouth met hers. And at first, the kisses were slow and lingering, continuing on for infinite minutes, until suddenly the pace changed. The kiss was like none they'd shared so far, honest and needy, filled with longing. To Hannah, it was like coming alive for the first time.

He lifted his head, then kissed each of her eyelids, the tip of her nose, the underside of her chin. He stood up, taking her hand and pulling her up before him. He looked down at her, his gaze intent upon hers. One finger set out on a sensual exploration of its own, skimming the slope of her neck, glancing across her collarbone, rounding the neckline of her dress, tracing the curve of her breast, leaving delicate tremors in its wake.

She murmured his name.

He gently turned her around and unzipped her dress, his hands shaking a little. Then he turned her to face him. His gaze followed the dress as it slipped from her shoulders and fell at her feet.

"You are so beautiful," he said hoarsely.

She began to shake her head, but he stopped her, brushing her lips with his. "Yes, you are."

And he proved his words with a series of feverish kisses that left her breathless. Her slip came next, leaving her standing before him in only the bra and panties they'd bought with the dress. And for some reason, there was none of the shyness, none of the awkwardness she had imagined.

With a boldness she would not have recognized in herself, she raised one hand to the neck of his shirt, lingering there for a moment, before reaching to undo the buttons with nimble fingers. He jerked the shirt free of his pants. She pressed her hand against his strong, wide chest, closing her eyes and savoring the hard, male feel of him. Meeting his gaze, she trailed her fingers across the width of him, then down across his washboard stomach.

He let out a low moan and shrugged out of the shirt altogether, loosening his belt buckle before sliding onto the bed and pulling her down beside him. "I want this to be perfect. I want it to be right for you."

"It already is. It couldn't be more right."

"Do you mean that?"

She nodded, aware that her gaze held all the love her heart possessed. "Yes. I do."

They fell back onto the bed, and Will pulled her to him, covering her mouth with his. Her hands wandered across his chest, up to his shoulders and to the back of his neck, where they tangled in the thick hair. She kissed him back, telling him without words how much she needed him. He still tasted of champagne. Champagne and desire. She didn't know which intoxicated her more. She pulled back and kissed the tip of his chin, her lips brushing across the whiskered skin.

He groaned and proceeded to return the favor, kissing her mouth, her breasts, the hollow of her throat. And for a brief moment, she remembered another time, another place, when this act had caused her pain.

As if sensing her hesitation, Will pulled back and looked at her with understanding eyes. "This is right, Hannah. I know it is." The kiss that followed was sweet and gentle, wiping away any thoughts of what had been, replacing them with the reality of what would be.

With his hands and his mouth, he taught her the way it should be between a man and a woman, making her impatient for more as the remainder of their clothes landed in a haphazard heap at the foot of the bed. She fitted herself against him, longing for the completion she sensed would come with the joining of two people who wanted and needed each other.

She ran her palms across his chest, cupped his jaw with one hand and kissed him, her mouth eager and seeking against his as she became consumed by feelings she had never expected to know.

He moaned and rolled her across the bed. Their surprised laughter rang out as they teetered precariously at the edge, a plait of naked legs and bedcovers entwined. Laughter again. Over and back to the center of the bed they went once more, he coming out on top with a low lionlike rumble of satisfaction, his clever knowing hands raising her own above her head, his body covering hers.

She ached for his touch. She tilted her head back and let herself savor each caress, his hand on her breast, her waist, the inner curve of her leg, the juncture between her thighs, loving, teaching. She could think of nothing but opening herself to him, letting him see the love that had settled so deeply within her.

Her mouth went slack with the magic his hand created, lifting her higher and higher until spasms of sensation rocketed through her.

"Oh, Will," she murmured, looking up at him through heavy lids.

"That's how it should be, honey. That and more."

And when the urgency became too great, he parted her legs and took her with an initial gentleness that made her wrap her arms more tightly about him, cherishing this binding of souls. As their bodies adjusted to one another, he set up a rhythm that made her ache with love and desire.

And it was beautiful, the dance for which this man and woman had been partnered. Heat and desire building... crescendoing finally on a single climactic note of joy.

Hannah knew in that moment a sense of home-coming like none she had ever experienced. Before this night, neither had been whole, living, instead, parts of lives for years. Now in that instant they were two pieces of a puzzle completing the picture, a lock clicking properly into place. They were one. Whole. Complete. At last.

CHAPTER TWELVE

A SHAFT OF MOONLIGHT illuminated the bed. On the streets below, a siren wailed. In the sanctuary of their room, Hannah lay curled against Will, her head on the pillow, her hair fanned out behind her. He rubbed her lower lip with his thumb, then leaned closer to press a kiss to her mouth.

She pulled back and said softly, "Would it have been like that ten years ago?"

He folded her closer. "I just wish we hadn't waited so long to find out."

Two hours later they climbed out of bed and got dressed in casual clothes, after they'd both admitted to starvation. Neither had done any justice to dinner. And they had since worked up something of an appetite.

They strolled through the lobby hand in hand, went outside and jumped in a cab. Will claimed he knew a place that was the world's best all-night bagel shop. Once there, they climbed up on a pair of stools and proceeded to tuck away half a dozen between them.

"You might have to carry me back to the hotel," she complained, resting a hand against her stomach.

"It'd be my pleasure, if the reward's good enough."

She sent him a look that had him wiping a napkin across his mouth, jumping off the stool and swinging her into his arms. He pretended to stumble a bit, then headed out of the shop in search of a taxi, oblivious to the looks of the other patrons in the shop. She laughed and knew a rush of joy more heady than anything she'd ever known.

Once back in the room, he ran a bath for her, ordered a bottle of champagne and then finally convinced her to let him sit on the edge of the tub while she soaked with bubbles up to her neck. He told her stories about the time his entire football team had spent the night in the same hotel only to leave when the manager almost suffered a nervous breakdown after one of the players let the tub overflow and leak through to the next floor.

She laughed and said, "You'd never do anything like that, I know."

He reached out and touched her cheek. "Only if my mind were on something else."

"Such as?" she asked a little breathlessly.

He leaned over and kissed her. "Such as the thought of climbing in there with you."

Years of modesty prevented her from extending him an invitation, in spite of what they'd just shared. She looked down at the thinning bubbles and said, "I doubt if we'd both fit."

He stood up and dropped the towel that had been draped around his hips. "Mind if we try?"

Hannah looked up at him, heat racing through her. "I, ah, I guess it can't hurt to try."

He slid in behind her, his chest to her back, pulling her into the V of his legs. She tilted her head to one side as his lips found the curve of her neck and his hands cupped her breasts. She sighed and said, "I think this will do."

"No complaints from this quarter," he murmured.

THE NEXT MORNING Will ordered room service for breakfast, and they sat there on the bed, sipping coffee and orange juice, watching the sun come up over the city.

They made love, slowly and without haste, intent only on enjoying one another. Hannah savored every moment, wishing they could stay here forever.

It was well after noon by the time they left the hotel. A typical spring day in the nation's capital. The cherry trees had begun to bloom. Joggers made their way up and down Pennsylvania Avenue. Everything seemed fresh and clean, new and wondrous.

The newness of that day was appropriate. For that was exactly how Hannah felt. As though she had been reborn into a woman who could feel, want, need. And even give.

They spent a few hours walking through the city, and it was well after five by the time they went back to the hotel, agreeing silently that they would spend another night together.

She didn't want to think about what might lie ahead. And so, she didn't.

"What do you say to room service for dinner?" he asked once they were back in the room and lying on the bed together.

"I say that sounds wonderful," she said, nestling into the crook of his arm.

They fell asleep like that, cocooned about one another. When they woke up, he ordered dinner, and they stuffed themselves on vegetarian sandwiches and sodas.

After that, they made love again. And long after Will had fallen asleep, Hannah lay there in his arms, staring up at the ceiling and wishing she could keep the future at bay for just a little while longer.

THEY LEFT THE CITY around ten the next morning. But the closer they got to Lake Perdue, the thicker the silence between them hung. Will reached for Hannah's hand once or twice, but he seemed as preoccupied as she was. She felt as though the separation between them had already begun.

Her mind shied away from thoughts of what lay ahead, and yet she knew she couldn't avoid them forever. He would soon be leaving Lake Perdue. That much was a certainty now. Dr. Edwards was in Washington. And that's where Will would be, as well.

She knew he would have to go. And a part of her had already begun to grieve at the thought of losing him.

When he pulled to a stop in front of her house that afternoon, he turned to her, his eyes asking questions he had not yet voiced. He reached across and rubbed a lock of her hair between his fingers, asking gently, "You want to tell me what's wrong?"

She focused on the roses by the front porch, unsure what to say now that the stretch of time that had been completely theirs had come to an end. She cleared her throat and reached for the door handle. "I know you'll be anxious to get home, so I'll—"

"Hannah," he said with a frown, reaching out to stop her. "You've barely said two words since we left Washington. What is it?"

"I—I should go now."

"Just like that?" he asked with a look of amazement. "You're planning to leave just like that?"

She glanced away, unable to meet that disconcerting gaze, seeing in it what they had shared, what she might never know again. "Don't you think it would be easier that way?"

"What would be easier?"

She leaned back against the seat and closed her eyes, voicing aloud what was only too obvious to her. "You going your way and me going mine."

He remained silent a moment before shaking his head and saying, "No. I don't think that would be easier."

"Our lives are about to take separate directions, regardless of what happened between us this weekend."

He tilted her face toward him and studied her for a long moment. "What happened between us meant everything to me, Hannah."

She looked down at the floor in an effort to hide the pleasure those words brought her. She believed that here and now, in this moment, he meant it. But that didn't change the fact that he had his own life to lead. When she looked up again, her voice held no indication of the turmoil taking place inside her. "It *was* special, Will. But I think we ought to step back for a day or two and see what happens. For the past couple of days we've been living in a sort of fantasy world. This is reality for me. Reality for you right now is Dr. Edwards. Go home and make your plans, and then we'll see where we fit in. Okay?"

He sat there and stared at her for several seconds. She could see the indecision on his face. The knowledge that what had happened between them this weekend was special. The further knowledge that he'd been handed an opportunity to prove to himself that he could be so much more than he'd ever allowed himself to believe. Finally he answered, "That's not how I want it."

"Things have happened so fast. How can you be sure?"

"I don't know. But I am."

She forced herself not to throw her arms around his neck. When she spoke, she struggled for a note of conviction. "We should take a couple of days. You need to think. And so do I."

He studied her for a long time before he nodded and said, "All right. We'll give it a couple of days. If you think that's what you need."

She swallowed the lump of emotion in her throat, blinked and smiled brightly enough to convince him she believed this was the right thing. He'd agreed. Wasn't that what she'd wanted?

"Thank you, Will. For this weekend. For everything." And with that she scooted out of the Cherokee, reached for her bag in the back seat and headed for the front door. She didn't want to give herself a chance to consider what she'd just done.

WILL DROVE HOME that night well under the speed limit. Down Main Street, past Tate's and finally over the little knoll that opened up onto Tarkington's Cove. He barely noticed the sights or sounds of Lake Perdue, this town he'd once again come to love.

Most people would have been bored stiff with it after living in one of the country's most vibrant cities. But not Will. He loved it here. The people. The space around him. The fact that he didn't have to worry about some kid pulling a knife on him for his tennis shoes.

Lake Perdue was not Los Angeles. And Hannah was not like Grace or any other woman he'd ever dated. But he'd grown to love both this town and the woman who'd been little more than a girl when he'd left so many years before.

Her name played over and over in his head that night as he lay in bed.

Hannah ... Hannah.

He'd never known anything like what they'd had. He'd had several lovers. But they'd never been friends first. He and Hannah had become friends. Two people who had something to offer one another. Two people with holes in their souls that had done a hell of a lot of healing in the past couple of months. And as lovers, the passion between them had been all the more gratifying. More than he'd ever imagined. Being with Hannah, he'd known a sense of belonging that he'd experienced few times in his life. Known the rightness that comes when two people touch, body and soul.

And now, just when he'd found that, he'd also been offered an opportunity to prove to himself that he could be more than a dumb jock whose career had ended. He could do something worthwhile, something that didn't involve football.

He lay there in the dark, knowing that he had to go to Washington, certain that he couldn't lose what he and Hannah had found.

For the first time in years, Will wished he could talk to his father about it. Like any normal son. Maybe he would try. One more time. What did he have to lose?

The next morning he drove out to his father's house shortly after nine. He'd been ready to go at seven-thirty, but didn't, not wanting his father to suspect how the situation troubled him.

He let himself in through the back door, startling Aunt Fan who let out a cry and then clasped him in both arms and squeezed. "Land sakes, what're you doing here so early, boy?"

"Smelled that bacon clear into town, Aunt Fan. Got any more?"

She grinned. "Won't take me but a minute to throw on a few more strips. You sit down. I'll call your daddy."

Will pulled back one of the bar stools and propped an elbow on the counter while she went to the kitchen doorway and yelled, "John! You come on down. Will's here."

She bustled back, opened the refrigerator door, pulled out a tupperware container of bacon and began forking strips into the already heating pan. "Haven't seen too much of you lately. What's been keepin' you busy?"

Before he could answer, John Kincaid strode into the room, a look of surprise on his face. "Will. I thought I must have heard Fannie wrong. What's got you out so early, son?" he asked uneasily as he finished knotting his tie.

"I wanted to talk to you, Dad, if you've got time."

John glanced at his watch and, with a nod, lowered himself onto the stool opposite him. "Got a few minutes."

Fannie looked at Will and then, wiping her hands on her apron, headed for the doorway.

"No, Aunt Fan, you stay. I want you to hear this, too."

She checked her steps, then went back to her bacon.

"I went up to Washington this weekend to see a doctor."

John's eyebrows shot upward in the first gesture of alarm Will had seen on his face in years. "What? About the knee?"

Will shook his head.

"You sick, son?"

Feeling awkward and uncertain now that the time had come to voice his problem, he decided to be straightforward. "I'm dyslexic, Dad."

The only sound in the kitchen was the sound of bacon frying. John frowned. "Dyslexic? Isn't that when people read backward?"

Will inclined his head. "Sometimes. I have a certain form of it. It's why I never learned as fast as others in school." He hesitated and then added bluntly, "It's why I never learned to read the way I should have."

Color suffused John's cheeks. "Never learned to read? What do you mean? You were just slower than—"

"No, Dad," Will said. "I learned enough to get by in school. That's all. After a certain point we stopped talking about it. I—I always felt you were ashamed of me. And I guess I was ashamed of myself, too. School was a nightmare for me. When I got drafted to play ball, I told myself I'd never have to worry about it again. Maybe that's why I was so driven by football. As long as I was a success in it, I didn't have to face my shortcomings. But that's when it all began, really. Paying off lawyers to keep my secret. Hoping I could trust the people I'd hired to handle my finances."

John Kincaid stared at his son with a look of open-mouthed shock. "You couldn't read?"

"Only to a certain level."

Will looked up to find Aunt Fan staring at him with love and sympathy. She moved the few steps necessary to pat his arm. That one gesture came as close to telling Will that everything would be all right as a whole book of words might have.

John's mouth worked silently, but he couldn't seem to push the response past his lips. He finally managed a hoarse "Why didn't you ever tell me, Will?"

"You want an honest answer, Dad? I was afraid of what you'd think of me. In sports, you were always proud of me. I didn't want to give you reason to be ashamed. So I guess it seemed easier to let everyone think I was the typical jock, too much in love with football to pay much attention to academic subjects."

John Kincaid looked away, his voice gruff when he said, "I always wanted you to have both, son."

"I know you did. That's why I felt like I'd failed you."

"So now what?"

"There's a doctor in Washington who specializes in this type of problem. He thinks he can help me."

"You'd live there?"

"For as long as I needed to, yes. I've got a lot of work to do on myself."

John looked down at the counter, but not in time for Will to miss the flash of guilt in his eyes. When he raised his head again, it was gone. "So when are you leaving?"

"There's a small hitch in the plan, Dad."

Puzzled, John said, "What?"

"I'm in love with Hannah Jacobs, and I want to marry her—if she'll have me."

Had Will announced he'd been chosen to run in the next presidential campaign, John Kincaid could not have looked more shocked. "You what?"

"Hannah was with me this weekend. She's the reason I went to see that doctor in the first place. We had a great time. But she thinks we ought to spend a couple of days apart and see what happens. It wasn't what I wanted, but I agreed."

"Hannah Jacobs?" John repeated as if he still couldn't believe he'd heard Will correctly.

"I love her, Dad." The words were firm, but he still wanted his father's approval. After all these years, he still needed it.

John's gaze remained steady as he said, "You sure that would be the wisest thing right now? Sounds like you'll need to be awfully focused the next few months."

Will nodded. "I'm not telling myself it'll be easy. But I know what life is like not being able to read. I don't think I want to know what it'll be like without Hannah now that I've found her." He looked up to find Aunt Fan beaming at him. The nod she sent his way went a long way toward making up for his father's negative reaction.

Tapping a thumb on the counter, John said, "Sounds like Hannah might be on to something. Give yourself a few days to cool off, and then if you feel the same..."

Will looked up at his father, realizing this was as close to a blessing as he was going to get. Leaving the bacon on his plate untouched, he pushed away from the counter and stood up. "I already know how I feel, Dad. But I guess I'll have to wait and see if she feels the same."

John remained silent.

"I'm going to L.A. for a couple days to get things straight with Dan and tie up a few loose ends. I'll call when I get back."

He got up and gave Aunt Fan a hug. She smiled and said, "You come back soon. And bring Hannah with you next time."

Will nodded and raised a hand at his father, wondering why, as he closed the back door behind him, the familiar sense of disappointment surprised him.

HANNAH LET HERSELF in her front door that night feeling as though she'd just run a marathon. She'd spent most of the day on the bookmobile, driving out by Silas Creek on the far edge of the county, making stops at the Methodist church and Sally's Food Mart along the way. She'd deliberately kept herself running at full throttle, determined not to dwell on the questions prodding her from every angle.

But despite her efforts, her doubts had sat like weights on her shoulders, pulling her down until she wondered if she might just sink beneath them. She imagined a thousand different scenarios of what lay ahead for her and Will. But the same theme threaded its way through each one. Will would leave Lake Perdue. He had no choice. He'd been offered an opportunity to turn his life around, to prove to himself that he was a capable, intelligent man.

How could she stand in the way of that?

She could not.

But did that mean what they'd shared this weekend had to end?

Her familiar self-doubts taunted her. She saw herself waiting here in Lake Perdue for Will to finish his program. Once in Washington, he would be back in the type of world he was used to. Glamorous restaurants, glamorous women. Women far different from her. Women more suitable for him.

She pictured herself as she'd looked this past weekend, dressed in the beautiful clothes Will had given her. Trying to be someone she was not. A wave of embarrassment washed over her. Did she really think those clothes changed her? Made her a different person?

For that little while, perhaps. But the truth was she was still Hannah Jacobs. Had she lost her senses in the past few days? Begun to think she could hold a man like Will Kincaid? A man who had seen far more of life than she could ever expect to see?

The questions sliced through her, every syllable an ax in her heart.

How foolish she'd been to think that her life had changed. To let herself think, even for a little while, that loving meant lasting.

HANNAH WASN'T SURPRISED three days later to find Will's Jeep Cherokee parked beside her car when she left the library. She'd been expecting him and preparing herself for this moment.

Her pulse leapt at the sight of him. She noted the defined cut of his jaw, the familiar wide shoulders. Had any man ever looked so appealing? She forced herself to take a steadying breath and said, "Hello, Will."

"Hannah." The way he said her name was more question than greeting. "I was hoping we could talk."

She took a deep breath. She wanted to get this over with. No point in delaying the inevitable. "Okay."

"Then let's take a drive."

A few minutes later, they were headed out of town. Will drove slowly, and Hannah kept her face toward the side window, afraid that if she looked at him, she would suffer an onslaught of sorrow that would have her pleading for some way to stay in his life.

When he reached across and took her hand, she gave a start.

"Hannah, I've done a lot of thinking the past couple of days—"

"So have I," she interrupted, desperate now to get the words out before she changed her mind. "I want you to know how grateful I am for everything you've done for me these past weeks."

Will frowned, "Hannah—"

"Please. Let me finish. As hard as this is for me to say, I . . . I think it would be best if we didn't see each other anymore." There. It was out. She felt suddenly weak, deflated.

"What?" He looked at her, sure he'd heard her wrong.

She studied the field outside the window and dug her nails into her palms. "I've thought it over, Will. I don't have to tell you we live in two different worlds. What we had last weekend was wonderful. But I think we both knew it couldn't last."

He remained silent, studying her as if looking for some physical proof she didn't mean what she'd said. When he finally spoke, his voice was wary. "Why can't it?"

She knew his weak point. She also knew that if he was to believe her, she'd have to use it. "We're too different, Will. We're not . . . we're not the same kind of people. We don't have the same interests. People don't really change. Our differences would eventually push us apart.''

He flinched, his face going pale. She saw that her arrow had hit home and she forced herself to go on. "So much has changed in the past couple of months. I've changed. There are certain things I want to do with my life. Things I need to accomplish."

The pulse in his neck beat visibly, but his voice remained even as he asked, "So what is it you want me to do? Step back and pretend that nothing happened between us?"

She flattened her palms against her skirt. "I want us to part friends."

"Friends?" His voice rose several notes, his eyes wide with disbelief. "After what happened between us, you expect us to be nothing more than friends?"

She looked down at her hands. She would get through this without breaking down if it killed her. She counted to five and said, "You've changed my life, Will. Made me face things I don't think I ever would have without you. You can't know how grateful I am for that."

Will slapped a hand against the steering wheel. "Damn it, I don't want gratitude from you, Hannah."

She went on as if he hadn't spoken, forcing herself to string one word after the other. "We've been through a lot these past weeks. And maybe...maybe we were drawn together because we both needed someone." She looked away and said, "It would be a mistake to read more into it than that."

He sat studying her for several seconds before saying, "Do you really believe that?"

She willed herself to find the right words. "It's time I stopped hiding from the world. And you, too. You have goals to accomplish. Dr. Edwards believes he can help you. And so do I. You'll need all your concentration for that."

He stared at her for a long moment. His voice wavered when he finally said, "Is this what you'd hoped for all along? That you could find someone else to help me? That you could stamp your debt of gratitude paid by showing poor Will Kincaid why he's been such an academic failure all these years?"

She shook her head at the pain on his face. "Will, no—"

"You don't have to tell me about our differences. I've been aware of them since the first day I laid eyes on you. I guess they're not all that easy to overcome, after all."

"Will, that's not what I—"

"But you're right about one thing," he growled. "I do have things to do with my life. So I guess the sooner I get started, the better." With his jaw set, he swung the Cherokee into a driveway, spun around and headed back toward town.

The rest of the drive was completed in silence. A silence that hung over Hannah like a wet quilt, choking the air from her lungs with its weight. A silence she could not bring herself to break. She bit the inside of her lip and kept her hands clasped tightly together. This wasn't what she wanted. But it would have happened eventually. He would have come to realize that the fragile bond the two of them had forged would never stand the test of two such different life-styles.

When he braked to a halt at her place, she opened the door and slid out. He kept his gaze straight ahead, refusing to look at her. There were so many things she wanted to say. *Will I ever see you again? Will you come back?* But she said none of those things. She blinked once, then merely said, "Good luck, Will. Please take care of yourself."

She stood there on the sidewalk as he pulled away and roared off down the street. Tears welled in her eyes and dropped one by one down her cheeks. She watched until his taillights disappeared, raising one hand to her mouth to prevent herself from waving goodbye.

CHAPTER THIRTEEN

WILL HAD NEVER thought love could feel like this. Crushing. Hopeless. He lay in bed that night wondering why he'd believed he and Hannah had a future. Life had set them out on different courses, and when it came right down to it, nothing had changed. They were two people with nothing more in common than a temporary need for company. He'd been right about their differences all along. Why had he ever let himself think he could overcome them?

There in the darkness he closed his eyes and let his mind replay the images he kept trying to push aside. Hannah beside him in the gazebo by the lake. Hannah jogging along behind him down Main Street. Hannah declaring him Extra Ordinary Apple Bobber. Hannah in his arms. In his bed.

His eyes flew open. His jaw clenched.

So what if Dr. Edwards could help him? Inside, he would still be Will Kincaid, not good at much of anything without a football in his hands.

The next day he drove out to Tate's to see Aaron. He climbed the steps to the old white store as he had a thousand other times, but this time, there was a finality to it. As though he might not return again.

Aaron came in from the back, his arms loaded with a box of canned goods, just as Will stepped through the front door. Will made the customary greetings to the regulars, then raised a hand to Aaron. "Got a minute?"

Aaron dropped the box and said, "Sure. Let's go outside."

Will followed him out the door to an old poplar tree, where shade and rocking chairs beckoned. A crow flew over, its cry echoing in the stillness. Aaron took a chair and offered Will another before lighting his pipe.

"Word's out you're planning to leave us again."

Will glanced away, grateful for his old friend's directness. "Looks that way."

Aaron leaned forward in the chair, one hand dangling between his knees. "Think it's the best thing, then?"

"I think so." He hesitated a moment, rubbing a thumb across the back of his left hand. "I'm going to be getting some help from a doctor up in Washington. It's a program for people with dyslexia. I'm going up there to learn how to read, Aaron."

The older man puffed on the pipe for a moment, then nodded slowly, his gaze steady with approval. "Glad to hear it, boy."

Will reached down and yanked a blade of grass from the ground beside his chair. "You don't sound too surprised."

"I'm gonna tell you something that I'm not sure it's my place to say. I wanted to speak up a long time ago. When Betsy had you in her class, she went to your daddy and asked for his permission to test you for a learning disability. She couldn't do it without his signature. But he wouldn't hear of it. He pretty much strong-armed her into agreeing not to bring it up again. She didn't even tell me until some years later.

She's regretted it ever since." He paused, then added, "I'm glad to see you're gonna do something about it, boy. That takes a lot of courage."

Will blinked and opened his mouth to speak, but no sound came out. When he tried again, his voice cracked. "Why would my father have done that?"

"Pride's a curious thing. That's something you and your daddy're gonna have to work out." Aaron took another puff from his pipe. "What about Hannah?"

Will's jaw set. He looked down and began rubbing the back of his hand again. "What about her?"

"You two get anything worked out?"

"There's nothing to work out."

"Didn't look that way to me."

"She's got things she wants to do with her life. We're like night and day, anyway. I always knew it. Guess I just fooled myself into thinking otherwise for a while."

"Sounds like you're feeling sorry for yourself."

Will's mouth thinned, but his voice held a note of resignation when he said, "She told me she didn't want me in her life. There's not much I can do about that, is there?"

Aaron shrugged and blew out a stream of smoke. "I don't know. Is there?"

"Damn it, Aaron, what are you saying?"

"Just seems to me that if two people want to be together, they ought to be. Simple as that."

Will got out of his chair and shoved his hands in his pockets. "Only it doesn't work when one does and one doesn't."

Aaron turned his pipe over and tapped out the remaining tobacco. "I guess you're right then. If that's how it is."

After leaving Tate's, Will drove out to his father's house. The back door was unlocked and he let himself in. There didn't seem to be anybody at home. Fannie had left a note on the stove saying she'd gone out to the grocery store and would be back in an hour or so. Will stood in the middle of the kitchen floor, his anger rooting him to the spot until the front door opened and footsteps sounded in the hall.

"Fannie?" Will called out.

John stuck his head in the doorway. "Will. Fannie's not here. I wasn't expecting you."

"I hadn't planned to come."

John crossed the room to open the refrigerator and pull out a jug of iced tea. "Get you a glass?"

"No. I don't plan for this to take long."

John set down the jug and turned to his son, his eyebrows drawn together. "What is it, Will?"

"When I told you what I'd found out from that doctor in Washington, why didn't you tell me Mrs. Tate had come to you years ago wanting to test me for that very thing?"

John went still. "Who told you such foolishness?"

"Don't," he said abruptly. "Don't even try to lie about it. Aaron told me. He should know, don't you think?"

John hesitated, then finally said, "I did what I thought was best. I didn't want you labeled. It could have hurt—"

"—my football career. That's all you ever cared about, wasn't it?" Will's voice rose sharply.

"I cared about you making something out of your life."

"But it was all right for me to grow up feeling like an idiot because I couldn't learn the way everyone else did?"

"Will, I didn't know—"

"You didn't want to know. You saw what you wanted to see."

John stepped forward, reaching toward his son.

But Will moved away, fumbling for the doorknob behind him. "You know, I actually came out here the other day hoping to get your blessing on my decision to ask Hannah to marry me. That was too much to ask, wasn't it? Don't worry, though. You got your wish on that, as well." He held his father's guilty gaze for a moment, then turned and walked out the door.

He met up with Aunt Fan on the front steps, wrapped his arms around her and hugged her, grocery bags and all, before saying, "Once I'm permanently settled in my own home, Aunt Fan, I hope you'll come live with me. You give it some thought, okay?"

Will left then, trying not to think about the look on his father's face.

ON THE DAY WILL LEFT Lake Perdue, he gave in to the need to call Hannah. He told himself it was the civilized thing to do. She'd said she wanted to part as friends. Calling to say goodbye was something a friend would do.

He'd convinced himself of as much until she picked up the library phone and said hello. He knew then that the only reason he'd called was to hear her voice one more time before he left.

"Hello, Hannah."

"Will," she said a little breathlessly. "I hadn't expected to hear from you."

"I won't keep you. I just wanted to say goodbye."

"You're leaving today. Someone out at Aaron's mentioned—"

"If you need to know anything, just check in at Aaron's place," Will said with an attempt at humor.

"That's right," she agreed softly.

Before he could stop himself, he asked, "Are you all right?"

"Oh, of course. Yes, I'm fine. I . . . I know—" She broke off and then in a stronger voice went on, "I know you'll do well, Will. This is the right thing for you."

The right thing. Then why was he so miserable when she obviously wasn't? He didn't say anything for a moment, just sat there with the receiver in his hand, wondering how the wall between them had gotten so high. Before he had a chance to blurt out something he might regret, he said, "Goodbye, Hannah," and hung up the phone.

SHE WAS SITTING at the front desk staring out the window when Jenny returned from an errand and said, "Hannah? What's wrong? You're white as a sheet."

Startled, Hannah glanced up and quickly wiped at the corners of her eyes. "Nothing. I was just—"

"Was that Will on the phone?"

"Ah, yes."

Jenny's voice softened. "I heard he was leaving today. Do I take it you two didn't work things out?"

"There was nothing to work out."

Jenny sent her a look of disbelief. "That's why you spent a weekend together, I suppose."

Hannah shook her head. "I could never fit into his world."

"Is that why you're letting him go?"

"He was never mine to let go."

"I've got eyes. I saw the way the man looked at you."

"It never would have worked."

Jenny frowned. "I know you didn't ask for my opinion, but I'm going to give it to you, anyway. I don't think you were ready for what Will Kincaid had to offer you. Somehow, some way, you've got to put what happened between you and Tom Dillon away for good. You haven't done that yet."

"Tom's gone, Jenny."

"That doesn't mean you've resolved it. He may be gone from this town, but he's not gone from your head. And until you work that out you won't ever believe yourself good enough for any man." Jenny reached for the bottom drawer and shuffled through her purse, then pulled out a newspaper clipping. Unfolding it, she handed it to Hannah. "I ran across this the other day. I thought you might like to read it."

Hannah's eyes skimmed over the paragraphs. "Jenny, I don't need this."

"There's a meeting next Wednesday night. You say the word, and I'll go with you."

Hannah scanned the article once more. She stared at it for a long time before folding it and sticking it in her purse.

The following weekend seemed like the longest Hannah had ever endured. She tried to keep busy, running in the morning, reading in the afternoon, but found that thoughts of Will kept creeping to the fore-front of her mind.

Had Jenny been right? Had she let her past get in the way of her future? There had been many times when she'd thought it was all behind her. But through it all, had she ever put aside the nagging belief that she didn't deserve any of it?

The thought played through her mind again and again as she drove up to visit Sarah on Sunday. Sarah was disappointed to see that Hannah had not brought "that nice young man" with her. Realizing her aunt's weakened state, Hannah could not bring herself to tell her that Will would not be coming back.

And so, she made up a story about why he couldn't come, hoping that next week her aunt would be stronger so that she could tell her the truth.

Hannah drove home that afternoon hating herself for lying to Sarah. It was wrong. But she hadn't known what else to do. And besides, she wouldn't have been able to get the words past her lips without dissolving into tears.

She thought again of Jenny's accusations. What if her friend was right? She reached into her purse and pulled out the newspaper clipping. The meeting was to be held on Wednesday night in Roanoke.

A support group for victims of date rape.

With a certainty she couldn't have explained, Hannah knew she would go.

THE MEETING WAS on the second floor of a downtown office complex. Hannah and Jenny had left work at five o'clock and made their way through the enormous doors of the building just before six.

Jenny squeezed her arm as they stepped into the elevator. "It's going to be okay. This is the right thing to do."

Hannah tried to ignore the churning in her stomach. The meeting was set up in a room just outside the elevator. A sign hung by the door that read Friends of Victims.

A woman with gold-rimmed glasses greeted them at the door. "Hello. I'm Tracy McDowell."

"I'm Hannah Jacobs," Hannah said, extending her hand. "This is my friend Jenny Dudley. She's here as my moral support."

"Good, I'm glad," Tracy said warmly. "Just have a seat anywhere you like. We'll get started in a couple of minutes." She looked at Hannah, her eyes gentle and understanding. "You may not feel this way right now, but I hope by the end of the evening, you'll be glad you came."

Hannah tried to smile, but her lips refused to move. The thought of sharing her experience with this group of women seemed just short of ludicrous. She didn't know them. Why would they care what had happened to her?

Promptly at six, Tracy stepped to the center of the circle and said, "Welcome, everyone. I recognize a lot of familiar faces tonight and see a few new ones, as well. I know each of us remembers the first night we gathered up the courage to make an appearance in this room. I'd like for everyone who's been here before to stand up now and introduce yourself to a face you don't recognize."

Chairs scraped against the wood floor. Hannah shook hands with a number of women who ranged in age from sixteen to sixty. Their faces were open and welcoming.

Raising her hand to quiet the room, Tracy began to speak again. "Thank you. For those of you new to this, I'd like to point out a thing or two. From the petrified looks on some of your faces, I'd guess you're thinking exactly what I thought the first night I stood before this group two years ago."

She smiled and let her eyes wander around the circle. "No, you don't have to talk about yourself if you don't want to. We hope you'll reach the point where you can. We believe it's a sign of healing. But if you choose not to, you never have to say a word. Just listen. That's all we ask. I think you'll find that some of the feelings you've been having are common among the women in this group. And now I'll sit down and be quiet so that someone else can get in a word."

Laughter rippled around the room, and some of the tension in Hannah's shoulders dissipated.

The group was silent no more than a moment or two before a middle-aged woman spoke up. "For you new arrivals, I'm Sue. And as for the rest of you, well, as you know, I told you last week that I had a date on the weekend."

Several of the women leaned forward and said in unison, "How did it go? Did you make it through it?"

"I did. And he was a very nice man. A little older. Quite handsome and entertaining. He took me to a nice French restaurant. I wanted to like him. And I think I do." She hesitated. "But somehow I can't bring myself to trust him."

Murmurs of understanding rose and swelled around the room. Hannah saw the woman's distress and wondered if she'd gone through the same ordeal as she herself had. The constant waves of self-doubt. The anger she'd repressed until it became nothing more than a hard knot somewhere deep inside her.

Sue cleared her throat and went on, "I want to. But how do you trust a stranger when you've found that you can't even trust someone you considered a friend?"

More sounds of sympathy came from the other women, making Hannah feel less like she'd been alone all these years.

And when Tracy said, "Would anyone new like to say something?" Jenny patted Hannah's hand. Hannah hesitated a moment, then stood.

"I—I'm Hannah Jacobs. In a way, I feel silly being here tonight. What happened to me took place ten years ago. I guess I somehow thought I was the only one in the world who'd been—" she paused "—raped by a date.

"The reason I came here, apart from my best friend's badgering—" she looked at Jenny and smiled "—is that I want to put it behind me. Maybe you all can help me do that."

IN THE DAYS FOLLOWING, Hannah came to realize the truth behind her statement. The next week she went to the meeting alone, although Jenny had assured her that she didn't mind going with her. But she knew she had to do this on her own.

"For the first time, I feel strong enough to face what happened, Jen. If it weren't for you, I might never have gone."

Jenny had put her arms around her and hugged her. "I'm so proud of you, Hannah."

Hannah began to be proud of herself. She listened each week as others relayed their stories, but she began to share her own, as well, even admitting at one point that she had pushed away someone she cared for a great deal. And at the probing of a few of the women, she admitted to them, and also to herself, that she'd never thought herself worthy of him.

At that point, she began to see hope for herself. She took a look at her life and realized that she had, indeed, blamed and punished herself over the years. Denied herself those things that she otherwise would have wanted in life—a husband, a family. She'd become a recluse, instead.

For the first time ever, she admitted the full extent of Tom Dillon's effect on her life. Because of him, she'd changed her plans of going to an Ivy League college. Because of him, she'd chosen to close herself off from people, preferring to lose herself in the pages of book after book, living other people's lives instead of her own. Because of him, she'd put herself inside that library every day, a place she still loved, but a self-imposed cage nonetheless. Because of him, she'd pushed away the only man she'd ever loved.

And although it still hurt to think of him, Hannah realized that she'd had nothing to offer Will a few months ago. Even though she'd changed during the time they'd been together, she still could not have offered him herself. Because she hadn't known who that was.

Now that was all changing. For the first time, she could look in the mirror and meet her eyes. *Really* meet her eyes. Not merely peer at the edges of her reflection. She no longer flinched at what she saw. She looked and acted a generation younger.

She bought a new car, reluctant to part with the "green boat," as Will had called it, but aware that it was time nonetheless. A Volkswagen convertible in a champagne beige fit the bill perfectly.

She kept up her running, and Jenny drove to Richmond with her one Saturday to buy some new clothes. The styles she chose were unlike anything in her wardrobe. Whitewashed jeans, a faded denim skirt and running shorts. Even a clingy little black dress, which Jenny said every young woman should have. Hannah felt really good about herself. About the person she had begun to rediscover.

At one point, she began wishing there was something she could do to help others who might have been through the same thing. And when Tracy suggested one evening that she go with some of the other members to meetings in nearby towns, Hannah agreed.

She shared her discoveries with Sarah. And one Sunday afternoon, when she'd worked up the courage, she told her aunt about Will.

The older woman's smile faded. "He won't be coming back?"

"I don't think so. But I've realized that I wasn't ready for what Will or any other man had to offer me. I had to come to terms with myself first. And I'm working on that."

Sarah stared up at her niece and said, "If only I'd done something about—"

Hannah reached out and pressed a finger to the woman's lips. "Shh. That's in the past, Aunt Sarah. I've put it behind me. It's time you did the same."

Sarah shook her head, her eyelids drooping.

"I'll go now and let you sleep," Hannah said lovingly. "See you next week, all right?"

BUCKETS OF ORANGE and yellow leaves dropped from the trees along the Washington streets until the branches were bare and skeletal. It was almost winter again, Will's least favorite season. But somehow the cold didn't bother him now. He had a goal in life, one he'd never imagined attaining. And as he moved closer to reaching it, he worked with a single-minded determination he'd never applied to anything in his life. Not even football.

He had, by now, settled into a routine. He'd rented a town house in Georgetown, a few blocks from Dr. Edwards's office. Despite Dr. Edwards's enthusiasm about what he could do for him, Will had been skeptical during those first couple of weeks. He'd failed often enough in his life that the possibility of succeeding was almost too much to imagine.

But the days of testing he'd undergone had revealed a great deal about his abilities and how he'd gotten as far as he had without revealing his secret. His was a relatively mild case of dyslexia.

The test results had revealed his reading skills to be around fifth- or sixth-grade level, which just happened to coincide with the time he got involved in football. Having learned these things about himself, he now knew why it had begun to sound to him like the rest of his classmates were speedreading. They'd progressed along at the normal rate, while he'd begun to fall behind. The dyslexia limited his ability to continue learning beyond that point, and his father's preoccupation with his athletic ability reinforced the belief that school wasn't as important as football.

Now as he pedaled his bike toward Dr. Edwards's office, he wondered at his progress. The psychologist had begun teaching him a different way of looking at things. His dedication had impressed the older man, who told him so every chance he got.

"I've yet to work with anyone as determined as you are, Will. You're really coming along. And that commercial you did for the Dyslexia Foundation will have a lot of influence. People need to understand that anyone can have a learning disability and that it can be overcome. You should be proud of yourself."

Throughout the duration of his football career, Will had received more praise than most people ever would. *Great play, Will! Terrific game, Will!* Somehow none of that had left him with the same sense of pride as those few words from Dr. Edwards.

He'd left the office that day torn between the desire to call Hannah and tell her what the doctor had said and the realization that she was no longer in his life. He knew that, and yet she was the one person with whom he wanted to share such moments of glory.

He couldn't seem to get her out of his mind. This city constantly reminded him of her: the bagel shop, the shops in Union Station, the Willard Hotel.

He wondered if her life had changed. Was she still jogging? Still working at the library? Did she visit Sarah every Sunday? Had she and Jenny finished teaching Henry Lawson to read?

In another couple of months, Dr. Edwards had said Will would be far enough along that he could seek help from more conventional routes. Will knew that after leaving Washington, he would continue learning through night classes or whatever it took. His education would be complete this time around.

The question now was what to do with the rest of his life.

Dan had kept in constant contact, setting up the commercial he'd done a couple of months ago for the Dyslexia Foundation. And, of course, he had a good long list of others to consider, as well. For the moment, they were of little interest to Will.

But something else had been tugging at the back of his mind. For some reason, every time he thought about what he would do with the rest of his life, his father's often-used term "worthwhile" came to mind.

Worthwhile. Will had his own definition of the word. And it didn't encompass touting underwear or light beer for the next five years.

Instead, he kept thinking about the kids he'd met through Dr. Edwards. He felt at home in those surroundings. He knew what those kids saw when they looked at the page of a book. He knew the frustration of feeling every bit as smart as the rest of the kids in class, but unable to prove it when the time came.

What would it be like to work with kids like that on a daily basis? Did he have something to offer them?

He thought about Tarkington's Cove and wondered if it was still in bankruptcy.

The idea hit him then with a clarity that made him realize it had been fermenting in the back of his mind for some time. Tarkington's Cove would be a perfect place for a school. A school for athletes with learning problems.

The old clubhouse could serve as the actual school. He could add on to it. And the condominiums could be converted to dorm rooms. It could function as a school for nine months of the year, an athletic summer camp the other three. Maybe he'd even work on building a football team.

He smiled to himself. A car honked as he cut across the intersection in front of it. Grinning like a kid, he raised a friendly hand at the vehicle and pedaled on. Maybe this was insane. Maybe he was crazy. And Hannah. What would Hannah say? The thought that this move would put them in the same town again gave the idea an appeal he couldn't deny. And for the first time since the night of the Superbowl that had ended his career, Will knew what he wanted to do with his life.

CHAPTER FOURTEEN

SPRING HAD PULLED OUT its paintbrush and begun to replenish the world with color. Tulips peeped up, the days grew warmer. In a lot of ways, Hannah felt as though she'd begun to bloom, as well.

Through her support group, she'd learned a great deal about herself. For that one night of the week, with that group of women, she belonged. They understood. They never judged. They simply listened. And by pouring out her thoughts and anxieties to them, Hannah began to realize life had more possibilities than she'd ever allowed herself to consider.

But she realized one afternoon that she'd been so absorbed in herself that she hadn't noticed Jenny's increasing unhappiness. A crash reverberated from the back office followed by the sound of Jenny sobbing.

Hannah jumped up from the desk and ran to her friend, finding her on the floor beside a pile of scattered books. She knelt beside her and put a hand on her shoulder. "Jenny, are you all right?"

The woman continued to cry, her reply delivered between sniffles. "Y-yes. I-I'm fine."

"You don't look fine. What is it?"

"Oh, Hannah. It's…it's Henry. I—I love him. The dad-burned old fool."

"But Jenny, that's wonderful," Hannah said with a smile. The past months had brought great success with Henry. He'd begun to read things he said he'd never imagined reading and had even signed up for a couple of night courses at a local community college. Hannah suspected Jenny had been tutoring him on the side.

Jenny sniffed again and said, "No, it's not. He's got it in his head that I'm somehow 'above' him. That since he didn't get a formal education, he's not right for me."

Hannah grabbed a tissue from a nearby desk and handed it to her. "Don't give up on him, Jen. You two do seem right for one another."

Jenny wiped her nose and said, "I—I don't intend to give up, but—"

"I'll talk to him." The words were out before Hannah even thought about them. Suddenly nothing seemed more important than making sure these two wonderful people had a chance together.

"I'm not sure it would do any good, Hannah."

"We'll never know until I try, though, will we?"

THE FOLLOWING AFTERNOON, Hannah went to see Henry Lawson during her lunch hour. She found him eating a sandwich by himself in the back room of the old brick building used by the town workers.

He glanced up from the book on his lap, obviously surprised to see her. "Why, Hannah. What are you doing here?"

"Hi, Henry. Do you have a minute to talk?"

"Why, sure. Have a seat," he said, pulling up a chair for her.

She sat down. "It's about Jenny."

Henry looked alarmed. "Is something—"

"No, no," she reassured him. "It's just that...she's been a little unhappy lately. Henry, she loves you."

He glanced away, his voice thick with despair when he said, "I love her too, but—"

"It'd be a shame to let that go to waste."

Henry looked down at his hands. "She could do an awful lot better than me."

"She's been looking for you all her life, Henry."

He shook his head. "There are too many differences between us."

"What? The fact that she was fortunate enough to get a formal education? And because you didn't, she wouldn't love you?"

The silence made his answer obvious. She realized then that she and Henry Lawson had a great deal in common. She'd pushed Will away because she'd been convinced that she would end up losing him, anyway. And she had. She didn't want the same for Henry and Jenny.

She stood up and put a hand on his shoulder. "If you love her, that's all that matters. Together, the two of you can handle the rest."

And as Hannah drove back to the library that afternoon, it occurred to her that maybe it was time she took her own advice.

THAT NIGHT Hannah was scheduled to speak to a group of women at a nearby college about date rape. A year ago, she couldn't have imagined finding the courage to take such a step. But being a part of Friends of Victims had shown her that, as a victim of the crime, she had a responsibility to others. To make the public aware that women were often too ashamed to report it and that they often felt responsible for what had happened.

The warmth and understanding flowing from the audience as Hannah finished her talk told her that this was the right thing to do. She lingered for a while after the meeting, sipping at a bottle of mineral water and chatting with Tracy McDowell. The talk had gone well and both women were pleased.

"I'm proud of you, Hannah," Tracy said. "You've come so far."

"I'm amazed at myself. I always thought role models were supposed to be flawless. I'm hardly that."

"You're a good example to these young women. It took you a long time to face what happened to you. But you did. And that's what's important." Tracy hesitated a moment and then said, "I've been asked to speak to a group in Washington this next weekend. Why don't you come with me?"

Hannah looked up in surprise. Washington. Would Will still be there? She was overwhelmed with a sudden longing to see him. So much had changed since he'd been gone. *She* had changed. And more than anything, she wanted to show him that.

"I'd love to go, Tracy," she said.

THAT SAME WEEK Will began making plans for his future. He'd been on the phone with the bank that held the note on Tarkington's Cove, discussing his proposition with the bank's president, Leo Coleman. Will had made an appointment to meet with him on Saturday in Roanoke.

Since the afternoon he'd decided to pursue the idea, he'd been going nonstop. He'd gone to see Jim Edwards the next day and pitched his idea to him. The doctor had leaned back in his chair and looked impressed.

"You're really serious about this, Will?"

"Yes, I am. I plan to continue my own education. But this is something I've put a lot of thought into. And I believe in it. Do you think it could fly?"

"I think it's a wonderful idea."

"Wonderful enough that you'd consider working there?"

Dr. Edwards's eyebrows shot upward. "Me?"

"I don't know where I could find a better headmaster. I want someone who'll show these kids some compassion, but at the same time pump them up with the desire to stick with it. I happen to know you're pretty good at that. Interested?"

"I'm flattered."

"I know how important your work is, Jim. And if anybody can appreciate your abilities, I can."

"I wasn't expecting this. But I have to admit the idea is appealing. Peg and I have wanted to get the kids out of the city for some time now."

Will smiled and stood up. "You think about it, all right? Discuss it with your wife. I'll call and let you know how things go."

JENNY WAS THRILLED to hear that Hannah had agreed to go to Washington. She and Henry had managed to work things out. Jenny all but glowed with happiness. "Henry told me you'd come to see him," she said one afternoon before leaving work. "Hannah, you know there's nothing that would make me happier than to see you and Will together. Why don't you get in touch with him while you're up there? I know he'd love to hear from you."

Hannah kept her decision to herself, but she called Fannie the next day and asked her for Will's phone number and address. Once she'd gotten it, Saturday seemed as though it would never come. Hannah volunteered to drive. They arrived at the hotel just before eleven, checked into their rooms and had a light lunch before heading for the meeting room. She sat and listened to Tracy's talk and then, at the other woman's urging, got up and made a few remarks of her own. The group welcomed her with clapping and smiles. By the time she finished her speech, Hannah was glad she'd come.

It was five o'clock by the time she got back to her room. With a trembling hand, she pulled out the scrap of paper from her purse and then picked up the phone to dial Will's number. She let it ring at least ten times, before placing the receiver back on the hook. She tried again before dinner and then again the next morning. When the phone continued to ring, she got up and dressed, leaving a message for Tracy that she'd be back by ten.

She drove away from the hotel and searched out the address she'd scribbled down. It was a beautiful old town house in the heart of Georgetown. She pulled up to the curb and fished for a piece of paper and pen from her purse, thinking for a moment before jotting down the message. The words were light and brief, basically just a friendly "Hi, how are you doin'," from one old friend to another.

She climbed out of the car and stuck the note in the door, wondering if she would ever have another chance to make it more.

IT WAS AFTER TEN on Sunday night by the time Will got home. His agent, Dan, was waiting for him on the front doorstep.

"It's about time you got here," Dan said as he shivered in the chill air. "A man could freeze his—"

"What the hell are you doing here?" Will interrupted with a quick grin, slapping his friend on the shoulder as he set his suitcase down.

"Got some things to show you. Figured I'd do better face-to-face."

"And I've got some news for you," Will said.

"What kind of news?"

"I've decided what I'm going to do once I finish here."

Dan's expression brightened. "Well, don't leave me hanging."

"I went to see a bank in Roanoke this weekend. Along with a couple of other investors I've managed to scrounge up, I'm buying a development on the lake. It's been in bankruptcy for the last six months. I'm going to turn it into a school for young athletes with learning problems."

Dan blinked. "You're what?"

"You heard me."

"Since when did you get the desire to be a teacher?"

"Since I learned there are a lot of kids out there who have the same problem I have. Since I realized I might have something to offer them. I've been working on raising the money. I sold the Ferrari. That was a start."

"Oh, man," Dan moaned. "What about these offers I've got for you? Ever since you did that commercial for the Dyslexia Foundation, they've been coming in nonstop. But if you don't soon jump on a few of them—"

"I intend to."

Dan stared at him. "You do?"

"Yes. I do. What have you got? Other commercials?"

"Yeah, and a couple of other things. Speaking engagements, personal appearances." Dan added suspiciously, "Why the sudden change of heart? This seems too easy. You know I'm wary of anything I don't have to bully my way into getting."

Will smiled. "I plan to put the money I earn into the school."

"Hey, that's cool. What you do with the money is up to you." Dan reached for his briefcase and then pulled a piece of paper out of his pocket. "Oh, by the way, this was on your door when I got here. I didn't read it."

Will unfolded the note, his gaze scanning the familiar handwriting. His heart quickened. Hannah. She'd been here.

"Too bad you missed her, huh?" Dan said.

He gave his friend a knowing look. "Thought you didn't read it."

"Thought it might have given some indication of your whereabouts," Dan said with a grin. "Guess she couldn't find you, either. Is she the little woman you've been keeping under wraps in Lake Perdue?"

Will ignored his friend's question, suddenly anxious to finish up their business so he could try to figure out what Hannah's visit had meant. "Let's go inside and you can show me what you've got, Dan."

"Translation, drop it," his friend said with a mock salute. "Nobody ever accused me of not being intuitive."

DAN LEFT sometime after midnight, headed for a downtown hotel where he'd booked a room. Will gratefully closed the door behind him and went upstairs to his bed where he lay in the dark with Hannah's note clutched to his chest, his mind filled with uncertainty and confusion.

He'd reread the note no fewer than a dozen times, wondering what the brief message meant. Had she changed her mind about their being together? The fact that she'd come here seemed like a step in that direction. But then, maybe that was only his wishful thinking.

In the past months his life had begun to come together in ways he never would have dreamed of. He owed a great deal of that to Hannah. But gratitude was the weaker of his feelings for her. Topping the list was love. And longing. He loved Hannah Jacobs. He longed for the closeness he'd experienced with her that weekend. Nothing that had happened during the past few months had changed that love. It was there in his heart, strong as ever, coursing through him with a sureness that made him realize now that, regardless of all the good things that had happened to him, she was the best thing in his life. Without Hannah, everything rang hollow. His progress with Dr. Edwards. The school he planned to build.

All of it meant nothing without her.

He thought about what Aaron had said the last time he'd seen him. *Just seems to me that if two people want to be together, then they ought to be. Simple as that.*

Will sat up then, fired with a certainty that what he was about to do was the only thing possible. Go to her. Convince her they belonged together. He swung out of bed and headed for the shower. He wasn't going to waste another minute.

A PERSISTENT KNOCKING roused her from a restless sleep. She'd dreamed most of the night, half asleep, half awake, and thought for a moment that the sound was only in her mind.

But it grew louder, and then a voice called out her name again and again.

She sat upright in bed, running a hand through her hair, her heart pounding in alarm. She glanced at the clock on her nightstand. Four-thirty? Who could possibly be at her door at this time of night?

She grabbed a robe and made her way tentatively down the stairs, wishing she had a dog or a gun or—

"Hannah?"

Her heart stopped thudding. Will. That was Will's voice.

She took the last few steps at a run, and without stopping to think she might be wrong, yanked open the door and stared at him. Just stared at him. Something inside her melted with the absolute assurance that as long as she lived she would never forget the sight of him standing there. He wore faded blue jeans, a white cotton shirt and his old leather jacket.

Just the sight of him made her throat tight, and she was overwhelmed with the desire to throw herself at him. It had been so long....

"Hannah?"

She didn't stop to think or edit her response. Instead, she followed her heart, launching herself at him with all the longing inside her. "You came," she said, half sobbing, wrapping her arms around his neck and holding on as if she'd never let him go again.

He folded her close to him, pressing his face to the side of her neck. "You knew I'd come, didn't you?"

She shook her head. "No. It never occurred to me. Until just now. Now I realize how much I wanted you to. Hoped you would."

He held her that way for a long time while she savored the steady thump of his heart, the reassuring feel of his body against hers. When he finally pulled back, he reached down and touched her cheek, his palm cradling her jaw.

She swallowed and said, "Come in. Please."

She led him into the den on shaky legs. He sat down on the couch beside her, looking as though he didn't know where to begin. "I..." He let out a sigh, closing his eyes for a brief moment. "I guess I should have waited until morning. But I couldn't. I needed to see you too much. Hannah, oh, God, Hannah, I've missed you."

He had missed her! she thought. Nothing had ever touched her more, meant so much. "I've missed you, too, Will. You can't possibly know..."

He reached for her hand, entwined his fingers with hers as though the gesture might merge their strength for the questions that lay ahead. "Then why did you push me away, Hannah?"

She looked down at their linked hands and struggled for the right words. "Oh, Will, so much has happened since then. I didn't see how I could ever be the kind of woman who could fit into your life. The kind of woman you're used to. So I said things I didn't mean, things I knew would hurt you enough to make you leave. I'm sorry for that now."

"Hannah—"

"Please. I want you to know." She hesitated, then went on, "I couldn't believe what had happened between us that weekend. I wouldn't allow myself to believe that it had been real or that it would last. I've since realized that I never considered myself worthy of you. Maybe I still felt somewhere inside that I deserved what Tom Dillon did to me. But now I've made some changes in my life. I've been going to this support group—"

"I know," he interrupted gently. "Aunt Fan's kept me posted. I think it was the best thing in the world for you to do."

She met his approving gaze and smiled. "It has been. I've made some wonderful friends. I think I've finally figured out I'm not so bad. I can't go on letting the past affect the rest of my life."

"And did you also figure out somewhere along the way that what we had was right, that it deserved a chance?"

"I realized how much I wanted you back."

With his other hand, he brushed her cheek. "You're one of the few people in my life who knows who I really am, who's seen all my imperfections and shortcomings. You know what I am. What I hope to be. And if you can accept that..."

"Oh, Will," she said, her voice breaking, "they aren't imperfections or shortcomings. You're the bravest man I've ever known. I'm so proud of you." She looked down and then added, "Fannie kept me up to date on your progress, too. She told me about the school. I love the idea."

He smiled. "She always was a busybody."

"She loves you. She also told me about your father...about his not allowing Mrs. Tate to confirm her suspicions about your dyslexia."

"My father's tried to run my life for a long time. I won't let that happen anymore." He reached out a finger and tilted her chin up. "And all that matters now is getting you to believe that nothing in my life means anything without you. You put the magic in my life. I love you, Hannah. And I'll do whatever it takes to show you that we belong together."

A rush of happiness washed through her. "Will, what are you saying?"

"That I want to marry you. I want to take care of you, live with you, make love to you, be the father of your children."

She swallowed, and her eyes filled with tears. She felt for a second as though she'd wake up any moment and find herself in her bed upstairs, mournfully aware that Will's declaration was part of a dream. But it wasn't a dream. He was here in this room with her. "I—" Her voice broke when she tried to speak. She swallowed and tried again. "Oh, Will, I love you so much. The thought of living another day without you..."

"Hey, you won't have to." He pulled her to him, his strong arms encircling her. "From now on, what matters most is what we feel for each other. And the rest will be okay, too, as long as we work on it together." He gazed down at her with love and understanding in his eyes. "I just want to look at you. Make sure you're really here."

"I'm here. I don't ever want to be anywhere else." She wrapped her arms around his waist and pressed her face to his chest. "Aunt Sarah's going to be so happy."

"You don't think she'll object to having me in the family?"

"There's nothing she'd like better. Maybe we could go see her today."

"Sounds like a great idea. I'd like to ask her permission to marry her niece," he said on a more serious note.

Hannah's throat tightened with emotion. "She would love that."

He pulled her to him and hugged her. She cherished this ability of his to know what she was feeling, to silently comfort her in a way no one else ever had. He leaned back and cupped her face in his hands, pressing his mouth to hers in a gentle kiss that smoothed away the pain of the past months, leaving in its place the certainty of a future they would face together. Side by side. Hand in hand.

"I'm not going to be very patient, you know," he said in a tender voice.

"About what?"

"Marrying you."

"Oh, is that so?"

His mouth found the vulnerable pulse at the side of her neck. "Two weeks at the most."

A shiver of anticipation went through her. "Two weeks, hmm?"

"That's it. I want you with me, Hannah. In my bed at night. By my side when I wake up in the morning. And speaking of that, where would you like to put that bed?"

"You'd need to be at the lake with the school, wouldn't you?"

"Some of the time, but if it's all right with you, we could keep your house, too. Since it was Sarah's.... Anyway, I always wanted a house in town."

Surely there could not be another man on earth like this one. Hannah pressed her face to his neck, cherishing the fact that he was hers.

He pulled back, looked down at her for a moment, then settled his mouth firmly on hers, kissing her with tenderness and an appreciation for what they'd found. She kissed him back, her heart full with the same gratitude and love.

A few minutes later, when he finally raised his head, she said, "Is this really how it will be?"

"This is how it will be. I promise," he vowed. "What would you think about having the ceremony in the gazebo at the lake?"

She smiled. "I think it sounds perfect."

His gaze became intent and searching. "And the pitter-patter of little Kincaid feet? What do you think about the sound of that?"

His face blurred before her eyes. She blinked away the tears of happiness then pressed her cheek to his chest. "The sweetest sound in the world."

They remained that way for a long time until he pulled back and kissed her with a tenderness that left her weak. And then suddenly the kiss changed, and she went weak with feelings of another sort. They were hungry for one another, mouths working desperately with the awareness that they had almost lost this precious gift. His hands found the neck of her nightgown, slipping the buttons loose, his lips skimming along the curve of her neck to the tops of her breasts.

Hannah's head fell back against the couch. "Oh, Will," she murmured. "I thought we'd never be like this again."

"Neither did I," he admitted. "We've got the rest of our lives to grow tired of one another."

"I don't think that's going to happen," she said with a smile.

"Then I fully intend to wear us both out trying."

Hannah laughed. She pulled his mouth back to hers, kissing him as a woman kisses a man of whom she is sure.

"What do you think about continuing this discussion upstairs?"

"Sounds perfect," she said.

He got up from the couch then and lifted her in his arms, heading toward the staircase that led to her bedroom.

She wrapped her arms around his neck, catching a glimpse of the Madam Butterfly rosebushes where they glistened under the rising spring sun outside the living room window, their blossoming petals eclipsing the thorns beneath.

EPILOGUE

IT WAS A WARM June day and Hannah and Will sat in the gazebo by the lake, gazing out over the sparkling blue water. "We did it, didn't we?" he murmured contentedly. "Just two more months, and it'll be open. I can't believe it's actually going to be ready."

"I guess we should both know by now that when you want something badly enough, you can make it happen," she said, thinking of how hard they'd both worked this past year to make the school a reality. She was so proud of her husband. And so grateful. So very grateful for this life they'd begun building together.

"I could never have done it without you. You know that."

The words meant everything to her. This first year of their marriage had been the happiest of her life, and more fulfilling than anything she'd ever dreamed of. She still spoke to women's groups every month or two, and when she did, he went with her, always supporting her. Jenny had taken her place at the library. Hannah and Will spent most of their time working together on the school. Eventually she planned to teach a class or two. In addition, she hoped to write a book for women who had been victims of date rape.

Life was good. So good that sometimes she still couldn't quite believe it.

She turned her face toward the morning sun, letting her head rest against the gazebo bench, cherishing the feel of Will's hand on her rounded belly. That was one thing she'd loved most about him in the past months, his constant need to touch her, to maintain a physical connection between the two of them and the child she carried. "I can't possibly get any bigger, can I?" she asked, glancing at him with a smile on her lips.

"I don't care if you do. You're beautiful," he said, fingering a lock of her hair. "I always thought pregnant ladies were special. They just look like they belong to someone. You belong to me."

She touched his cheek with her palm, letting her eyes take their fill of this man who had brought her such incredible happiness. "The way he's been kicking, I have no doubt who he's taking after. I think he's already wearing shoulder pads."

He laughed and kissed her, a long lingering kiss full with love, appreciation and respect. "I love you, Hannah Kincaid. Did I tell you that today?"

"As a matter of fact, you did," she said, resting her head on his shoulder. "But I don't mind hearing it again."

They sat there in the sun, summer sounds echoing around them. Hannah put a hand on her stomach, and said wistfully, "I wish Sarah could have been here for this baby."

"Me, too, sweetheart."

"I'm so glad she was there when we got married." They'd had two ceremonies, one at the church in town and one in Sarah's room. The national papers had carried the story of their wedding, and they'd received so many flowers that they'd finally asked the florist to deliver them to patients at Lake Perdue Memorial Hospital.

"It meant a lot to me that she trusted me to take care of you."

"She knew you would."

"And I will," he promised, tilting her chin up and placing a soft kiss on her mouth. "You and that little kicker inside you."

She settled back into the comfort of his strong, loving arms, her cheek against the soft cotton of his shirt. "If he turns out to be a she, would you mind if we named her Sarah?"

Will hugged her to him and said, "I wouldn't have it any other way."

Hannah pressed a kiss to his chest. Life was very good, indeed.

HARLEQUIN SUPERROMANCE®

VERONICA SATTLER!

This September, critically acclaimed author Veronica Sattler comes
to Superromance with her first contemporary romance:

Wild Cherries

Francesca Valera has been schooled in a convent, where nothing
prepared her to deal with her new bodyguard, all-male, all-hunk
Rafe O'Hara. When a plane crash strands them in the Sierra Madre,
her education begins for real. Pursued by her father's enemies, she
becomes a three-way pawn in a very dangerous game. There's only
one man she can trust...or can she?

**Join us for the adventure of your life with Superromance.
Wherever Harlequin books are sold.**

VS-1

This summer, come cruising with Harlequin Books!

PORTS
OF CALL

In July, August and September, excitement, danger and, of course, romance can be found in Lynn Leslie's exciting new miniseries PORTS OF CALL. Not only can you cruise the South Pacific, the Caribbean and the Nile, your journey will also take you to Harlequin Superromance®, Harlequin Intrigue® and Harlequin American Romance®.

♦ In July, cruise the South Pacific with
  SINGAPORE FLING, a Harlequin Superromance
♦ NIGHT OF THE NILE from Harlequin Intrigue
  will heat up your August
♦ September is the perfect month for
  CRUISIN' MR. DIAMOND from
  Harlequin American Romance

So, cruise through the summer with LYNN LESLIE and HARLEQUIN BOOKS!

CRUISE

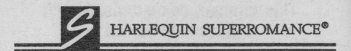

HARLEQUIN SUPERROMANCE®

Superromance Showcase is proud to present
award-winning author

Karen Young

The Promise, the last book in the O'Connor Trilogy, is the
story that started it all.

At last you get to meet Kathleen Collins and Patrick O'Connor
in the first flush of youth and passion. Their panoramic story
will take you from the shores of Ireland to New York to
Savannah. Separated by tragedy, each goes on to forge a new
life. But nothing can keep them apart forever—not even
Caroline Ferguson, whose father makes sure she gets
everything she wants....

The Promise. A story so special, it had to be showcased.

Look for *The Promise* this September, wherever
Harlequin Superromance books are sold.

SHOW1

This September, discover the fun of falling in love with...

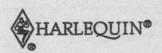

Harlequin is pleased to bring you this exciting new collection of three original short stories by bestselling authors!

ELISE TITLE
BARBARA BRETTON
LASS SMALL

LOVE AND LAUGHTER—sexy, romantic, fun stories guaranteed to tickle your funny bone and fuel your fantasies!

Available in September wherever
Harlequin books are sold.

⬥HARLEQUIN®

LOVEL

HARLEQUIN®

Don't miss these Harlequin favorites by some of our most distinguished authors!
And now you can receive a discount by ordering two or more titles!

HT #25525	THE PERFECT HUSBAND by Kristine Rolofson	$2.99	☐
HT #25554	LOVERS' SECRETS by Glenda Sanders	$2.99	☐
HP #11577	THE STONE PRINCESS by Robyn Donald	$2.99	☐
HP #11554	SECRET ADMIRER by Susan Napier	$2.99	☐
HR #03277	THE LADY AND THE TOMCAT by Bethany Campbell	$2.99	☐
HR #03283	FOREIGN AFFAIR by Eva Rutland	$2.99	☐
HS #70529	KEEPING CHRISTMAS by Marisa Carroll	$3.39	☐
HS #70578	THE LAST BUCCANEER by Lynn Erickson	$3.50	☐
HI #22256	THRICE FAMILIAR by Caroline Burnes	$2.99	☐
HI #22238	PRESUMED GUILTY by Tess Gerritsen	$2.99	☐
HAR #16496	OH, YOU BEAUTIFUL DOLL by Judith Arnold	$3.50	☐
HAR #16510	WED AGAIN by Elda Minger	$3.50	☐
HH #28719	RACHEL by Lynda Trent	$3.99	☐
HH #28795	PIECES OF SKY by Marianne Willman	$3.99	☐

Harlequin Promotional Titles

#97122	LINGERING SHADOWS by Penny Jordan	$5.99	☐
	(limited quantities available on certain titles)		

	AMOUNT	$
DEDUCT:	10% DISCOUNT FOR 2+ BOOKS	$
	POSTAGE & HANDLING	$
	($1.00 for one book, 50¢ for each additional)	
	APPLICABLE TAXES*	$ _____
	TOTAL PAYABLE	$ _____
	(check or money order—please do not send cash)	

To order, complete this form and send it, along with a check or money order for the total above, payable to Harlequin Books, to: **In the U.S.:** 3010 Walden Avenue, P.O. Box 9047, Buffalo, NY 14269-9047; **In Canada:** P.O. Box 613, Fort Erie, Ontario, L2A 5X3.

Name: _____

Address: _____City: _____

State/Prov.: _____ Zip/Postal Code: _____

*New York residents remit applicable sales taxes.
Canadian residents remit applicable GST and provincial taxes..

HBACK-JS